W9-BUK-651

A House of Men

A HOUSE OF MEN

SUMNER WILSON

FIVE STAR
A part of Gale, a Cengage Company

Farmington Hills, Mich • San Francisco • New York • Waterville, Maine
Meriden, Conn • Mason, Ohio • Chicago

LIBRARY OF CONGRESS CATALOGING-IN-PUBLICATION DATA

Names: Wilson, Sumner, author.
Title: A house of men / Sumner Wilson.
Description: First edition. | Waterville, Maine : Five Star Publishing, a part of Cengage Learning, Inc., [2017]
Identifiers: LCCN 2017022959 (print) | LCCN 2017032274 (ebook) | ISBN 9781432834456 (ebook) | ISBN 1432834452 (ebook) | ISBN 9781432834425 (ebook) | ISBN 1432834428 (ebook) | ISBN 9781432834487 (hardcover) | ISBN 1432834487 (hardcover)
Subjects: LCSH: Dysfunctional families—Fiction. | Interpersonal conflict—Fiction. | Vendetta—Fiction. | GSAFD: Western stories.
Classification: LCC PS3623.I585815 (ebook) | LCC PS3623.I585815 H68 2017 (print) | DDC 813/.6—dc23
LC record available at https://lccn.loc.gov/2017022959

First Edition. First Printing: December 2017
Find us on Facebook–https://www.facebook.com/FiveStarCengage
Visit our website–http://www.gale.cengage.com/fivestar/
Contact Five Star™ Publishing at FiveStar@cengage.com

Printed in the United States of America
1 2 3 4 5 6 7 21 20 19 18 17

To my wife and best friend, Linda.

CHAPTER ONE

And a man's foes shall be they of his own household.

Matthew 10:36

Witness Tree Station 1878

Steel Fixx rode up the lane that led to the fabulous three-story colonial-style house of brick and marble that his cousin, Honus Rust, had built several years ago for his wife, and, Fixx felt sure, to confirm for himself his great success. He saw little of the splendor of the impressive structure, torn apart as he was by the seriousness of his mission. He boiled over inside because Rust's son had impregnated his daughter, Molly. The boy, Jorod, had treated Molly as if she were an object that he used and tossed away. Fixx's pride pushed him along, although he wouldn't admit pride had anything to do with the whole wretched matter. What's more, Jorod had taken her by force. Fixx truly felt this. Molly had told him so, and she had never lied to him. What hurt Fixx worse was that Molly and Jorod were second cousins.

Fixx's wealthy cousin had no compunctions about cheating any man he dealt with. In fact, he had the reputation of being a crook, although a rich, important crook. In the past, his grand house had been the scene of social gatherings attended by politicians and other men of significance not only in the county but in the state as well. Many of these men possessed fewer morals than did Rust, and the majority of them were wealthier.

He stepped from the saddle at the foot of the immense house's wide, steep steps, and felt his anger growing. He tied the horse to a banister and stepped upward toward the wide porch. Passion plants bloomed upon the banisters, winding in and out on each side of the steps. Bees buzzed about the blue and white flowers, unconcerned with the insignificant matters of men. Steel Fixx saw none of this, nor heard the sleepy drone of the bees as they buzzed about the flowers gathering pollen. He conquered the steps and crossed over to the door.

He rapped on the door and soon the housekeeper, Joan Murphy, answered. He informed her of his desire to speak to Honus, and she scurried off to fetch her boss. Honus Rust poked his head out of the door. He saw his cousin standing there, and stepped outside and closed the door behind him. They stood awhile and stared at each other like cur dogs with their tails curled over their backs as if laying groundwork for a scrap.

Rust's mandibles were as thick as a bulldog's. He looked flushed from lugging around his tremendous bulk. He wheezed and struggled to breathe. Heavy rolls of fat lapped over his shirt collar and bounced off his collarbone with each movement of his massive head. Large drops of sweat lay upon his broad, ridged forehead.

Fixx heard Rust's labored chest wheezes and squeaks, and figured they had come about because he'd grown fat over the years. Rust had always been somewhat heavy, but had breathed fine before he grew obese and cumbersome, Fixx recalled.

He must think he's a gentleman-rancher, Fixx told himself, as he studied the man's garb.

Rust wore a full suit, vest and all, made of gray English tweed, with a pale red silk tie of the latest fashion, and his eyes were blood red.

Fixx hated the man's airs. He noticed the glass monocle that dangled down onto his chest, one he'd likely picked up on one of his trips to Europe, and he forced down the urge to laugh, and swallowed it with difficulty.

"Just a minute," Rust said.

He opened the door, stepped back inside, and returned seconds later with an expensive tan beaver hat in hand.

"Now, let's take a little walk. I need the air."

They descended the front porch steps, which were in bricks in a herringbone pattern, and up a pathway that blazed white in the sun, trimmed in green. They mounted the steps, and entered the shade of the overhead wooden canopy, made in imitation of a child's carousel. Rust sat down at a small white table with matching green trim on the legs. The same invasive plant that lined the steps to the house's porch was in the act of overrunning the gazebo, and bees buzzed about the blooms as thick as a swarm of flies on butchering day, but much noisier.

Fixx drew out a chair and sat across from the enormous man. They took up the identical bluff stance they'd employed on the porch before Honus had decided that he needed to fetch his hat, although he hadn't donned it. The hat now sat upside down on the tabletop.

Rust drew out a cigar. His chair squeaked loudly when he leaned back and lit up. His eyes followed the rise of the smoke to the ceiling where it hovered in a fat cloud.

"What do you want here, Fixx?" He asked the question as if Fixx were a rank stranger instead of his cousin.

The attitude Rust had decided to assume angered Fixx. He let it pass, and said, "I want to talk to that boy."

Honus swiveled in his chair and looked over a shoulder, as if the "boy" might be somewhere nearby, maybe even somewhere in the yard itself. He turned back to Fixx, and said, "Hughie? Well, that boy stays busy. I 'spect he's out somewheres in one of the pastures right now."

"It ain't Hughie I need to talk to. I mean your least one."

Mrs. Murphy's seven-year-old daughter, Irene, passed by on the pathway toward the house. The pathway was lined in red roses, in a faint now from the drought. Rust saw Irene. He reared up and said, "Tell your mam to fetch my drink out here, girl."

Irene nodded, quickened her pace, reached the steps and ran up them, and crossed the wide porch as if she were late for an engagement.

"You talking 'bout Jo?"

"How many boys you got, Honus? Did I miss one?"

"Why, Jo ain't here, Fixx. I sent him on a trip."

"A trip?"

"Yep. Sent him up to Nebraska. He's checking out some horses I intend to buy. That is, if they're suitable. That boy's got an eye for a filly." He revealed his teeth, as yellowed as the keys of an ancient piano, in a sly smile.

The slur punched Fixx in the face. His skin shivered frantically up his spine. Somehow, he held himself back.

"You took to raising horses now, have you? They'll grub up your pasture. Then what'll you have? Nobody I know eats horses, Honus."

"I 'spect I'll worry about that my damned self, Fixx."

"You better start worrying about something more worthwhile than horses, Honus."

Joan Murphy mounted the steps of the gazebo. She carried a wide tray with a pitcher of water, a glass and a bottle of spirits with which Fixx was unfamiliar. She placed the tray on the table, and he attempted to read the label, but the script was in a foreign hand.

The woman set the glass in front of the huge man. She placed a flat, pointed spoon-like affair with slots in it in the form of vines in a decorative pattern across the mouth of the glass. She poured green liqueur over the spoon, and it drained down the sides of the glass. Then she took a lump of sugar, set it on the spoon, and glanced with cautious eyes at Rust. Fixx saw she was fearful she might make a mistake. Rust nodded. She poured a small amount of water onto the sugar, watched until it dissolved, removed the spoon, and filled the glass close to the top with water. She stepped back and waited.

Fixx watched the liqueur make a transformation. It turned from green to a milky white, venting an aroma he decided might be anise. He could smell its strong odor in the air even from across the table.

"I can drink this stuff straight, Fixx, but it's sometimes bitter. I sugar it down now. Tastes better this a way."

He nodded to Joan Murphy. She turned to leave. He set a large flat hand against her backside, patted her there in a gentle slap and added, "That's the way folks in Europe drink it."

The flushed-faced woman stumbled on a step as she descended, but grabbed onto the rail with a free hand and righted herself. Her face grew so bright it might have lit up the sky, had it been nighttime.

Rust sipped, set the glass back on the table. He wiped his broad, graying mustache, and sighed as if sitting on the front porch of heaven itself.

"Quit drinking whiskey have you?"

"Picked this up in Europe. Kind of liked it, bought up a batch and brought it home with me. Sort of grows on you. Has wormwood in it. Know what that is?"

"No."

"Wormwood's what they sometimes got drunk on back in the old Bible days."

"News to me. Didn't know folks in the Bible got drunk. Thought they were all pretty much pious folks."

Honus Rust studied his cousin with critical eyes, as if he were attempting to see if Fixx was making fun of him. He puffed his fat cigar, blew smoke toward the sky, swatted at a bee, and unable to contain himself any longer, tossed back his head and roared with laughter. When he subdued the laughter, he wheezed out large squeaks from his lungs, took up the cigar again, and puffed at it as if he and it had a grudge to settle.

"Thought at first you was trying to have a go at me. I see now you wasn't. Don't read much do you?"

"Still talking about the Bible, Honus? No, I don't read no more'n I have to."

"You're still living back in East Tennessee, ain't you, Steel? Still got them old hill ways of doing things. You'd been better off settling in northwest Arkansas or southwest part of Missouri instead of here. Been more at home up there . . . in the hills . . . with the rest of them brush apes."

"That ain't what I come for, Honus. I think you probably know that."

"I can't help it your little girl's knocked up, Steel. She should've kept her dress tail down." He caught up his glass again, and sipped slowly, but for all his caution still succeeded in making a gross sound.

Fixx's soul leapt once again. He longed to unleash upon his cousin all the fury that hell had forgotten it possessed. All the tension he'd been under since he learned of his daughter's pregnancy demanded to be released. He wanted to murder this grotesquely overweight man. Honus Rust, he felt, had become flawed by his success, the wealth he'd earned by honest means and of all he'd stolen.

"It seems to be her fault, Fixx. I ain't one to worry over things I can't do nothing about."

"Oh, but this here's something you *can* do something about. I'm asking you now to do what's right in the matter. Talk to the boy. But if it embarrasses you too much, let me do the talking."

Fixx saw a decided calm settle over Rust, which replaced the vague sense of unease he'd felt in the air when he first met him on his porch. It was as if Rust now figured he'd found the right path to take, and meant to do just that. His eyes were no longer bloodshot, but had turned again to the clear, pure blue Fixx recalled from childhood. The man's chest expanded with what Fixx took to be confidence. He was in command now, and wasn't about to allow his cousin to ruffle him, as had been the case for most of his life in their squabbles and competitions.

Rust said, "You know that old woman—Felipe Reyes's old woman? She has a way with herbs and healing. Kind of like a root-doctor back home. She can fix it for your gal, if you want. That bunch has been a thorn in my side since I come to this country and tried but failed to buy 'em out. Might as well get something out of 'em, I reckon."

This proposal turned Fixx to stone. "You know what you said, Honus?"

"Well, it's one way, Fixx. What the hell, this here's not the first time a gal's got herself knocked up."

"You mean to say you'd go along with the killing of your own grandchild? A part of you? You'd allow someone to kill one of your own?" Rust's mother, Fixx's Aunt Emma, still lived in Rust's eyes, and Fixx couldn't even call him a son of a bitch for fear of dishonoring her memory. "And besides, I hear Felipe's wife died during the winter."

Rust puffed his cigar, set it on the lip of the table, took out a handkerchief, honked into it, returned it to a rear pocket, and sipped his drink again. When he set the glass down, he leaned forward, his massive arms at rest on the tabletop. Cigar smoke still curled a long trail toward the ceiling of the gazebo. "Are you proposing them two marry, Fixx?"

"That's exactly why I rode over here, Honus."

"Why, Jesus Christ, man. Them two are cousins."

"And that shocks you? But killing your own grandchild don't?"

"Why, hell's fire, yes. It does shock me. Close cousins don't marry. Not out here they don't. Damn it, I said you should've settled in southwest Missouri. I see now I was right. Them two share great-grandparents, Steel. Them kids are too close."

"It happens," Fixx said. "And besides, your mam and my pap would have called 'em third cousins. How many times you seen someone marry his second cousin, thinking them to be third cousins, and them not counting the in-betweens? The once-removes?"

"Well, hell, I don't know. But one thing's for sure, it damned well won't happen in this here house."

Fixx's spirit stiffened. He was through talking. He reached to his side and drew from a sheath a knife he'd fashioned from a spring of an old Studebaker hack. He grasped the knife by the handle in his rough, knobby fist and drove it into the table to a sizeable depth. He leaned back in his chair, and studied Honus Rust's face. The man had taken on a new strength since he had met him on the porch. He figured the liqueur lay behind it. Still, he doubted Honus would go for the knife. But, in a way, he wished he would. He felt this despite what his father might have said had he a way of knowing, being dead for many years and buried in far-away Banner Cemetery.

"One of us might die today, Honus. You been baptized?"

"You know I was. In the same damned creek you was. What the hell're you doing, Steel? This here's crazy . . . you know it, too."

"Yeah? Ain't nobody going to make my child pregnant and not marry her. Not and me still breathing. I came here today to receive some sort of reassurance . . . satisfaction will do, I reckon. So if you won't talk to your boy, your only way out is to go for that knife. I'll not be made the fool by you nor no man alive."

"Still ain't got over that Tuffy dog, have you, Steel?"

"I mean what I say. I'm going to slit your damned throat, and bleed you like a hog . . . else you talk to that boy of yours."

The bee buzzed about Rust's mouth. He swatted it out of the air to the floor. The large man's eyes bulged, and emotion fired up the soul behind them—one that had grown perverted over the years. Fixx saw his cousin longed desperately to grab up the knife. Fixx had always beaten him when it involved dexterity and speed. Rust won only when he brought his strength into play—his overpowering weight and muscle. But Honus wasn't ready, no matter how much he wanted it. Honus Rust, he saw, was not quite ready to die.

"Go ahead on. Grab it up. Be rid of me. Give it a spin. Hell, you might beat me today." Fixx straightened on his chair, and added, "But I doubt it. I see you do too."

He sat there and watched as the sweat that'd been resting on the man's forehead began to drip over the lip of his eyebrows and seep into his eyes.

Honus shook his head to clear his eyesight, then chuckled softly. "Aww, go to hell, Steel." He attempted to make it out to be a joke, the way he always had as a child when Fixx had outflanked him.

"This is no laughing matter, Honus. I mean for you to speak to that boy. I ain't never been so serious about a thing in all my life. If you don't, well, that means I'll have to. You can bet I won't be near as liberal with him as you've been all his born days."

Rust picked up the half-smoked cigar, puffed at it, watched the rise of the smoke again, and attempted to give the impression of deliberation, not willing, as it looked to Fixx, to give up in a rush. After a time, he dropped the cigar to the floor, crushed it out, picked up his glass, and downed the liqueur in a gulp, as if it were lemonade.

"I'll talk to him, Steel. This ain't no matter to break up our families over."

Fixx reached out and plucked the knife from the wood, and placed it back into its sheath. He stood up and pushed the chair back at the same time. "No, sir, I don't see no reason to break up our family relationship over this here." He walked down from the stage of the gazebo. At the bottom step he turned again to Rust and said, "Nor to die over, neither."

He strode back to the steps of the porch, took to his horse, and mounted up. Before leaving, he leaned forward in the saddle, with both hands on the pommel. "Better watch out Adair Murphy don't hit you over the head with his anvil. I doubt he'd appreciate the way you been abusing his wife."

He spurred the horse, rode from the yard, and left Rust there to sit and think. He felt his cousin's eyes on him all the way up the lane to where it turned into the Hazlett Church Road that headed north toward Witness Tree Station.

Fixx waited for the boy to come to the house, waited for him to ask his permission to marry Molly. Jorod wasn't such a bad kid, he figured. His father had pampered him. This was his main weakness. They both were young, Molly and Jorod. The boy still had plenty of time to accept responsibility. Maybe he'd grow up after the child was born.

Fixx waited awhile longer, waited and waited until he could wait no more.

Clive, his eldest boy, was eighteen. Redman was seventeen. Redman seemed mature beyond his years, serious and reliable. Clive was a joy to talk to and be around. Everything to him seemed to be a laugh—life, a song he should sing with his head thrown back. But he was as big, at eighteen, as strong, as was

Fixx. He needed to push him though, show him the way. He in no way had a weak spirit, but was of good nature and joyful.

Redman was a lean hound who could tackle a wolf. He couldn't match Clive in strength, but could wear him down, and out, from sheer determination.

Fixx figured the memory of the gazebo talk had receded in Honus's mind. His cousin hadn't bothered to talk to the boy, of this he felt certain. He was aware of Jorod's habit of going off to town on weekends. So he sat and waited until one Sunday at midday. He called for the boys to saddle three horses. They rode off toward Witness Tree Station with his wife, Olivia, watching from the porch. His young son Enos stood with his mother. He waved, and they returned the wave as they rode out of the barn lot headed for town.

CHAPTER TWO

A wet-weather spring bubbled up out of the earth three miles from Witness Tree Station. A large copse of willows ringed the spring. The Fixx men stopped there, and while their horses were drinking, Fixx cut three long, keen switches with a pocketknife. Both sons looked on with wonder, unable to question their father. When the bellies of the horses sloshed with water, the men mounted up, and rode slowly the rest of the way into town.

Late in the afternoon, Fixx, seated on a bench in front of the courthouse, spotted Jorod as he staggered out of the apartment of the widow of a merchant who was a year dead. At least he hadn't been in the arms of a whore, for whatever small consolation that might bring Fixx. Jorod lurched to the back door of Big Boy Hines's tavern to buy Sunday spirits, the way most of the men in the area did. Minutes later, he reappeared, a bottle of whiskey tucked beneath an arm. Fixx and the boys watched him enter Henry Ives's livery barn.

A few minutes later, he emerged from the barn on a chestnut gelding. They watched him cut up the street at a slow trot, taking an occasional swig from his bottle. Fixx held tight for five minutes more, and when Redman appeared to grow impatient and about to give up, Fixx rose from the heavy oak bench on the courthouse lawn, snapped his pocketknife shut, slipped it in a pocket and walked to his horse. The boys followed. Both of them by now, he realized, had figured out by observation what he had in mind.

The Fixx men lagged back out of sight save for an occasional glimpse of Jorod, as he crested a treeless ridge. They passed the wet-weather spring and rode on. They paced Jorod, staying a quick gallop behind, then rode on past the lane that led up to Fixx's home, following him still. They met several buggies headed to church for the evening services in the small community of Hazlett. The church was nothing more than a small Baptist church and meeting place, serving as a polling site as well, which saved the outlying ranchers from traveling the extra distance into Witness Tree Station to vote. Fixx nodded to the churchgoers, apologized for being in a rush and explained that he couldn't stop to converse, which was their warmest desire, as he was well aware.

In sight of a tall, post oak tree forty feet off the road, Fixx got up his horse in an easy canter. The boys kicked up their own mounts, caught up to him, and rode alongside. Sunset loomed red with a sharp edge to it upon the horizon, announcing another pretty day tomorrow. Ahead of them, Jorod's head lolled to the side, jerked erect again, then after a few seconds, lolled again to his chest.

"Grab his reins, Redman," Fixx said. He turned to Clive. "If Jo fights, you'll have to help me with him."

"Sure, Pap."

"You can handle him, can't you?"

"Always could. I don't see where nothing's changed."

Fixx kicked up his horse. The animal leapt ahead in a full run, dead on toward the rider napping in the saddle.

Jorod jumped awake when his chestnut gelding tossed its head high. It nickered, startled and shied. Jorod attempted to turn to the men. Redman latched onto the horse's reins, and brought the creature to a quick halt amidst a violent dust storm that the horse had kicked up.

"Redman?" Jorod said. He looked at them with surprised eyes, as startled as the gelding. "What the hell? Uncle Steel, what's going on?" Jorod had called Fixx "Uncle" since childhood.

Fixx said, "Been expecting to see you over at the house, Jo. Olivia's been expecting you too . . . and Molly's kind of been looking forward to seeing you again."

"Lord, you scared me shitless. I been too awful busy for socializing here of late."

"We were seeing quite a lot of you there for a while. Must've had more time on your hands back then."

"Yeah, well, things've changed. Pap keeps me busy. He's been doing a lot of traveling. Me and Hughie've got our hands full. I'll be back over there soon. I kind of miss Aunt Olivia's cooking. Mrs. Murphy ain't much of a cook."

"You're right about that, Olivia's a fine cook. I 'spect if we went up to the house right now, she'd be happy to set an extra plate."

Jorod attempted to take back his reins, but Clive jerked his own horse up against the side of the gelding, and Redman held Jorod's reins in a tight fist.

"Give me my reins, Redman. I got to go home. What'n hell is this, anyhow?"

Fixx's cigarette had burned down almost into his bushy gray mustache. He spat the stub from his lips, and said, "Haul your sorry ass down out of that saddle, Jorod."

An explosive fire of panic flamed up in Jorod's eyes, and he attempted to kick up his animal. He couldn't move his legs, though, clamped in tight, with a horse on each side of his gelding. The tetchy animal threw its head, reared up, and came close to unseating its rider. Then, when its front feet struck earth, Jorod Rust's "uncle" backhanded him full in the face with one of his work-hardened hands.

Jorod struck the ground flat on his back, unable to sit up, breathe, or likely even wonder at the full extent of the danger staring down at him from the saddle as he attempted to gasp air into his deflated lungs.

Fixx and Clive dismounted, and one on each side, dragged Jorod through the dust of the road, to the lone post oak tree, the one tree of any size within a half-mile.

"Stretch his arms around the tree, Clive," said Fixx. He drew from his rear pocket a length of leather pegging string.

Fixx tied Jorod's wrists together, binding his arms to the tree. He brought out another string, and tied his ankles to the tree as well. He stepped back, breathing heavily from the exertion and the tension, and from a fair amount of remorse.

"I reckon when we're done here, Jo, you'll have a different way of looking at things."

"You ain't going to leave me out here, are you, Uncle Steel? Don't go off and leave me tied out here aside the road."

"Naw. I ain't going to leave you out here. We'll boost you back on your horse in a bit, and send you home."

Fixx stepped to his horse, untied the willow switches, and took them back to the tree where his cousin once-removed stood bound tight. He dropped two and kept one in hand.

He took a practice swing with the switch.

The air filled with a shrill scream as the switch slashed through it.

The realization of what was clearly about to happen to him cut through his whiskey-dulled mind. Jorod said, "Uncle? Jesus now, Uncle Steel!"

Fixx struck the boy, using the strength of his shoulders, his full weight behind the swing.

Jorod released a startled sigh before the full awareness of pain cut through to his senses, then cried out in amazed protest.

"Jesus. Uncle Steel. Jesus."

"You ain't hurt yet, Jo," Fixx said. "Not as much as you're going to be."

He brought the switch back behind his shoulder and launched it forward. He staggered when it struck Jorod, his knees buckling from exertion as the switch slashed deeply into Jorod's back.

"Jesus. Jesus. Jesus!"

"Yeah," said Fixx. He spoke through lips, gummed now from stress, doing a job he allowed should've fallen to the boy's father years ago. "I 'spect you should call on the Lord, Jorod. He's the only one I know can help you now. Pray I fall down dead. That'd help you some, I reckon."

He lashed out again with the switch, and after each strike, he stood back to assess the damage. Once more, the switch struck Jorod's back. Then again, and again. Jorod trembled from pain and shock. He would've fallen to the ground if not for the leather that bound his arms to the tree.

At length, the switch grew frayed. Fixx tossed it aside, bent to where he'd dropped the other two, and stood erect with a fresh one. Later, the second one broke as well, and Jorod's body quaked and trembled like leaves in the wind.

The third switch was the most fearsome of the three. It seemed indestructible.

"Please, Uncle Steel, please. I'll do right. I'll do right now." His head slumped hard against the tree, and he passed out.

Fixx struck the boy twice more after his concession. He looked at the switch in his hand as if it were a live snake, tossed it away, went to the boy, and cut him down. The savage caning had torn up Jorod's shirt. Rivulets of blood flowed down his back onto his hips. Fixx saw several large ridged welts pop up beneath what remained of the shirt.

Fixx had no water with which to revive the boy. But when he looked to Jorod's gelding, he saw the neck of the whiskey bottle protruding from the saddle bag. He fetched it. It was practically full yet. He poured whiskey into a cupped hand, and bathed Jorod's face until at length he opened his eyes.

He allowed Jorod Rust to regain some of his senses, for he wanted to impress him with the gravity of what he had to say. Jorod awoke. He sobbed in misery and pain.

"Can you hear me, Jo?" Fixx said.

Jorod continued to sob, to moan.

Fixx took him by the shoulder. He shook him until he opened his eyes again. "Can you hear me, Jorod?"

"Yessir." He spoke through wet, slobbering lips. His chest heaved and bowed now, like a bank-tossed fish.

"I mean for you to come to the house next Sunday. You hear me?"

Jorod Rust nodded with vigor.

"What'd I tell you?" Fixx said.

"Come to your house next Sunday."

"You're going to ask me and Olivia for Molly's hand in marriage. I guess you heard that there too, didn't you?"

Jorod nodded. "Yessir. Ask for Molly's hand in marriage. Yessir. I did. I heard that."

"You want a drink of this here whiskey?" Fixx offered.

"No . . . sir."

Fixx sniffed down the neck of the bottle. "Any time you need whiskey, come to me. No need for you to drink this here shotgun-whiskey."

"Yessir."

Fixx still held the bottle in his hand. "Two weeks from today . . . week after you ask for Molly's hand, we'll have the wedding. Have it at the Hazlett Baptist Church. How's that sound? I hope you ain't busy that day."

Jorod failed to answer.

"Speak, now! My aunt's memory would never allow me another night's rest if I killed you."

"No, sir. I won't be busy." Jorod grew more alert with every second that passed.

Fixx said, "Because, if you got plans other than marriage, I reckon you better change 'em."

"No plans. No, sir. No plans, other than marrying Molly. That's the very thing I want to do."

Fixx turned to his sons. "Boys, put him in his saddle."

Clive and Redman jumped and lifted Jorod back into the saddle. Fixx stood and watched. Then with the bottle still in his hand, he sniffed again into its neck, made a disgusted face and tossed it into the weeds.

Jorod sat in the saddle, reins in hand. Fixx walked over. "After the wedding, I 'spect we'll all meet back at my place. We'll have us a fine time. I'll hire some fiddlers and a caller and have a dance. Be plenty of fine food, plenty of whiskey. Might have to exercise a little caution drinking, and not act too rowdy. Some of Olivia's friends are hellish on religion."

"Yessir," said Jorod Rust.

Fixx stepped to the side. "I 'spect you can go home, Jo. We've settled everything. Go on home. Sleep easy. Daylight comes early this time of year."

"Yessir." He got up the horse in a slow, easy trot, lolling again in the saddle, from pain this time, riding up the road toward his father's ranch.

Fixx heard the sound of his sobbing for quite some time, listening, with his sons alongside. Jorod faded into the approaching darkness.

CHAPTER THREE

Eight Years Later

The ranch hand, Batch, had worked on the Rust place since he was thirteen years old, six years ago. His mother had died when he was twelve. He'd never known his father. After his mother died, his grandmother, a widow woman, took the boy in with the intention of raising him. Fate, as it usually does, took a hand in the matter, though, and she too died within a year of the death of her daughter. Afterward, the boy fended for himself on the streets in the town of Staley.

Hugh Rust, Honus Rust's elder son, full grown and well respected in the area, with the reputation of being a man who knew ranching like no other, heard of Batch's dilemma. He took him in. Now, after many years, everyone knew Hugh regarded the boy as his best hand.

Batch watched the blacksmith, Adair Murphy, finish shoeing his gelding, his own personal property, one of the few things in the entire world he actually owned. The sky was filled with snow, although it'd been clear when he'd rolled out of his bunk to start his day. It started snowing a short time after breakfast, and now the wind picked up strength and blew snow into the faces of the two men, where it stung their unprotected skin. The gelding's tail blew about in the wind, like a flag on a pole.

Adair Murphy's enormous bicep muscles rippled and Batch

watched them roll freely beneath the man's heavy, long-sleeved shirt.

"I figure this snow might amount to something," Murphy said. He stood up, finished. He placed an arm over the flat of the horse's rump, and peered at Batch on the other side.

"Yeah. You're likely right," Batch agreed.

He heard the front door of Honus Rust's enormous house slam shut. He looked over the back of his animal, over Murphy's head, and saw the young girl, Sarah Ellen Rust, Jorod and Molly Rust's eldest daughter, running down the steps. He took this as odd. Sarah Ellen wasn't a girl given to frivolous activity, except in play, which was seldom.

Adair slapped the horse on the flank, and stretched the kinks out of his back. Sarah Ellen came on in a run. Batch saw her hair stream out long behind her as she ran.

"Something must be wrong up at the house," Batch said, his eyes on the girl.

Both men stood and watched her run straight for them, bareheaded, without a coat, even though the cold blowing snow and sleet bit with fierce teeth.

"Mam's sick," the girl said, before she reached them. She thrust her hands out to them to beckon them forward. "She needs help . . . quick."

Batch listened as Murphy, who'd realized the seriousness of the moment, ordered Archer Payne, the horse wrangler, to saddle up and strike out for Witness Tree Station to search for Jorod, the little girl's father, for everyone on the ranch knew the missus expected another child at any hour.

Batch took the girl by the hand. She was seven or so years old, he was never sure, and walked her back to the house, although he had no idea what help he might provide. But he was ready to assist if he could. As they climbed the steps toward the porch, he looked and saw Payne flogging the sides of a chestnut horse into a gallop toward Witness Tree Station.

They entered the house and he shut the door behind them, moving into the marble-floored hallway, which led into the front parlor. He heard Molly Rust cry out urgently for her husband. He guessed she'd mistaken him for Jorod, and detected a note of relief in her voice, as if now she might at last receive help.

"Jorod," she called. "I need help. Fetch Dr. Hance."

He entered her bedroom with caution, and felt he'd stepped inside a place forbidden to him. When he stood at her bedside and saw the bloodied bed sheets, the rumpled bedcovers cast to the floor, he came close to freezing in place. Molly's face looked white as milk, robbed of its fat, left with a pale, almost-blue color. She was sprawled abed, face covered with heavy drops of sweat. Her lips, usually pink in health, looked tight, and were the color of an eggplant. A wide white ring of tension and pain encircled her upper and lower lips.

He couldn't speak, just stood there, unprepared for the scene he'd barged into.

In a weak voice, she said, "Mr. Batch. I thought you were Jo. Do you know where he is? I need him . . . bad."

"No, ma'am, I don't." He felt incapable of telling her that Jorod was in town drinking.

He watched the hope that'd flared in her face fade away. She brushed her hair with a hand, which too was bloody. As if all hope had flown, she said, "Then would you go and fetch Leona for me? Leona Reyes?"

"Yes, ma'am, I'll fetch her right now." He started to leap for the door, but she stopped him.

"On your way, please take my children to Mrs. Murphy. I can't take care of them in my condition. They're too young to see me like this." Her voice sounded weak and faded to him.

"I will, ma'am. I'll do that too." He hurried off again into the parlor.

He gathered the children, helped them on with their coats, which were thin and threadbare as if they were the youngsters of a destitute man, instead of the grandchildren of the richest man in the county. When finished, he herded them out the door, holding Honus in his arms, the youngest child, named for his grandfather.

"Molly asked me to carry these youngsters to your wife, Adair," he said to the blacksmith as he rushed past the shop. "Hitch a horse to the hack for me. She wants me to fetch Leona Reyes."

Adair hopped to then, and rushed toward the corral, directly behind the shop bordering the edge of the north pasture, for the horse. Snow blew frantically about him as he hurried. The wind-driven snow leapt from the ground and soared high into the sky.

By the time Batch dropped the children off at Joan Murphy's door and returned to the shop, the hack stood ready. He hopped aboard and cut the reins over the back of the animal, and they fled the yard at a fast pace and passed on into the curtain of snow that'd taken to falling harder.

Batch stepped to the ground in front of the small house Rust had often referred to as "that shack." A dozen thin, underfed cats rushed at him as if he had food for them, but parted like water before a boat, as he hurried straight through them toward the front door.

After bidding him to enter and on hearing Batch's request, the old man, Felipe Reyes, studied him with distrustful eyes through a thin screen of yellowish smoke from the cigarette he sat and smoked. "Why should I allow Leona to go with you?"

Felipe looked unknowably ancient to Batch. His eyes narrowed to thin slits as if he were a man of the Orient. He sat in a rough chair, straight-backed, the paint faded to the point where it could be any color except white, which Batch guessed had been its original color. The chair looked even more ancient than the man who sat upon it.

"She's dying, Señor."

"It's *Mister*," the old man said. "I've spoken English longer than most men in this area have been alive. If you speak to me in Spanish address me as *Señor*. Never in English."

Batch had heard of the old man's sensitivity in this regard from other men, but this was his first encounter with him, and his frankness took him aback. He nodded. "Yessir."

"Now, since you're not a doctor, how do you know she's dying?"

Felipe Reyes sat beneath stalks of drying tobacco, chilies and other herbs Batch couldn't identify. The herbs hung upon a string between two open ceiling beams. Behind Reyes, in a wooden frame of a deep walnut color, gilded by what Batch took to be gold, hung a faded painting of the Holy Mother. Reyes, himself, looked to Batch to be posing for his own painting.

"She looks to me like she is, that's all I can say."

"Because Rust now has an illness in the family, you feel you can come to my house for help. Honus Rust has nothing for me but contempt. There's a doctor in town. Dr. Hance'll be glad to do this service for him. With Rust's wealth, I'm sure he can pay with little hardship."

"Sir," he replied, "the missus—Jorod's wife—is bleeding to death. She's trying to have a baby."

Leona Reyes stepped into the room. She wrapped a heavy shawl of dark wool about her shoulders then pulled the hood atop her head like a cowl. She picked up a small bag that Batch figured held herbs, which she slung over a shoulder.

"I'll go with him, Father. A baby isn't responsible for the sins of its father, grandfather or of anyone."

The old man nodded and continued smoking.

Leona wouldn't allow him into Molly's bedroom on their arrival back at the ranch house. He was glad of this, for he'd seen more than enough the first time. But he had no trouble hearing Molly Rust crying out in pain. This hurt him as he sat upon the hearth, stirring the fire with a poker—nervous work intended to keep him busy.

Leona Reyes had told him to stay nearby in case she needed him for some chore, and so, he sat there, poised to jump up and assist her.

Once, she asked him to draw a fresh bucket of water and to fetch a clean drinking mug from the kitchen. This task eased his tightened nerves, but afterward, he sat alone with nothing to do, eager for it to be over. A heavy silence fell over the house. He hoped this was a good sign.

Later, he heard Molly cry anew, stronger than before. Leona Reyes rushed from the room. He watched her race down the long hallway into a back room. Shortly, she reappeared again in a run, arms laden with bed sheets, and disappeared into the bedroom. He kept an anxious eye on the hallway, and expected any moment for her to call out for him.

He waited another half hour before he heard any more. Then, he heard a weak, lamb-like cry. It sounded as if Molly was too weak to cry any louder than this brief whimper.

Minutes afterward, the front door burst inward, and bounced off the back wall. Jorod Rust, wide-eyed, staggered inside.

"What the hell're you doing here in the house, Batch? What's going on that's so urgent Murphy sent Payne to fetch me from town? Why ain't you out with Hugh and the boys? You on vacation?!"

Batch got to his feet and removed his hat in a sweep of deference to the son of the ranch owner. He smelled whiskey on Jorod's breath, as well as perfume. The man's eyes looked raw and inflamed.

"It's your missus, sir."

"Well, what about her?"

"She's having a baby."

"A baby? Hell, I already knew that. That's why I went to town in the first place."

Batch braced himself. "I think she's dying."

This cooled Jorod's blood for a time. He swept his hat from his head, allowed it to fall to the floor. "Dying? Are you sure?"

"No, sir. But she looks to me like she is. You bring the doctor?"

"Hell, no. Wasn't nobody told me she was dying. Who's with her?"

"Leona . . . Leona Reyes. Supposed to be great at these matters."

It grew ominously quiet in the room. Batch heard the wall clock tick off every second. He took to counting them, and when he reached twelve, Jorod stepped up into his face.

He was shorter than Batch, but possessed cruel, spite-filled eyes. Batch couldn't maintain his gaze, shamed that Jorod had stared him down.

"Who brought that woman into this house . . . ? She's a goddam Mexican witch."

"I did. I brought her here. Your missus asked me to fetch her."

Jorod placed his finger on the tip of Batch's nose. Batch allowed it to remain there, which acknowledged his employer's right of ownership, his own servitude.

He felt like knocking the man down, drawing his pay and leaving, but didn't. Instead, he stood there in all meekness, with Jorod's finger upon his nose.

"If my wife dies, Batch, you sonofabitch . . . if Molly dies, it'll be on your head. You hear me?"

31

"I heard you."

Jorod swung about, strode quickly down the hall and into his bedroom.

Moments later, he hustled Leona Reyes out of the bedroom. He held her by one arm, half dragging, half leading her. He paused at the front door, and stared at Batch with eyes filled with hatred, venomous as a copperhead snake.

"You fetched her here, Batch, drive her home . . . or let her walk. I don't give a damn which." He shoved Leona out the door. Leona had to run to keep on her feet. She ran across the porch, stumbled all way down the steps, but managed to keep from falling.

At the bottom, she swung about and presented a defiant face. "Molly'll die if someone doesn't help her. You have no idea what you're doing."

"I reckon that there's my own damned business, and none of yours." He flung her bag of herbs at her.

CHAPTER FOUR

Batch returned from taking Leona home. He found that Jorod had left again. The five Rust children were back from the Murphys'. They stared at him from where they sat upon the hearth of the fireplace. Their eyes were haunted with doubt, the terror, the odd events they'd heard inside their mother's bedroom. He felt Sarah Ellen, the eldest, was capable of glimpsing a tiny bit of the truth of what was taking place in there, much to her misfortune.

"Where's your father, Sarah Ellen?"

She stared at him from frozen brown eyes, transfixed with sorrow.

"Sarah Ellen?"

"He fetched us back from Mrs. Murphy's then left for town, sir."

"Who's with your mam?"

"Mrs. Murphy. But I think she might be sick. I heard a loud noise. I was too afraid to look."

He knelt alongside her, patted her shoulder. She caught him about the neck in a death grip. Soon all the children clung to him, and sobbed in muffled voices, all except for the boy, who stood back and stared into space from unconcerned brown eyes.

"You youngsters had anything to eat today?" He tried to keep his voice as carefree as possible, which was difficult to do when he looked into their faces. Batch was a man shackled to an exceptionally tender heart. He wasn't far from tears himself.

Sarah Ellen shook her head.

He helped them all on with their wraps, and hurried them out the door.

At the blacksmith's he turned the children over to Murphy's daughter, Irene, fifteen years old, who stood with downcast shy eyes in his presence. He'd noticed her observing him curiously ever since she'd turned fourteen.

"And see you feed them, Irene," Murphy told her. "Batch says they ain't had nothing to eat today."

Batch watched Irene lead the children off toward the blacksmith's house on their second trip there today. The Murphy's house stood fifty yards behind the blacksmith shop. The wind and snow trundled them along as if they were made of down. The snow swallowed them whole. The wind screamed now in long, drawn-out tortured waves.

"Sarah Ellen says she heard a loud noise in Molly's bedroom," Batch said, as the two men mounted the steps of Honus Rust's house. "Said she thought your missus was sick. She was too afraid to go look. I couldn't go in . . . they hung all over me like little possums."

"Joan's too damn nervous for such as this. I told Jorod as much when he come to fetch her. Lordy me, I'd sooner have Irene care for me as her. She's always been spooky. Can't help it. She has a squeamish nature."

"I 'spect by now, Molly's probably dead. So much blood—I was fixin' to puke."

"Well," said the blacksmith, "I figure Joan passed out. She can't abide the sight of blood. That's what them kids heard that spooked 'em. She's passed out and fell down."

"Well then," said Batch, "who'll clean up Molly for burying? Jorod and Honus won't allow Leona Reyes back on the place. Somebody'll have to go fetch Mrs. Fixx."

"Be a cold day in hell, when Honus allows any of them Fixxes back on the place. Since Fixx beat Jorod's ass that time, they're even less welcome than Felipe Reyes. I'll do it, I reckon. We'll have to say Joan did it, though. Jorod finds out I cleaned up his wife, he'd can me right away."

"You're right about that. Fact of the matter, I'm likely canned my own self, 'cause I fetched Leona."

"You found this job, didn't you?"

"It sort of found me, Mr. Murphy."

"A decent hand won't have to look long, Batch."

Molly Rust was dead when they entered the bedroom. Joan Murphy had fallen from her chair onto the floor, dazed. A small bruise showed on her forehead where she'd cracked it as she fell down in a faint. They helped her into the parlor and sat her down in one of Honus Rust's large leather-covered easy chairs.

"Molly died, Adair. I couldn't take it. I fainted. Molly never did have no chance ever since she entered this house."

"Somebody'll have to clean her up, Joan."

"You'll have to fetch Leona Reyes."

"Nope. Jorod's done run her off once today. That's why the job fell to you. I 'spect I'll have to do it myself."

Joan Murphy sat with her hands folded in her lap, head bowed. At length, she lifted her eyes, and they shone with the fire of a newfound strength.

"You can't do that, Adair. It ain't right for the girl."

"Somebody's got to do it," Murphy said. "If you'd drink it, I'd fetch you a cup of whiskey. I 'spect that'd give you the courage. Would you do it, Joan? If not, I'll have to clean the girl up myself. It's up to you."

She sat for a time in silent prayer then raised her eyes to Adair. "You scout about this house, and find me some whiskey. I ain't never swallowed no strong spirits in my life, but if that's what it takes to do this job, then, Amen, sir. That's what I'll do."

Adair brought her a flesh-colored coffee mug filled with reddish whiskey, passed it to her, and she sat as meek and quiet as one awaiting a long-gallows walk. She sipped, made a horrible face, and blew out her breath, shocked by its intensity.

It took her half an hour to finish the cup of whiskey, but when it scattered out through the breadth of her brain, she arose on sturdier legs, clearly buttressed, and entered the bedroom. Not once did she look back at the men. Batch figured she knew they both sat and appraised her, but was determined now to clean up the woman with the dead child still inside her.

Later, Batch prepared to mount to the saddle at the foot of the steps of Honus Rust's splendid house. He peered through squinted eyes at the fall of snow up in the orchard. Men up there were digging the grave that was to be the final place of rest for Molly Rust.

"Where're you going, Batch?" asked Honus Rust, the ranch owner. He'd approached from the rear yard, where he'd likely been on some misson. He stepped up with snow blowing in a mad swirl all about him. He caught onto Batch's saddle horn. "You got chores to tend, I 'spect. Ain't you?"

Batch never felt comfortable around the old man. He knew Rust disliked him for some reason.

"I figure somebody owes it to the Fixxes to tell 'em. . . . You won't, or can't. Whichever way, it 'mounts to the same thing."

Smoke from Rust's cigar blew away on the wind. He relaxed his jaws, removed the cigar from his teeth, and attempted to browbeat Batch into submission with a look.

Batch had allowed Jorod to browbeat him earlier. He stiffened his spine, determined to prevent it from happening to him twice on the same day.

"If you go," Rust said, "you'll go afoot. You ain't going to ride out of this yard on one of my mounts."

"This gelded horse's my own personal property, Mr. Rust."

Rust turned his enormous bulk to Murphy. Murphy stood nearby in the snow, hat in hand, with the wind about to tear his hair out by the roots. "This here's my animal, ain't it, Adair?"

Murphy squirmed in his boots. He said, "No, sir." He spoke fast, as if he wished to purge his brain of the words as fast as possible. "That creature belongs to Batch, sir."

Rust turned back to Batch, started to speak, changed his mind, stared angrily at Murphy for a second, then dropped his hands to his sides. He mounted the steps, entered the house, and banged the door shut behind him.

Batch and Murphy stared awhile into each other's eyes.

Batch coughed from nerves. "I'll be back later for my junk, Adair. If you would, I'd appreciate it if you'd go to my bunk and gather up my outfit. I got my mam's Bible in there. It has a bracelet of her mam's hair inside tied in a bow. Hate to lose that Bible. Has a couple of letters from my mam's pap in there. I don't much care about them ragged-assed clothes, but I'd hate to lose that Bible, them letters, and my grammam's hair-bracelet."

"I'll gather your outfit, Batch, and your last pay. Keep it all safe for you till you return for it."

Batch reached the Hazlett Church Road quickly. He looked skyward. The storm clouds swirled stronger and bucked wilder than earlier. Ugly gray skies sat level with the puny, low ridges. Snow stood above the gelding's hock joints and was falling much harder. He turned the horse into the blowing snow, and had second thoughts about the chore he'd undertaken.

CHAPTER FIVE

At nightfall, in the bitter cold, Batch stepped down from his horse to walk alongside his animal in the deepening snow. The snow slammed down so savagely he lost his way. Soon, he admitted he was lost. The wind ripped through the air and flung the snow in his face with the strength of a gale blown in without mercy, without let up, and displayed brutality that did not concede. It screamed like a tortured animal. Each hard brittle flake felt like a knifepoint as it struck his face. He'd underestimated the strength of the storm, and by the time he realized he should've stayed home, it was too late to turn back. His hands were stiff and wooden. His toes were numb as well.

He figured old man Fixx would find him in the spring or one of his boys, Clive or Redman. Stumble upon what the coyotes left of him.

He tried to beat down such thoughts, but found it difficult with the wind in his face, cursing him. The area ranchers always hung lighted lanterns from their bell poles in storms like this. If he struggled on, stayed erect, he'd find a house by accident, if nothing else.

Since he left the saddle to lead his horse, he felt warmer. This could be his imagination, but he clung to the thought. He peered into the heavy snow, but it was like trying to look through a solid wall that shifted its shape with every blink of his eyes.

Wind whistled sharply through the hair at his ears, and occasionally sounded as if far-off voices were pleading for mercy somewhere out there in the storm.

He now trudged through snow above his knees. When he'd left the Rust ranch, it'd been a fraction over the hock-joints of his animal. The storm had caught him out. An early storm. He'd known storms of this magnitude before, but couldn't recall one this savage this early in December.

The worst weather always came in late January, early February. This one, though, he felt was one of a kind. But he'd been compelled to make the trip. Any worthy man would've done the same, wouldn't he? He'd heard this call to help, failed to think twice about it, went ahead, and did what he felt his grandmother and mother would've cheered him on for.

Steel Fixx deserved to know his daughter was dead, killed by a neglectful husband. Molly had suffered at Jorod's hands. Rust had spoiled Jorod for so long, there'd been no way he would ever grow up straight, and he hadn't. Batch had seen Jorod let his few duties at the ranch go. He lived for nothing more than going into Witness Tree Station, to drink and whore about town, and when he did come home, Batch had watched and heard him terrorize his wife and children. All the hands had turned a blind eye to this mistreatment because they needed the job, and did nothing to stop it, as if it were none of their business.

After a time of blind blundering about, Batch brushed against something in the murk and chaos of the storm. He couldn't see what it was for sure, but it gave slightly when he brushed it. It was living. He wondered if he'd stumbled into Steel Fixx's cattle herd.

He felt hope spring up in his heart. The Fixx herd always rode out bad storms in a growth of cedar trees near their barn. He knew this and figured he was close to the Fixx place. He stopped, and stood still. The horse at his neck snuffled. The animal had noticed the same thing he had and much earlier, he figured. If he hadn't been so lost in thought, he might've discovered it sooner by watching and listening to the creature.

He felt another brush-by. He bumped against something, a straight-on encounter. He reached out, felt the snow-covered back of a cow, and his mind battled with his emotions. He heard many animals as they shuffled about and bunched up tightly. The wind in the tops of the cedars rushed away, a unique sound, like the earth itself mourning. Truly, he'd stumbled into the cedar growth.

He squinted. Saw a dark hump in the snow, then another, and another. Soon, the sound of so many cattle breathing in such a closed space grew machine-like the deeper into the herd he penetrated, low, faintly distinguishable above the roar of the charging wind in the tops of the trees, but there, steady as a clock at work.

He banged into a tree, stopped, and rested his forehead against it. Relief spread throughout his worn body, his nerves relaxing. The cattle emerged one by one from the storm that hid them, diffuse but visible in the swirl of the snow. Steam arose from their backs.

The great furnace inside each of them propelled them, pumped life into them with miraculous force. Their internal furnace demanded so much fuel that in winter they grazed without cessation in order to maintain enough heat to prevent freezing.

He wondered how long it'd been since they'd been fed. Steel Fixx, his boys—the two grown boys, that is—were savvy to harsh winters, had learned long ago how to read the signs that foretold storms, a trait Batch had ignored in his haste. They must've fed the herd before the storm hit. But it might be that they, like him, were surprised, felt it too early in the season for such a storm to strike.

He figured that if they hadn't fed the cattle before the storm, they'd now have to wait. No wheeled wagon could roll through snow this heavy. Some of the drifts he'd struggled through were four-foot deep in places. All the ranchers had sledge runners they attached to their wagons in heavy snows, of course, but it took time to swap wheels for runners.

Batch recalled that the Fixxes owned three huge wagons for use during haying season, as well as to feed the cattle in snows of severe depths or long duration. They also had three spans of oxen with which to haul them. That would do the trick, but they would need to repeat it in a couple of days. Cattle lost so much weight when left to fend for themselves that by spring, what few that survived, would be practically worthless, and likely would never recover all their lost weight. So Fixx needed to feed them until the storm broke, until the thaw, or until the hay ran out, whichever came first.

It was hard to believe the Fixxes would run out of hay, though. Their huge barn—a combination barn and warehouse— held an enormous quantity of hay. But Batch couldn't survive until the boys came again to feed. He knew that. If they hadn't fed already, it might be morning before they swapped out the wheels for runners. By then, he'd be stiffly frozen.

He couldn't survive much longer. As soon as he warmed himself a bit, he had to strike out for the Fixx barn. He lifted his head from the tree, staggered deeper into the herd. A short time later, he saw cattle all about him when the wind blew the snow away for a brief time.

It'd be warmer in the center of the herd. He headed there, drew the gelding along with him, reins tied to his left wrist.

As he neared the center of the herd, he saw a large dark mass rear up, and knew in an instant that it was one of the Fixxes' wagons. He saw a second dark mass, to his left, smaller than the first one. He staggered over to it. The Fixxes had forked the hay out onto the snow. Then farther off to his right he saw another dark mass, another hay pile, with a large group of cattle amassed about it, feeding.

He spoke aloud his thoughts through frozen lips, "Storm surprised 'em. Tried to beat the snow, hadn't changed out the wheels. Left that one wagon, took its span of dumb brutes, hitched 'em together. Pulled the other two empty wagons home like that."

Even with the extra span of oxen, he figured it must've been a tough haul. He saw in his mind the undercarriages of the wagons as they clogged and balled up with snow. It must've been much like hauling the earth itself.

"They was forced to do it, to drag them other two wagons home. Else these cow-creatures would all freeze to death."

His heart skipped a beat with hope. Maybe they'd left recently. He might've missed them by a few minutes.

He drew the horse along, stepped deeper into the herd for the warmth, to allow his animal to feed. If the men had left recently, he might find their tracks.

The gelding raised its head from the hay, snuffled low, full now with hay. He drew it back out of the herd then trudged off, in what he guessed was the direction of the barn. The heat of the herd had warmed him a bit. The time had come to move on, to find the ranch, to fulfill the rest of his sad mission. He slogged through the snow halfway around the herd in search of any drag marks left by the wagons. As he began to doubt himself, he found wagon-wide wheel marks in the snow. To his eyes, they looked more like the tracks of children at play in the snow than what they really were. The discovery filled his eyes with tears, but at the same time, he chuckled under his breath from the joy of it.

"Too blamed close," he muttered. "Could've missed them as easy."

But he hadn't. No use to fret over what might've happened, he figured, and the tears froze on his cheeks. As soon as he left the herd, the cold leapt back into his bones, only much worse.

He mumbled to himself, "It's colder'n the grave."

The horse stepped closer. He gave a little as it bumped into him. Man and beast shared body heat as they lunged on through the snow.

He grew watchful so he wouldn't get knocked down. The wind howled like the pathetic protests of condemned souls. It created large whirlwinds of snow, thick and impossible to see through. He set his mind, and battled straight on through the whirlwinds. The blown snow covered the front of his coat. As the wind screamed in his ears, he had nothing but the vague, distant hope of survival to sustain him.

Chapter Six

Enos Fixx, fourteen years old, youngest child of Steel and Olivia Fixx, emerged from the house, bundled in a heavy fur-lined mackinaw a tad too large for him, handed down to him from Redman, his older brother.

Earlier, as he pleaded his case to his mother to allow him to join his father and brothers in the barn, he'd peeked outside and saw where the blown snow had drifted up against the immense barn in drifts of seven and eight feet, which gave the structure the appearance that it was low-built to the ground. The footprints that his father and siblings had created earlier, as they trudged to the barn, were mere ghosts, nearly hidden by the heavy snowfall and the drifts of the battering-ram gusts of winds.

Redman would yell at him when he got inside, he figured. Enos oftentimes thought Redman yelled at him more than did his mother, but his father would welcome him. His older brother, Clive, clung always to a cheerful mood. He was one to laugh and joke. His father had often said that Clive spoiled Enos. At times, his father rebuked Clive, saying he would ruin Enos, set back his mental maturation. But Enos noticed that none of this ever cut through Clive's delightful behavior. He was always bursting with happiness and joy like a seedpod with split seams, its fluffy seeds spilling out in a hefty breeze.

He saw the honey-colored glow of the lantern, swinging away, attached to the bell-post in front of the barn. The wind whipped it about with savage force as though someone stood below it beating it with a stick. The muted glow of the lantern looked pretty to him, soft yellow and misty, as it swayed back and forth in the whistling gale. A light left out as a guide in a nighttime storm would warm the heart of a traveler with hope. He imagined the elation it would bring someone lost in a storm.

Enos was tall but still the snow reached above his knees, and the hard walking tired him. He crossed drifts as though crossing a stream nearly thigh-high. By the time he reached the barn door, he huffed and puffed heavily from exertion.

He lifted the latch to open the door, eager to escape the storm. The wind, though, seemed to sense its chance. It ripped the door from his hands, and slammed it back against the barn's outer wall. The impact sounded like a close boom of thunder. He lurched for it, to set things right before his brothers, or his father, beat him to it. He dreaded what Redman would have to say.

But the force of the wind held the door trapped to the wall, and he was unable to move it. Soon, as he feared, all three men from inside the barn appeared. They shoved him inside then shut the heavy door.

"What on earth are you doing out here, Enos?" Redman said. He was mad, as Enos figured he'd be. "It sounded like the hinges sprung when the door slammed against the side of the barn that away."

"Leave my partner be, Redman," said Clive. "We're tight—me and Enos. Ain't that right, Enos?"

Enos smiled as best he could, but he still chafed from Redman's anger. Clive knocked Enos's hat to the floor, and gave his head a brisk drubbing with the knuckles of a fist.

"Well, the boy ain't got no business being out here in this weather," Redman said.

Steel Fixx spoke from where he'd resumed work on the

wagon, "We're about done, anyhow. We'll all soon be in out of it. Quit fussing, and help me with this flange."

Enos looked about the barn, scanned the work area by the light of lanterns hung from nails driven half-length into heavy beams that bore the weight of the upper floor and the roof. They'd finished converting one of the wagons into a sledge, and all the second one lacked was the one flange that'd given them the trouble Fixx had referred to.

Enos took down a lantern and left them to their work. They'd brush him aside as always, and he didn't feel like butting heads with Redman. He walked deeper into the barn where the mules stood, heads up and alert to every movement. The saddle horses were grinding away at oats in the manger, and the dull brutish oxen peered at him briefly with eyes that seemed to lack curiosity, fear, or any other emotion.

When he reached the end of the long row of stalls, he opened a door and entered another room. This was the large room where the family stored lumber and white oak staves for the making of barrels for the aging of the whiskey that Steel Fixx distilled. A tall copper pot stood inside the large room, too, as well as the vats where the corn, barley and rye fermented. The whiskey itself aged here, in barrels in racks against the far wall.

This room belonged to Enos. For neither of his brothers showed any aptitude for whiskey making. His father took great pride that he had a talent for the work. Enos even enjoyed making the staves, a chore the older boys looked on with distaste because of the numbing repetition required. The boy worked at it with the thought in mind of what the outcome would bring.

He had the required patience for the job, and not merely the making of barrel staves, but for all things connected in the process of making whiskey. He had a nose for the vats, could tell by smell when the grains were properly fermented, and always watched the bubbling, fermentation process with the eye of a mother hen watching over a brood of chicks. In this room alone, he became the equal of his brothers. His father had already informed him the whiskey business would one day fall to him, and he learned all he could from his father, who made the best whiskey in this land. Folks traveled from as far as fifty miles and more to cart back home with them a barrel of Steel Fixx's whiskey. Enos intended to be ready for the day when he'd carry on the tradition, one that'd been handed down from father to son, since the first members of the Fixx family entered the new world back in the early eighteenth century.

He glanced up to where the whiskey rested—aging in white oak barrels. Then right away, he turned his attention to the small hideout he'd built in the wall several years ago as a place to hide away by himself. He no longer used it, had outgrown it, but so far hadn't sealed it up.

"Enos," he heard his father yell. This drew him back from his daydreams. "Come on. Let's go to the house. We're finished out here."

He took a last look about the room, and left, making sure to shut the door tight behind him.

He saw his brothers snuffing out the lights when he returned to the main room of the great barn. He blew out his own lantern, and re-hung it. Only one lantern remained lit. It cast dark shadows about the room that threw the images of his father and brothers up against the north wall, giant-like.

"Come on, Enos," said Clive. "Mam's probably got supper on the table. You don't want to make us late. She'll pinch your ears for you . . . after Redman's done with you, that is."

With the work finished, even Redman spoke up in a dandy humor. "Yeah," he said. "And you know how much a frozen ear hurts when you pinch it."

"Yes. I do," said Enos. "You won't fool me on that one again."

Redman grabbed for one of his ears. "Aww, come on. Let me

show you again."

Enos thrust aside his brother's hand, and appealed to his father. "Pap."

Suddenly, the barn door sprang open with a tremendous crash, as if the world was ending. It banged loudly against the outer wall, the same way it had when Enos had entered.

A creature stood in the doorway. The glow of the lantern as it swung from the bell-pole backlit the intruder. The creature looked to be of a different breed than any the boy had seen before. No one spoke, not even the creature, snow-covered from head to toe. His mustache was white with frost, so were his eyebrows. They all stood and stared at the newcomer as if he'd fallen from the sky. The wind screamed and blew snow inside the barn.

The boys' father must've recognized it as a member of the human family. He stepped forth and said, "My word, man. How long you been out in this?"

The man seemed to lack the strength to speak. He stood and stared dumbly as if he'd entered a new, unbelievable dimension, free of snow and wind. Enos couldn't believe his eyes. Soon though, he recognized the man—Batch, from the Rust place.

"Shut the door, boys," Fixx said, and stepped forward, took hold of Batch, and tugged him inside, with the horse right behind him.

By the time the boys shut the door and reentered the barn, Fixx had freed the reins from Batch's wrist. He located a couple of horse blankets and wrapped them about the shoulders of the specter.

"Drag the saddle off that animal, Enos," Fixx said. "Brush him down. Massage them legs right sharp."

As Enos worked on the horse, his father guided Batch to the tongue of the wagon they'd transformed into a sledge. He pushed him down onto it, untied the handkerchief from beneath

Batch's chin, stiff from the frozen breath he'd expelled, and then removed his hat. Fixx set to work massaging the wanderer's face, his neck, going gently over his ears. He rubbed briskly in his hair, his scalp, to bring back life and warmth to the snow-covered man.

Enos finished rubbing down the horse, and stood erect.

"Enos, run to the house," his father commanded. "Tell Mam to heat up the bricks. We got to get this man in a warm bed, right away. Tell her we'll be along, soon as possible."

"Should I come back, Pap?"

"No," said Redman. His voice left no wiggle room.

"Help your brother with the door, Redman," Fixx said.

Enos plunged back into the storm, and made what haste he could as he leaned forward into the wind, slogging through the snow toward the house, two-hundred feet away.

Later, the men reached the house, and entered the large room with its huge fieldstone fireplace. Batch saw the cheery-red flames of the fire lick high into the chimney. He wanted to go to the hearth and sit there, gaze into those flames, soak in the heat, and summon life back into his body. The men attempted to prevent this, though, for they intended to put him in the bed Mrs. Fixx had prepared for him, hot bricks at its foot, beneath the heavy covers and the upper feather tick.

Batch grew insistent. He tugged against them, motioned toward the fireplace, and indicated his desire to sit there. At length, they conceded, assisted him, and sat him down on the wide hearth.

The frozen man stared into the welcome, bright red flames, and shucked the weight and burden death had placed on him. He felt for the first time he'd actually survived the storm.

The difficult part had now begun, though. He knew this, and wondered how he'd ever be able to spout the terrible words he'd traveled so far in this horrid weather to deliver.

Mrs. Fixx appeared with towels in hand that steamed from the heat of the kitchen range. She wore a pair of gloves, which must have belonged to the boys, so she wouldn't burn her hands. She reached him, shook out the towels, tested them by placing them an inch from her own face, and set them gently against his cheeks, and around his neck. He shivered from the delightful shock of such luxurious warmth.

Her tender touch, her kindness, traveled the length of his body. How, he wondered, could he ever summon the courage to tell this gentle woman her daughter was dead?

Olivia Fixx massaged his ears with the warm towels.

"I know you've brought us pain, Mr. Batch. No man travels in such a storm to chat."

With those words, having battled death and won, and facing such compassion that he felt springing from the woman's breast, he broke down completely and wept. He saw the men all turn away. Through his tears, he watched them seek out places to divert their eyes. Olivia Fixx left the room. She reappeared moments later with a cup of coffee so hot steam lifted from it in a cloud, like a long tail that drug along behind it. Batch's hands had cramped into knots from the cold. He couldn't clasp the cup. Mrs. Fixx held it to his lips. He sipped slowly. The warmth, the pleasing scent alone, was nearly enough to crumple his backbone. The heat of the fire behind him soaked into his very bones. This forced him to chuckle and cry at the same time.

He finished the second cup and started to hand it back to Mrs. Fixx. He felt his hands slowly loosening up.

"I 'spect that there's as fine a drink as I've ever had, Mrs. Fixx. Thank you . . . from my heart."

His voice croaked from lack of use and his condition, but he worked to strengthen it to deliver his message. The missus suspected bad news, as she'd already said. Still, it wouldn't be easy.

"Hold up your cup, Batch," Fixx told him.

Batch did as commanded. The mister poured bourbon, red-tinged and malt-scented, into the heavy enamel cup. He sipped the rich whiskey-flavored coffee. It had a mild scent of vanilla that caused him to think of Christmas, and of eggnog.

"I 'spect you might soon turn me out, Mr. Fixx. For the news I've brought you—ain't pleasant." Now the whiskey set to work coating his insides with a fine, slow-moving warmth.

"Most news ain't, Batch—to bring a man out in a storm. We'll have to live with it, I reckon. It's about Molly, ain't it?"

The ranch hand still found it difficult to speak. Olivia Fixx's honest concern for his well-being touched the softest spot in his psyche. He was unused to such kindly treatment. For a time, he almost grew angry, and felt he could've dealt with this much easier if not for their kindness.

"She's dead, sir. I found her trying to have her baby. Alone, save for her kids. I took 'em all to the blacksmith's house. Later Jorod fetched 'em back to the house.

"Earlier, I went over to the Reyeses' house—that Mexican Honus has tried to run off the place for years. Carried his daughter, Leona, to the house to see what she could do to help. Molly had asked for her. Leona tried real hard. She'd made some headways, but—"

His emotions overran him again, and brought him to an abrupt halt. He attempted to fight off the hard lump in his craw, but lost out. He felt the shame of tears hot on his cheeks. He spoke in a mighty rush to empty his burden, "If Jorod hadn't run Leona off, Molly might've made it. She was a comfort and aid to her. I felt sure."

"He run the woman off?"

"Yessir. Got mad at me 'cause I fetched her to his house. I

knowed Honus and the Reyeses was having problems, but Molly'd asked me to fetch her.

"That old Mexican man owns that little scope of land, right in the center of the Rust place, and he won't be bought out nor scared off. So Jorod didn't dare leave that man's daughter in the house to tend to Molly, and later have to explain it to his pap. But he didn't act none too concerned for her as it was. It wasn't nothing for a man to see. Nor a woman either, I reckon, far as that goes."

A bright hot fire rose in Fixx's eyes. Batch saw the man's fists ridge high with wide, knotty knuckles. He dropped his eyes from Fixx's awful gaze.

"I took the Mexican woman home. Time I got back, Jorod'd already left for Witness Tree Station again, after he'd brought in the blacksmith's wife. Mr. Rust's still mad over what you did to Jorod that time. Didn't want you to even know Molly died."

"Where were them grandchildren of mine all this time, Batch?"

"Sitting in the parlor by the fireplace, on the hearth like ducks in a row. They was staring hard, with huge round eyes.

"Tore my heart out, watching them youngsters. They knew something was amiss, but didn't know for sure what. That eldest one, though, I fear she knew. The least one, that boy, was mostly asleep but the rest of 'em was wide awake."

Redman went in a quick circle about the living room. His boot heels rang out loud upon the oak floor. After a time, he stopped, threw his hands high and in a shaky voice said, "Let's go, Pap. Let's go now."

Steel Fixx ignored him, dug out a paper and tobacco, and set about to roll a smoke. He stared into the flames as he built it. When finished, he stood with it in his mouth for a time, one hand at rest on Batch's shoulder, and at last, brought forth a match, struck it on a stone of the fireplace and lit up.

"What'd Honus say, when you told him you was coming here?" He pitched the matchstick into the flames of the fire, where it crackled and snapped, as it protested its demise.

"Pap," the ignored son said in a determined voice.

Batch swallowed the rest of the whiskey. "He said if I went, they wasn't no need in me coming back, for I'd no longer be working for him. I feel bad about this 'cause I still feel I owe the Rusts. Especially Hughie. He took me in, a starving boy over in Staley, six years ago."

Redman strode to the wall, and kicked over the hat rack in frustration.

"Redman," Olivia said. "No need to tear up the house."

"But, we got to do something," he said. Redman looked to Batch to be suffering from a pain far past his tolerance.

Fixx spoke, "Go to the kitchen, Redman. Let me hear this in peace."

Redman stormed off in a rage.

"You made a fine ride, Batch," said the rancher. "I want you to know you got a job—a home—on my ranch for as long as you live, if you want it. I appreciate your courage with all my soul. I don't intend to forget it."

"We got to put you to bed, Mr. Batch," said Fixx's wife. "Need to see about your toes, that they ain't frostbit."

"We'll put you in Enos's bed. He can bunk with Redman," Fixx said. "Come on now, and let's get you out of them clothes and to bed."

Fixx and Clive helped him into the bedroom and put him to bed.

Batch peered up from deep within the bedcovers. His toes on the right foot flamed up with pain, and throbbed with each beat of his heart.

"This ain't good," said Fixx, when he saw that Batch's entire left foot was turning black and had already swollen to twice its normal size.

Olivia abruptly slanted her eyes away from the frozen foot.

"Will they be all right? They'll be all right, won't they, once they thaw out?" He'd seen the reaction on Mrs. Fixx's face, and this frightened him as nothing else ever had.

When Olivia avoided his eyes and looked instead to her husband, the tough old rancher said, "It's bad, Batch. I'll not lie to you. You're a man, and should know the truth."

He tried to rise higher on the pillows but gave up. He sighed and fell deeper into the covers. "I should've got down sooner and walked. My own laziness might've done me in."

"You ain't one I'd call lazy. Man make a ride like you did." Fixx turned to Clive, who stood watching over his mother's shoulder as she spread a thick, black ointment over the toes of Batch's feet. "Fetch him another cup of whiskey, Clive."

Clive sprinted from the room.

"Feels like Satan is poking me . . . all over my whole body with his pitchfork," he said. He rolled about in bed from the pain.

"Can you feel your feet?" Olivia said.

"I can feel the right one. I don't think I can feel much in the left one. But, that right one hurts enough for both of 'em."

Clive returned and handed the cup of whiskey to his father.

"Drink this down, Batch," said Fixx. "It might help you rest some. It ain't much to relieve the pain, but it's all we got."

The whiskey sloshed over the tipped side of the mug. Batch battled it for half an hour before he conquered the entire cup. By this time, the whiskey kicked in, and granted him a bit of relief. Then in less than ten minutes after he'd drained the mug, he fell asleep.

In the parlor, Fixx spoke in a gentle tone to his wife, "I mean what I said, Olivia, about that boy having a home here for as long as he'll stay. Remember that if I die, and someone wants to run him off."

"Yes, sir," she said. "But it ain't nobody would ever want to do that."

"You hear, Clive, Redman . . . you too, Enos? That man in there in that bed has a home here for life if he wants it."

Clive said, "Yessir, we hear." He, as the eldest son, spoke for them all.

The matter looked settled, signed and sealed for all time.

"In a few days, I'm afraid he'll lose that left foot. He can't even feel it right now."

Fixx got to his feet, and strode off in search of the meat saw, file and whetstone. He needed to sharpen the saw keenly for what he had in mind.

CHAPTER SEVEN

Two days later, Batch's frozen foot had turned completely black. It was impossible for the doctor from Witness Tree Station to make calls in the terrible weather, even though the snowfall had slackened enough that a body could see all the way up to the pasture above the house where heavy snow-rollers were propelled across the fields by the strong winds.

The wind still roared around the corners and beat against the Fixx house and the sky was filled with shifting, blown snow all day long.

Batch's toes on his right foot were much better, requiring rest and time to heal. The left one, though, looked much worse, swollen in the grotesque exaggeration of a child's black ball. Olivia applied more black ointment upon the toes, being careful, going in between them to reach the webbing. She then wrapped them in clean rags torn from an old bed sheet she kept to use as bandages.

"Still can't feel your toes on this foot?" she said. She figured the foot would have to come off. "Your left foot, I'm talking about?"

Batch lay awake. He appeared so worn out to Olivia's eyes that he might've been a hundred years old, and his every word emerged slowly and painfully. "No, ma'am. I feel like it don't even exist no more." His head lolled and fell on his chest. Though he'd slept for more than twelve hours, he still looked exhausted, groggy and hung-over. He still needed sleep.

"Are you hungry, sir?" Olivia said.

He shook his head in answer, as if this were all he could do.

"I'll be in after a bit. You sleep now. You'll be hungry later. If you're anything like my own boys, that is." She shut the door with a soft click, and left him there already asleep, as if the earth had fallen out from under him.

"How's the foot look, 'Livia?" Steel Fixx said. Olivia had returned to the parlor. Steel, and the three boys as well, looked up from their fireside chairs, feet propped up on the hearth-stones, with the least son trying hard to emulate the actions of his elders, pushed forward in his chair, stretched out to his greatest length to touch the hearth with his toes.

"It don't look any better, Steel."

"Worse, then?"

"Much."

Fixx held the bone-saw he'd sharpened to a bright edge up to the light of the fire. The edged metal blade caught and turned the firelight, which ricocheted and flashed about the room with each roll of his hand.

He set the saw on the floor alongside his chair, dropped his feet from the hearth, drew out the makings and rolled himself a smoke. He worked to build the smoke with slow fingers, deliberating each move, each roll of the tobacco within the paper, deep in thought. He longed to be anywhere else but here right now, facing this chore, but he kept his face calm and proud. He realized his family looked to him for strength in these situations. He found he couldn't stare down the cigarette or the problem, that if he had to do it, he must strengthen his mind for the job. He continued to slowly roll the tobacco and paper with fingers hampered by a buildup of calluses on their tips, and idly thought that soon he'd have to pare them back if he wanted to continue crafting cigarettes or to perform any other fine work. Finished, he fetched a match from a vest pocket, struck it on the rigid leather sole of a boot and lit up.

Clive had gone to the barn earlier, brought back a flat piece of thick metal, and rigged up a handle from a pair of forge tongs. The metal plate set there now, in the fire, glowing red-hot, ready when needed.

Olivia went to the kitchen, and returned directly with a mug of coffee that she handed to Fixx. He took it, blew steam across the rim of the mug, and watched the fire, as he fought back the pain of losing his daughter, fighting the near terror because he must saw off Batch's foot. He managed to set aside his grief over Molly for the time being.

He told himself it'd likely be the same as cutting through the bones of a hog or a beef, but so far he hadn't quite made himself believe this. Eventually, he wore out all the possibilities, thinking about the accidents an operation like this might have lurking beyond the scope of his knowledge. He tossed his cigarette stub into the fire, stood up, and drained the coffee cup.

"Clive, you and Redman fetch the kitchen table in here." He noticed his youngest son attempting to act grown-up, and added, "You too, Enos. Go with 'em, lend a hand."

"I'll bring in the extra lamps," said Olivia. "You'll need plenty of light."

The boys set up the table, then located a long roll of new trace leather purchased months ago from the harness and boot maker in town. Redman cut the leather into short strips to restrain Batch because of the pain he'd need to tough out.

The table was ready. The lamps were lit and placed at the foot of the table. The leather straps ran beneath the heavy oak table, passing through metal rings screwed far into the underframe. The bone-saw, too, lay ready at hand upon the table. Fixx brushed the hair back off his forehead, and said, "Let's haul him in, boys."

Batch awoke as they lifted him from the bed. "What're you doing, Mr. Fixx?"

"We got to carry you into the parlor. It's lighter in there and warmer."

Batch saw the kitchen table set up in the center of the room, the leather straps, the bone-saw, and flung himself backward in an attempt to tear free of their grip. They were strong men, though. They held him firm.

"You ain't going to cut off my foot. No, sir. I forbid it."

The men placed him flat on the table, and Fixx said, "We got to, Batch. You already got you a fever. We can't allow the poison to build up no more'n it is already."

Batch clutched Fixx's shirtsleeve. "Give it more time. It'll soon be better."

"No. It's got to come off . . . now. If we wait till tomorrow, and it's worse, it won't matter if we take it off or leave it on—you'll die from blood poisoning in a few days. This way, all you'll lose is a foot."

"This the thanks you hand me? This how you repay me for riding over here, freezing my feet? You ain't cutting off my foot." He strained against the men again and again like a skittish horse.

"You have many years left in you, son. Don't be in such a hurry to jump into the grave. You'll be there soon enough as 'tis."

This stopped him for a time, but reluctance was still set hard upon his face.

"What's a ranch hand supposed to do with only one foot? I won't be no help to nobody. Not even myself. I beg you, Mr. Fixx, please don't cut off my foot."

Fixx watched heavy droplets of sweat pop like magic to the surface of Batch's forehead. Again, he wished he were anywhere but right here. But he banished the thought, feeling that negative thoughts often led to failure. For the boy's sake, he had to banish them . . . and he did.

"I told you, son . . . when you arrived, you got a job here, a home, as long as you want it. Don't trouble your mind about that."

Olivia washed Batch's forehead with a damp washcloth, tears in her eyes, but with her lower lip as firm and strong as ever. She shushed him with a soft purring voice, half song, half warm, gentle breath.

"You can't go this alone, Batch." Fixx poured a cup of whiskey. "Take this here, and drink it down. We'll get you as drunk as possible. We don't have nothing stronger, so Steel Fixx's whiskey'll have to do."

Batch accepted the whiskey, reluctance firm in his eyes. He stared at it for a second.

"Go on now," said Fixx, "before I take it away from you and drink it myself. Lord knows I need it bad 'nough."

Batch lifted the whiskey cup to his lips. He tipped the cup, and nearly drained it all. He gagged and came close to throwing up. When he could speak, he said, "Hard liquor ain't in my ever'day diet."

"Now," said Fixx, "I'll not be asking your referral of my whiskey. Not if you react to its taste in that manner. Drink it slower. Take all day . . . all night, if need be."

"Sorry. I sort of let it go down the wrong way."

Enos fetched him a cup of water. "Drink this. It'll go down better if you do. It'll taste better."

Batch accepted the water, sipped it, and said, "You an old-head whiskey drinker, Enos?"

"I'm too young. Pap won't allow it."

"Enos is my master-distiller. Has a fine knowledge of how it's made and an instinct for it. Now, drink up."

Batch downed the remaining whiskey and handed the cup back for a refill.

After he emptied the second cup, Fixx saw the ranch hand had become mildly inebriated. "Drink a few more. Let us know when you think it's safe to fasten you down. I advise you to get blind drunk, though."

"Drunk as a pig," said Redman, with a serious face.

Batch caught up his cup now with mounting strength and fearlessness. Redman's comment struck him funny. "I ain't never seen a drunk pig. Have you, Redman?"

"Nope, I ain't. Heard people make that reference though."

Batch downed half the cup, took it from his lips, and laughed, light-headed. "Drunk as a pig," he said. "Lordy me, I'm about to drift off to the ceiling." He laughed with an outrageous strength of humor.

"I did," said Fixx.

"Did what?" Batch said. Fixx's whiskey had waylaid his attention.

"Saw a drunk pig. When I was a youngster, one got into the old man's vat, and got drunk on it."

"Drunk as a pig?" Batch laughed in an uproar again that sounded like swift, running water.

Fixx laughed too, sensing the boy was about ready. "Drunker'n a pig. That pig was drunk as a hog."

Batch sipped again, and the wisecrack caught the whiskey between his mouth and the point of no return at the edge of the long slide down into his gullet. He laughed, and snorted whiskey out his mouth and nose at the same time. This time, though, he was equal to the strong drink, and conquered the gag reflex. He said, "Wish I had me a smoke."

Redman rolled one up, placed it between Batch's lips, stuck a lit match to its tip, and said, "That's all I can do, Batch. You'll have to puff it your own self."

Everything grew funny to the boy, leaning back on shaky elbows, smoking, laughing even when there was nothing to laugh at. He sipped the whiskey now and again. By the time he'd downed half of another cup, he tossed back his head and roared out an old hymn. Olivia joined in. Soon, they were all singing hymns.

In the middle of a song, Batch said, "Wonder what happened to that pig. The one got drunk."

"Why, it made the old man so mad he knocked it in the head with a sledge, slit its throat and we butchered it right there. It wasn't yet butchering weather, though, so we called in all the neighbors and had a feast of pig meat so it wouldn't spoil. Fiddlers and callers came and we had a fine time, almost everybody got drunk on the old man's whiskey and sleepy on his pig meat."

"Drunk as pigs?"

"Yeah. Some even drunker'n pigs."

"And hogs?"

"And hogs too. Sure enough."

Every time he lifted the cup, Batch spilled whiskey on himself and the bedcovers. After he finished the fourth cup, his head lolled about on his shoulders as weak-muscled as a newborn. The room had filled clear to the rafters by this time with the sweet aroma of whiskey.

"Still feel sort of tortured in mind by going against my employer. Hughie treated me square. Took me in, give me a home, and made me a ranch hand," Batch said in a surprising moment of lucidity. He dropped the cup, fell back on the table, released a loud, pent-up burst of air, and passed out.

"Took a while," said Redman. His impatience had no boundaries.

"He's out cold," Clive said. "Might not feel a thing."

"Don't count on it," Fixx said, realizing it'd take more than mere whiskey to numb a man to the point where he wouldn't feel his leg being sawed off. "He'll feel it all right. How much, I can't say. He's young and that bone is plenty strong."

Olivia prayed aloud softly. She prayed for the Lord to guide her husband's hand in the operation. She prayed Batch would feel little pain. She prayed for the soul of her dead daughter and the baby she'd attempted to bring into existence. She prayed too, for those souls that'd died before baptism. She prayed for all those who'd given their lives in the late war.

She soon finished, and Fixx stood with bone-saw in hand. He motioned for Olivia to go to the hearth, where the handle of the flat, heated plate poked up out of the fire within easy reach.

"You char the veins, 'Livia," he said. "I hope it's hot enough where all you need do is put it close to the wound and it'll close up them veins right tight.

"Clive, you hold Batch's shoulders in case he starts fighting. Redman, help hold him down. Tie the leather around his leg now, Enos," Fixx added. "Make sure you wind it tight as possible."

Enos tied his free leg down, and looped another leather strip around the damaged leg where his father indicated. He tightened it down, then took a long tube of rolled iron out of a rear pocket, nearly equal in size to his middle finger. He hooked it between the leather and Batch's skin, forced it upwards until it protruded above the leather, midway of the tube's length, which would provide him enough space for a handgrip on each side. He looked up at his father.

Fixx said, "Now, when you got that thing tight enough it squeaks, try to give it one more wrap, then we'll be set."

Fixx looked about him and, satisfied everyone stood in place, he said, "Now, this saw's sharp as shattered flint. It won't take but a second to cut through the bone. But I figure he'll try throwing you boys clear out the door when the saw cuts into the marrow. A man's spirit for life has the strength of a beast. You must hold him down. If Enos loses grip on that iron bar, blood'll shoot clear to the ceiling. We got to be ready for everything."

"Yessir," muttered Clive. "We'll hold him."

"All right then. Tighten it down, Enos."

Enos twisted the leather, holding tight to each side of the roll of iron. The leather, though, kept giving. But when it was tight enough, it would surrender, and he'd wrap it more. After a bit more turning, the leather spoke up in loud, shrill squeaks. Fixx figured he was really close.

"Ready, Pap," Enos muttered. Sweat stood out on his forehead, and rolled down into his eyes.

Fixx spoke in a voice so calm he might've been at the breakfast table instead of ready to saw off a man's ankle and foot, "Try to give it one more, Enos. Then hold it with all you got."

The boy tried but couldn't budge it. Everything stood in order and ready.

Fixx caught hold of Batch's knee. He felt the power of his entire body gathering in his arms and hands. The veins on the backs of his hands stood out in knotted ropes. He placed the edge of the blade on the leg at a point a few inches above the anklebone, confident this'd be above the poison. He sighed, and took an enormous breath. His wife stood at the fireplace, hand already upon the handle of the homemade suturing plate. He heard her praying again.

He let it all go then like a man forced to plunge into an icy river. With one stroke, he set the blade deep into the bone. Again, with all his weight upon the handle, he forced the blade deeper into the bone. He felt the bone concede, and bright crimson arterial blood seeped onto the blade.

Batch screamed like a wounded animal as the blade cut into the marrow. The boy reared up as high as the leather straps would allow him. His body bowed now in an arc, like a fish flapping onshore. He screamed again, like one of the wild cat-

creatures Fixx had heard in the dark wilderness as a boy back in East Tennessee, and then passed out and lay in frozen silence.

The saw cut clean and made neat, quick work of its assignment, slicing through the large bone, the tibia, and then through the smaller one, the fibula.

" 'Livia," Fixx said.

Olivia leapt across the room thrusting the glowing plate far out in front of her, its bright glow fading even as she ran.

Fixx drove the saw one last time through all that remained of the meat of Batch's ankle, and by the time Olivia reached the table, the foot and stubbed-off ankle fell into the ashcan below. He heard it land with a dull, lifeless thump.

"Now," he said and stepped to the side.

The offensive odor of burnt hair and flesh clung tight to the hairs of his nostrils, filling the room, but he saw that Olivia wasn't deterred any by the intense smell. She held the makeshift suturing-plate close to the bone. Nearly instantly, the puckered edges of the veins browned-up the way sugar hardens in fire, curled as they shrank, and then closed up. When they darkened to a deep shade of brown, nearly black, he nodded, and Olivia removed the plate, carried it back, and set it back into the fire, in case she needed to use it again.

Fixx waited a few more minutes, and then said, "Loosen it really slow, Enos. Them veins got to be shut up tight."

Fixx saw no leaks, no seeps. "It's all right, Enos. Turn it loose all the way."

Olivia set to work. She applied huge gobs of black ointment on the ugly, unnatural-looking wound, and when she'd fully covered the stump with the salve, she wrapped it in clean bed sheeting.

CHAPTER EIGHT

The men placed Batch back in the bedroom, returned to the parlor, and gathered about the hearth. They sat in silence for a long time. At length, Olivia got up and walked off into the kitchen.

"Never seen nothing like it," Redman said. "I saw how you did it, Pap, but I ain't right sure I could do the same, to save me."

"Could if you had to," Fixx told him. "That was the first time I did it, and the first I'd seen it done. I made a go of it. You could too. All of you could. It was a matter of have-to. They ain't nothing a man can't do when he's made to do it."

Olivia returned with coffee mugs that rose with heavy mist like steam off a butcher's barrel. She passed one each to Fixx, Clive and Redman. They sat and talked, and enjoyed their coffee. When Fixx's cup sat empty on the floor at his side, he got up, found the whiskey jug, poured his cup full, and set it aside. Then he took Clive's cup, filled it, and poured one for Redman.

He said, "I ain't ashamed to tell you I was one surprised man, when I cut through that big bone and found another one there for me to have a go at. I should've expected it, from all the butchering I've done in my day, but it sure set me astir there for a time."

"You didn't let on any I could see," said Clive.

He sipped his whiskey, experiencing relief nearly as high as a dense flock of passenger pigeons passing overhead.

"The last thing I needed was to look like I didn't know what I was doing."

They all laughed then.

"I sure hope that boy'll be all right," Olivia said.

He took her hand to his lips and kissed it. "We've seen about all there is to see in this old world, ain't we, Olivia?"

She took back her hand, and ran it through his hair, fingers at work like the teeth of a comb. But, she didn't speak. Fixx read the sadness on her face, and guessed she was grieving for her dead daughter.

"I've had to learn carpentry and cabinet-making, farming, working with cattle, done masonry work galore, was born a whiskey maker, but never in my wildest dreams did I ever figure I'd make a surgeon, and do it without ever stepping inside schoolhouse one."

"This proves," said Clive, smiling behind a whiskey glow, "some things're damn sure overrated."

"Clive Fixx," said his mother. "If that's how that whiskey's going to make you talk, you better pass it on to someone who can handle it."

Clive jumped to his feet, caught up his mother, and whirled her three times about the room, before setting her back on her feet. "You're forgetting that I'm a big old boy, now."

"Yes. Well then, try acting like one. Don't be going around cursing like you was in a gin room."

He placed a hand on his mother's shoulder, drew her close, and said, "Mam, how do you know what kind of speech they use in a gin room?"

She slapped his shoulder, half in jest, to let him know he was still a mere child to her. She said, not quite able to put on a hard face, "I was raised with seven brothers. I reckon I know what goes on in them corrupt places."

Fixx passed his cup to Enos. A few dregs of whiskey

remained. "Fill this for me, son."

Enos took the cup, and said, "But, Pap, there's still some left."

"Well, then, see if you can make it disappear." He watched the boy's eyes grow round in surprise. He watched Enos down the whiskey, without a wrinkle on his face.

When Enos finished the few drops of whiskey, he rolled his tongue about inside his mouth. "I taste the corn, and the barley."

"What do you think, distiller-man?"

"Needs more barley."

"Steel," Olivia said. "You'll learn that boy to be a drunkard."

"I was drinking by his age, Olivia. I ain't never made a drunkard yet."

"Oh, well, sure—you stop it right now. I ain't having it." Her lips knitted in tight frown lines.

"Yes, ma'am." He sat up straight in an exaggerated pose.

She slapped him on the shoulder as she'd done Clive earlier, whirled her skirts, and stalked off toward the kitchen. "I know when I'm not needed. I'll wash up and pinch out the supper biscuits."

Fixx took up his cup again, and told Enos what a fine job he'd done today, and watched the boy try to take it without squirming in embarrassment.

"You did a man's job today, Enos. Looks now like I live in a house of men." He saw the boy's chest expand with pride, and he felt a wave of satisfaction spread throughout his being.

Later, Fixx ordered Enos to take the ashcan to the barn. When he was ready to step outside, he said, "Put that boy's foot inside that large iron pot out in the barn, set the lid on it and lay something heavy atop it. We don't want the cats to eat it."

Enos's head must've still been a-swirl from the whiskey, Fixx figured, for now the boy said, "Can't I leave it inside the ashcan out at the barn, put a piece of metal over the can?"

Redman and Clive whooped in hearty laughter. But Fixx just looked at him with calm eyes. "Then, what'd you use to carry out the ashes in, son?"

Enos left fast. He watched him depart, the boy trying to hide his embarrassment.

"That boy's still got a lot of growing to do, Pap," Redman said, "before he makes a man."

"He's learning, though," Fixx told him. "Enos'll do fine. I'd bet on it."

The three men talked low at the fire. Once in a while, one of the sons—usually Redman—got up and tossed more wood into the jaws of the ravenous fireplace. The younger men couldn't hold their whiskey. They both fell asleep toasting their feet against the heat that sprang from the fireplace.

Enos had long since returned from his barn chores and sat now in the kitchen with his mother.

Fixx sat alone with his thoughts, old memories of his childhood, doing so more and more these days. He thought of his mother, of the hardships she'd endured. He thought of his father—feeling that he still wasn't the man he'd been, not even close. He thought of his brothers, his sisters, his home place up on Little Pigeon in Sevier County in East Tennessee.

He sipped his whiskey, and concurred with his youngest son—it lacked barley. He thought of many things while he waited for his wife to call him to supper, but couldn't think of the one thing he longed to think of—the loss of his daughter.

His thoughts were dark spirits of the past, of things left undone, of things done that should have remained undone. Olivia called out that supper was ready. He drained his cup, stretched, shook the boys awake, and strode off toward the kitchen.

★ ★ ★ ★ ★

The earth rolled over and fetched nighttime in its backwash. Fixx felt they'd done all that was possible to do for Batch. Fixx found himself alone in the bedroom with Olivia. She sat at her dresser—one he'd made for her many years ago—in front of the small mirror hanging on the wall at the back of the dresser. She drew a brush through her long hair—hair she kept atop her head in a high bun in the daytime hours, but allowed to fall free at night. Her hair had several thin, gray bands scattered about, but for the most part, was still a rich chestnut color.

He sensed it. She was in a blue sulk. When his boots stood upright at the side of the bed, he walked across the floor to her in his stockinged feet.

"Steel Fixx, if you knew how hard I work keeping your socks up in decent shape, you wouldn't wear them out on this old rough floor."

This was a pet peeve of hers, he knew. But he was too aware that this wasn't what really bothered her right now. He was to blame. He felt his guilt grow. He sat back on the edge of the bed, removed his socks, then went again to her side. The cold from the floor soaked into the soles of his feet as he placed a hand atop her shoulder. She shoved it off in a cat-like swipe, and continued brushing her hair, its color rich and alive in the lamp's yellow glow. He placed his hand again on her shoulder. This time, she allowed it to remain there.

At length, she said, "It ain't fair, Steel. You can sit with the boys and drink, but what've I got as a comfort? Nothing."

He saw no way to combat this remark, and wouldn't have done so had there been one. What she'd said was a statement of fact. Nothing he could do about it. Let her talk. This might provide her some small consolation. He recalled she often found peace in this way. She needed to empty her spleen. She deserved relief from it all.

Tension stood heavy between them. Fixx always felt this when she was in a *mood*. He might as well have been walking about with an anvil tied around his neck. At times, the weight nearly overwhelmed him. Right now, he felt about ready to collapse under the weight.

When he attempted to place his other hand on her shoulder, she struck it with her hairbrush, and whirled upon her chair. "You know it, don't you?" Speaking too loud, he felt, fearful the boys might hear. "It's your fault, Steel. . . . I still don't understand why you made Jorod marry her. We could've made out with her here . . . her and her child. You know you were wrong, don't you? Is Molly better off now? We should've kept her home. Her and the child!"

"It *was* my fault," he said. He'd do anything to help her find peace. "I'm sorry, Olivia. That's all I can say." He knew she was right. He'd been wrong.

"That how you expect to resolve this? It's not a small matter of soothing my anger, my unhappiness. It's more this time. You placed our girl in danger, years ago when you flogged Jorod, and made him marry Molly. You couldn't bend to your pride. Could you? No!"

She dropped the brush, raised her hands to her eyes. She bent over at the waist, her head about in her lap. She cried with such pain, Fixx thought, she might feel that she was the last human alive. He stroked her back. She allowed this. Still, she wouldn't lift her head to him. After a time, she spoke, but her words sounded muffled as she spoke into her nightclothes, "I'm sorry, Steel. I'm sorry. I shouldn't have said those words. I'm so lonely . . . so sad."

"It's all right, 'Livia." He stood above her, stroked her back, while she cried herself into submission.

He lifted her when he sensed she would allow him to, carried her and placed her in bed. He pulled the covers up to her chin, removed his clothes, and by the time he got in bed beside her, she was asleep. "I was wrong, 'Livia," he said. "I wish I could undo what I did back then."

CHAPTER NINE

Batch remained in a sorry state of health for several days after Fixx amputated his foot. On the fourth day, he awoke feeling a little more the way a man should feel. Those first few days had been afire with pain. Old man Fixx had poured whiskey down him but even that did little to ease the pain. He couldn't abide the mere thought of food at first, but today, he felt hunger all astir in his gut.

He lay awake and attempted to stare through the darkness of the room. About all he made out for sure was the large chifforobe against the north wall. He gazed at it, and pretended to make of it a cathedral like he'd once seen in a newspaper. It had all the right ridges and crests, angles cut to make it come to life in his mind, but then even that illusion escaped him in the darkness of the room. He lay there and toughed it out until he heard someone building a fire in the massive fireplace in the parlor.

The scraping in the fireplace stopped, and Olivia poked her head into his room. She stood in the doorway, backlit by the fire that roared in the fireplace.

"How're you this morning, Mr. Batch?"

"Some better, ma'am. Thanks for asking."

"Feel like eating this morning?"

"Yes, ma'am. I might be able to put something down this morning. If it ain't no kind of trouble."

"It won't be any trouble at all," she said. She turned and left, leaving the door open. Batch lay watching the flames leap up the throat of the fieldstone fireplace until she returned with a tray of food. He ate with enthusiasm, even the oatmeal, which he usually didn't like.

He was sitting up in bed, pillows heaped high against his back, holding the tray of food on his lap, and eating with great attention. He heard boots upon the floorboards, looked up and saw Fixx enter the room. The old man took up a straight-backed chair, sat easy, and watched on until Batch finished eating.

"Must feel better this morning, Batch."

He watched Fixx roll a cigarette, staring at his slim silhouette cut by the light of the fireplace in the living room. He pushed the tray to the side, sat up, and sipped away on his cup of coffee. "Yessir. I figure I might make it now."

"How's the pain?"

"It feels like somebody cut off my foot with a bone-saw, Mr. Fixx."

"Had to be done, Batch. You'd be in a fine pickle by now if we hadn't cut it off." He rose from the chair and stepped alongside the bed.

"I know. Still don't make it no better . . . much nohow. What'd you do with it?"

He accepted the cigarette Fixx had built.

"It's in an iron pot in the barn. Enos'll bury it soon as the ground thaws."

Fixx's fingers dived into a shirt pocket, produced a match, struck it on the tight cloth of his jeans on the underside of his right thigh, and touched the flame against the cigarette in Batch's lips.

Batch inhaled. He felt dizziness slap him hard from going so long without nicotine. He leaned back and rested against the pillows. "I 'spect there's no hope you'll be putting it back on any time soon, is they?"

Fixx chuckled.

"Nope. I only take 'em off. You'll have to find somebody with more skill than I got to put it back on, I reckon."

Batch sat enjoying his smoke, riding the nicotine's pleasure with a welcome heart, and a warm sensation of comfort.

Fixx asked him to repeat his story of how Molly Rust had died. When he finished the sad tale, Fixx said, "You say Jorod ran off the Mexican's daughter?"

"Took her by the arm the way a bartender treats a drunkard who makes too much of a fool of himself. Shoved her down the steps.

"He wasn't having her in his house. Said she was a witch. She might've been one for all I know, but one thing's for sure in my mind . . . she eased Molly's pain some. You could tell her suffering had eased a bit . . . wasn't making such a fuss. It's hard to talk about this, Mr. Fixx. The right words to describe her pain. You wouldn't have wanted to hear her. I'm trying to save you some. I know you got to be suffering. But, it was bad, that's 'bout the only way to describe it and do it with kindness."

"Appreciate it, Batch."

He watched Fixx stand, and walk toward the door, heard him say over a shoulder, "I meant every word I said, Batch . . . you got a home on this ranch long as you want it." He passed on out of the room, and left Batch alone again with his thoughts, which were becoming easier and easier to live with, despite the loss of his foot.

The snow lingered. Fixx and the boys took hay to the cedar grove, and fed the cattle holed up there. Later in the week, the snow still hanging on with a firm grip, they went again to the cedar grove. This time they brought back the wagon they'd abandoned when the snow first set in. This time it was easier to keep the wagon wheels in the tracks the sledge had cut out.

Fixx wanted the wagon in the barn lot in case they received more snow, for this last one seemed to be hanging around long enough for another one to come along and cover it up.

Fixx tolerated Redman, as his middle son often queried him about when or if ever they were going to avenge the death of Molly. Fixx silenced the boy, with a stern, fearsome look of his dark eyes. Afterward, Redman didn't trouble him again over the matter and kept his mouth shut.

The snow continued bowling across the pasture above the house in enormous snow rollers. The large balls of snow ultimately grew too heavy for the wind to push any farther, and they stopped, lined up like toys of a giant's playful son. Fixx monitored them until the activity turned tiresome and no longer held his interest.

Olivia forced Enos to wear his overshoes for so long Fixx allowed the boy had forgotten what it was to go without them. He watched as he removed them after a night of completing his barn chores. Enos stepped about with a light foot as if he were weightless and might float to the ceiling.

Fixx grew inward each evening, staring into the fire, a glass of whiskey propped on his stomach, untouched at times until he got up and went off to bed. The boys—even Clive—ceased to talk without reserve as they liked to do, and Olivia became the lone recipient of any utterances from him not of a sharp nature.

After a time, Fixx noticed that Batch was fast on the mend, for he'd taken to sitting in the parlor. As he sat there, he watched Batch work away on a board with his knife—a flat board Enos had fetched from the barn. When he asked what he was working on, Batch would smile, peel back another slender splinter of wood from the board, and pitch it into the fire where it snapped and crackled away its life in the flames.

The snow hung on, and the skies were seldom any other color than a boiled gray. The mood of the entire household grew heavy with the weight of sad, dismal thoughts.

The board Batch worked on must've helped him pass the time, Fixx figured, occupied his thoughts, and kept his mind off his own disorder and unrest. After many hours of diligent carving, Fixx saw that the board was slowly turning into a foot, or rather, a fair resemblance of one. Then, not just Fixx but the entire family saw what the ranch hand had in mind.

Enos brought Batch a few leather scraps from the burn-barrel in the barn, as well as a handful of brass rivets. Everyone grew excited by the foot Batch was creating. They all sat and watched, at times even giving advice. But Batch must've had his own design for the foot and stuck to it.

Then came the day, having already rigged the harness of leather to be strapped around the stub the bone-saw had made of his ankle, he took up his boot and attempted to fit the foot inside. He found it still too large. So he removed it from the boot, and set to work again with his knife until it fit snug, but not too tight. With some effort, he managed to slip the board foot inside with the right amount of room to slide in and out with fair ease. Fixx fell under the spell as Batch worked to attach the leather ankle harness to the foot using the rivets to secure it in place.

The entire family stood about when he first attached the foot to his anklebone and stood up. With this accomplished, they shouted out congratulations.

Batch clacked about the house upon his new foot for a week, and gained more and more confidence daily. "I guess I'll have to learn to wear the thing without the boot first," he said, and grinned with pride. "Then when I can maneuver some with the thing, I'll try it out with the boot on."

He overdid it and a huge blister appeared upon his ankle. At this point, Olivia took over. She applied her famous, thick black salve to the blistered ankle, then bound it again in a bandage.

As the household waited for the ankle to heal, Olivia sat at the fireplace of an evening, constructing a circular pad of soft leather, lined with dense cotton, meant to fit around Batch's ankle where the blister had flared up. The ankle healed, and Olivia fitted the pad into the leather harness.

"Now, sir," she said, "give that a try."

It worked wonders. Two weeks later, he started wearing the foot inside his boot. He lumbered like a drunken sailor ashore, but learned more and more each day how to use his new foot.

"Soon as that pad begins to wear out," Olivia said, "you be sure to tell me. I'll sew up another one for you."

The snow lingered. The wind howled in the rafters of the barn and screamed. Enos heard his father say he couldn't recall a harsher winter. That this was the longest he ever remembered snow to stay on the ground. The cold, snow and winter winds continued into early March.

One night, though, the wind swung around, and blew warm up from the south. Enos sat up in bed, awakened at midnight by the sound of melting snow running off the house like a spring thundershower. By the time he finished his oatmeal and bacon that morning and looked outside, he found the heaped snow banks had all caved in on top like fallen cakes.

"This snow'll be gone in four more days," he heard his father say, and Enos watched him sip his coffee, talkative for the first time in weeks. "We can go back outside then, and find something to do."

Once again, Enos sat up in bed, awakened at midnight or thereabouts, on the third day of the thaw. He'd dreamed he was in the cedar grove helping his father search for a calf. The calf bore a star in the center of its white, curly forehead. The cattle kept crowding around him and his father, bawling, preventing them from entering the herd. The deeper inside the herd they pushed, the louder grew the sounds of protest from the cattle, until it woke him up.

He lay still, listening to the racket of the herd for perhaps five minutes then decided he was awake and was no longer dreaming. He jumped from his upstairs bed where he'd taken to sleeping since Batch's arrival. He rushed to the window, and when he saw them in the light of the full moon, milling around the barn lot, he cried out, "The cows. They've come to the barn."

This awakened his brothers, and they too came to look.

One week later, the men removed the runners from the wagons and replaced them with wheels. In a festive mood, the entire family, except Batch, rode into Witness Tree Station. Olivia's sister owned a dry-goods store in town with upstairs living quarters. The sister and her husband, Henry Ridenour, had lived in those quarters until their children were married off. Afterward, they moved into a small house in the residential district of Witness Tree Station. As a result, the space upstairs stood empty, which provided the Fixx family with a place to stay while in town on an overnight visit.

Olivia visited with her sister on their stay. She vented all the pain and grief that'd built up since Molly's death. The two of them spent hours together in the kitchen, and in the parlor while they sat sewing, talking, reminiscing.

The long period of winter confinement, the death of her daughter, struck to the quick of Olivia's heart, and she hadn't been aware of how genuinely filled with the blue-miseries she'd become until she sat with Bernadette. It all came out then in heavy gushes. Her sister held her, allowed her to sob away much of this pent-up despair and agony upon her shoulder, the same way she'd done when they were children.

They spent two days in town, restocking their food supplies; sugar, coffee, flour, spices, nutmeg, vanilla, lemon extract, and all of the condiments Olivia needed to keep a household of men from revolting by alternating the table menu. On the wagon trip home, she sang a blissful tune in her high voice, a song filled with joy, ending happily in love arrived at after a struggle that occupied most of the many verses leading up to the resolution.

She became a stranger to her children—younger, and more carefree than they'd seen her all the long winter. There'd been little singing in the Fixx household during their time of wretched sorrow.

The daffodils had erupted in bloom while they were in town. They filled the yard with their yellow righteousness at the foot of the steps, and around the sides of the house. Their lovely yellow heads bounced in the brisk breeze of the forenoon, held erect by healthy, sturdy green stalks. The bridal's wreath bushes were swollen with buds as well, although not yet in bloom. The purple crocuses were up, had been, even before they'd left for Witness Tree Station.

So once more, it appeared, the Fixx family had survived another winter, and this one most harsh, nearly unforgiving.

The following Saturday, Fixx sat at the breakfast table with Olivia. The meal was over, and the younger men were outside already, occupying their hands and minds with whatever work came to hand. He sat, drank coffee, and smoked.

"I think it's time we went to visit Molly's grave. Maybe see the grandchildren. What do you think, 'Livia?"

"Oh, Steel, I was just now thinking the same. When can we go?"

He smiled, putting his teeth into it. "Why, today, of course. Tomorrow never comes. I think you know that, Olivia."

He hitched the horse to the Studebaker hack, and set off with Olivia to visit the grave of their daughter. Out on the Hazlett Church Road, not far past the lone post oak tree Fixx had tied

Jorod Rust to years ago, they came upon a small hollow, a gulch, where a tiny grove of redbud bushes stood in full bloom.

"Stop here, Steel," she said. "Cut some of those redbuds to place on the grave."

When he handed them to her, she sat and held them upon her lap, along with a large bouquet of daffodils she'd cut from her yard. They traveled the rest of the way to the lane, which led up to the large three-story house with wide-porches, which belonged to Fixx's cousin, Honus Rust.

The day had filled up with soft sunlight, and the red bricks of the house rose like magic from the treeless plain. It sat there, a ship at sail on a brown sea, a sea that would soon change to a brilliant green before the advent of full summer, when the sun would bake it all to a crackling brown, then wear it down again with age.

Adair Murphy stepped out of his blacksmith shop into the sunlight as Fixx pulled to a halt in front of the building. Murphy stood blinking at the harsh sunlight that'd settled in his eyes and blinded them.

Fixx climbed to the ground. When he turned to meet him, Murphy thrust out a wide, work-toughened hand.

"Mr. Fixx."

Their hands came apart, and they stood and stared into each other's face.

"Well, sir, I 'spect it's sure 'nough a fine day," Murphy said.

"Yes, 'tis. That's what brought us out. Come to visit the grave."

Murphy's face fell. His eyes traveled reluctantly across Fixx's face. "I never did feel so bad in my life as I did when that girl died, Mr. Fixx. Molly was a fine girl . . . and like my wife, Joan, says, she never had no kind of chance since the day she come to live here."

"Where's she buried, Mr. Murphy?"

Murphy pointed with a blunt, forge-blackened finger toward the north, where the buds of the apple trees were swelling with life, yet unborn—the dead woman lying in the ground beneath their wide limbs. "She's up there. In the orchard. I set up a stone I found in the creek. Ain't much, I guess, but it's better'n what was there, which was nothing."

"You mean to say Jorod didn't set her up a stone?"

"Said he'd get around to it. We did have a bad winter. Kept most folks in close to the fire."

"Did it keep Jorod in by the fire? Or did he manage to ride to town on occasion?"

"He was in and out . . . most of the time."

Olivia leaned forward, and said to Murphy, "Are the little ones here, Mr. Murphy?"

Murphy dipped his head in a slight bow to her. "No, ma'am. Honus took them up to Lily."

"To Lily?" said Fixx. "Why to Lily?" Before Murphy could reply, Fixx answered his own question, "Oh, that's right. His sister-in-law lives there. Mrs. Brewster? Rose's sister?"

"Yessir."

Olivia said, "How long, Mr. Murphy? How long have the little ones been up to Mrs. Brewster's?"

"Since right after your daughter, Molly, died. Honus took 'em out in that god-awful blowing snow and cold. Had me put on the runners for him, and off they went, snow blowing across in front of 'em . . . it's a wonder he didn't lose hisself. Would've too, except that nigh-side mule was born in Lily and knew the way. Thought he was going home, I reckon."

"I was counting so much on seeing the children," Olivia said. "It's a shame they ain't here. No telling how they're being treated."

"Mrs. Brewster I believe's a fine woman, ma'am," Murphy said. "I'm sure she's taking good care of 'em."

She nodded in agreement, and swung her gaze to the orchard.

"Well, we'll drive on up there and visit the grave, Mr. Murphy." Fixx swung up again into the hack, picked up the lines and added, "I got Batch living with me, Mr. Murphy."

"Oh, great. I was wondering did he make it in that storm."

"He made it . . . most of him, anyways. Lost a foot to frostbite. Anyhow, he asked would I pick up his outfit."

"Yessir," Murphy said, "I'll dig it out and have it for you when you decide to leave."

They swung back up the road, crossed the pasture and up the slight rise to the orchard. He helped his wife down from the hack and felt a mild breeze blow into his face. The day had turned warm, and his shirt was sticking to his back.

Olivia asked him to fetch the flowers they'd brought along, and place them on the grave.

He did, and when he set them on the mounded earth, they stood out bright against the drab grass that surrounded the scar in the earth that was his daughter's grave. He straightened back up and felt his heart constrict like a hard blow to the back, not only with grief, but from guilt as well.

"It's so beautiful here, Steel," Olivia said. "A right beautiful hill."

Fixx nodded.

"So beautiful," she said again. "And God saw fit to give us such a gorgeous day."

He watched her sway, likely from heavy grief.

"Aww, Steel," she moaned. She flung herself into his arms and cried as if to shake the earth.

Her tears were hot upon his chest, and this increased his guilt. That tiny point of guilt grew larger and larger until it swelled to the size of the planet. He gritted his teeth, bit back tears, banished his guilt, and created hatred from it, bitter as lemon rind.

They stayed several hours on the rise. Olivia dreaded to leave, he saw—couldn't bear to leave Molly there by herself in her lonely grave. A good deal later on, she turned and rushed off to the wagon, boarded, and sat there grim and granite-faced.

"It's time to go on home, Steel," she managed to say.

When he accepted from the blacksmith the battered canvas-shipping bag, containing Batch's possessions, he placed the bag in the small storage area behind the seat, and when his hand returned to view, it held a gallon jug of his whiskey, as if he'd caught a critter by the tail. He handed it to Murphy.

"Why, Mr. Fixx. You needn't have done that." But from the look he saw on Murphy's face, it would've taken a man of most uncommon strength to wrestle the jug from his hands. "Come with me. I'll put this here up."

Inside Murphy's shop, the fire in his forge had dropped its bright edge and the coals were fast turning gray like the hair of Fixx's sideburns and mustache. The blacksmith placed the whiskey on a high shelf, amid his many tools, and Fixx saw the seriousness in the man's face as he turned to him.

"Mr. Fixx?"

"Yessir?"

"I'm afraid that Honus Rust. . . ." Murphy paused for a second, as if his way lay burdened with snares and traps. "I do think that man's losing his senses."

"Honus? How so?"

"Well, he's changed. When first I come to work for him, I couldn't ask for a better boss. He was more or less like the rest of us working here. Know what I mean? But he started taking them trips overseas, and changed.

"Started putting on airs, I guess you'd call it. Wearing fancy clothes and all. That thing in his eye."

Fixx recalled the monocle his cousin had taken to wearing. This'd been a short time after one of his European trips. He recalled as well that Honus had started drinking fancy European liqueurs.

"There's times I been woke up by loud singing coming from inside his house."

"Well, I recall he always was kind of a singer, Mr. Murphy. Even when we was kids."

"Yessir," the blacksmith said. Fixx figured Murphy was trying his best to impress him with the change he'd seen in his employer. "But, to do so at all hours of the night? Sometimes all night long?"

Fixx cast an eye back outside, where his wife waited for him in the hack. The large house loomed behind her like a mountain of bricks. "Well, if I had to live alone in that house I might sing all night too, on occasion."

"No, sir. I got to tell you, Mr. Fixx . . . there's something wrong with Honus Rust."

"You saying he's lost his mind, Adair? That there what you're telling me?"

"Yessir . . . more or less, and trying to do it nice, since you're his kin. Worse, I asked for Batch's last pay, and he cursed me. Said Batch stole a horse off his property, and he was keeping his pay. Hell, it only 'mounted to seven dollars—Rust with more money'n he knows how to spend."

Murphy's words lingered in Fixx's mind all the way home.

CHAPTER TEN

Calving season arrived. Enos walked each day into the herd with his father. He begged Fixx to let him pull a calf. After a long wait, his father conceded. This swelled his pride, for all in his family, and all those he knew of, often sat back of an evening, talking ranching, calving and the stubborn births they'd assisted in.

Then one day, he nearly fell over from shock. He saw the head of a calf, being squeezed from its mother's birth canal. The mother had grown tired, it seemed, for the calf had hung up. Enos's father must've seen the cow was in no real trouble, but was somewhat lazy, this being its first birth, and allowed the boy to pull the calf. She'd labored for some time from the act, and had lain down.

Enos seated himself on the ground behind her as he'd often watched his father do, and set his feet upon the animal's rump bones. He caught hold of the front legs of the tiny cow-creature in a firm grip. He expected a great battle, as he'd sometimes observed making the rounds with his father. He bunched his shoulder muscles to give a great tug, but to his surprise, the calf fell between his legs at his lightest touch.

He looked up at his father with puzzlement in his eyes, then back again to the calf at his feet. He rose himself, to allow the cow that by now had shaken off its laziness and was rising to its feet. When it did, it nosed the calf around until it stood upright on its own with unsteady legs.

"It goes that way sometimes, Enos," said his father. "Sometimes you'll work up a sweat, and tug until your muscles are 'bout wore out before they drop. Other times, like now, they just fall out at a mere touch. This cow here's young. Her first calf. I don't 'spect she'll decide to lay down next time. She's a lot like you, son . . . still a little green."

The cow got busy licking its calf with a long pink tongue. At length, she finished cleaning the tiny animal. Enos saw that the tiny creature's coat stood out a sharp reddish-brown, with a stark white, curly forehead, and sitting in the exact center of the forehead was a small, neat star outlined in a darker white, nearly gray color.

"It's the calf I seen," said Enos. "It's the one we was searching for."

"Now what nonsense is this, Enos?"

"We was looking for this calf," he said. Excitement fired his eyes like two small chunks of shiny coal. "The other cows wouldn't let us inside to it."

Fixx stopped the boy, and made him tell him the entire tale, which he did.

"Can I take it to the barn, Pap? It'll be no trouble. Its mam'll be there with it."

"I'll tell you what," said his father. "We'll drop back by here before we go in for supper. If that cow's still up and around like she ought to be, and if you can lug the thing, I guess it won't be no harm to have a pet about the place."

Later, their rounds complete, they returned to where they'd left the cow and the calf with the starred forehead. The mother stood grazing in the young greenery, where wild onions grew this early in the season. The calf lay nearby, and looked on from wide eyes of complete innocence.

Enos's father handed the calf up to him in the saddle. They arrived home late for supper. Enos placed the calf on the straw-strewn floor of an empty barn stall. The cow entered behind them. She checked to see if it was safe. Satisfied, she turned about, left the stall, and returned outside, and started grazing on grass that grew in lush abundance, a mere shadow's toss from the barn.

Enos and his father strode up the path toward the house. Enos looked back to discover that the calf had followed them outside, had found its mother's milk, and was busy now butting its head against her bag.

Fixx placed a hand on Enos's shoulder, and said, "It'll be all right, son. Let's go in to supper. I imagine your mam'll be upset you kept me out so long. She don't like to keep supper in the warmer until it dries out, you know."

The pride of his day's accomplishment spread across Enos's face in a broad smile that remained there all the way to the house. He smiled and smiled, until by degrees, his mother drew the story from him, although it required no threats on her part.

Enos finished the telling and looked at his mother, the smile still on his face, the beam in his eyes. "You'll be calling the thing Star, won't you?" said Olivia Fixx.

A small dark look of dashed plans flashed across the boy's face.

His mother laughed, along with her husband, and said, "Well, what on earth else would you name the thing with a star on its forehead?"

"That's a bull calf, son. We'll have to castrate it. Unless you'd rather trade it to one of the neighbors for another one later on."

Enos, the old-head cattleman by now, said, with great confidence, "I figure we'll keep him, Pap."

His spirits ran high for several days after he helped birth the calf. He wore his hat pushed back off his forehead, his chest thrust far in front of him, striding about the barn, and watching the calf romping in play.

When the ground warmed up enough that it would work up with ease, his mother said Fixx should hitch their oldest mule to the plow, and set Enos to breaking their garden. This small act of servitude tended to place his hat back where it belonged. Enos soon learned that following a mule, who expelled sour gas in great quantities, was a mean chore.

Still, of an evening, he always reverted. He'd sit with the men, hat pushed back, legs crossed, and feel he'd arrived at last. All he needed for true "arrival" was a cigarette dangling from his lips, for all the men there had them as though growing from their faces. The men allowed him to make comments at times, although, since the blunder he'd made regarding Batch's foot in the ashcan during the winter, he made careful review of his words before he spoke. Enos was learning.

For the past several nights, he noticed his father's face had grown more somber and silent, as though he sat with half a mind on the conversation, half on thoughts that were likely far off and dark.

No one spoke of Molly these days. Redman had even given up his pursuit of the topic. However, one morning, right after breakfast, Fixx went to the closet and returned with his .30-30 rifle, his hat on his head and his denim jumper slung over a shoulder. When he reached the front doorway, he turned to the boys, who sat watching, faces filled with wonder, too cautious to make an inquiry.

"Well," he said, "you two going with me? I'm riding over to visit Leona Reyes. See what she has to say about Molly's death."

Redman jumped to his feet so fast he upturned his chair, and Clive arose too, but with more reserve. Enos stood up to go along as well, but his father said, "Not you, Enos. You stay and help your mam make the garden."

Enos slumped back down in his chair, and it looked to Fixx

like someone had kicked him flush in the chest.

"Stay or go with us, Batch," Fixx said. "Suit yourself, and rest assured you're in no way obliged to go."

Batch rose to his feet. "Sure. I 'spect I might enjoy the ride."

When Fixx departed the barnyard, the boy stood on the porch waving. Enos looked so disappointed he felt sorry for him. Then seeing him striding toward the barn for the old mule, Pal, to disc over the garden, he smiled. Olivia would keep him busy all day long. Enos, he saw, was growing up.

Fixx was moving down the wrong path. He felt it truly, hard and hot in his guts. His nights, though, were a torture of tossing and turning, sweating, dreaming crooked dreams when he did sleep, which was uncommon enough, until he arrived at his decision. Then, even though he knew it the wrong one, he felt it the only path that might offer him even a small measure of relief. Right or wrong, he'd made his decision. He meant to stick with it to the end. The alternative was too horrendous for him to contemplate, let alone to act on.

CHAPTER ELEVEN

Honus Rust sat tortured by his own thoughts. His sleep, filled with dreams of monsters with reddened eyes—half human, half demon—plagued and chastised him. He'd also come to a decision, but his came two days before his cousin, Steel Fixx, arrived at his own. He knew now—revealed to him in a dream—that the Mexican and his witch daughter were behind all his miseries. They'd have to go. In the process, he'd take over the small portion of land the old Mexican claimed as his, which was all that remained to Reyes from an enormous land grant given to his ancestors many years ago by Spain, or so the old man had often bragged.

Reyes claimed that the North Americans had chipped away at his grant a small parcel at a time until this tiny island sitting in the middle of Rust's enormous acres was all that remained. Felipe Reyes, Honus Rust decided, would never part with his land of a free will. He'd already tried everything in his power to purchase the small strip of land, but all to no avail. Money couldn't buy it from the stubborn old man.

Rust shoved back in his chair, pushed away his glass, half-filled with the liqueur he craved now after one of his European trips. This drink, he'd been told, was filled with magical properties, and was jade green while in the bottle—in the glass, too—but when added to with cold water, turned milky and pale.

He called out for his son, "Hughie. Hughie Rust, come up here, right now."

A few minutes later, his tall, slender son, as darkly handsome as Satan, entered the room, heeding the call of his father. Honus lifted his red eyes up to the boy, and found he was staring at his youngest son, Jorod. He shook his head in wonder at how Hughie had become Jorod. He gave up the thought, fearful his head might split into two different halves if he somehow happened upon the answer.

"Hugh's out in the pasture, Pap," Jorod said. "What do you need?"

"Well, I need Hughie to go into Witness Tree Station for me. That's what I need."

"I could go instead."

"No. Hell, no. If I sent you off to town, you'd hook up again with some old whore and not return until next week or thereabouts. You *could* go out and hunt Hughie up, though, if you would. Tell him I need him to run into town for me."

"Well, sir, by the time I hunt him up I could be in town and back, Pap. It'd be faster to go on into town."

Rust felt as if he ought to throttle Jorod. He realized he'd spoiled the boy but saw in him a superior being, one nearer to the stars than other mere mortals. He knew if he'd been a young man and had pulled half the stunts this boy had, his father would've beaten him nearly to death, and would've been justified in doing so. But all Jorod need do in winning him over was smile that wide, full-of-shit smile of his. The very next moment, Jorod's face broke into a broad smile, and when he saw it, Honus Rust conceded. "Well, go ahead on then. And see you return."

"What is it you want from town, Pap?"

"Go to the sheriff's office. Bring that no-account Pleasant Rathaus back with you. I need him and right away. Tell him if he don't come on out here right now, he'll be looking for another job come election. We're going to Felipe Reyes's place.

92

I'm bound to reclaim that land for myself."

The day turned out windy, and blew cold out of the north in an attempt to make a mockery of the spring-blooming flowers on Rust's lawn, flowers that bobbed in the wind, ducked and dove like children on a playground.

Honus Rust was much too heavy and far past riding horseback these days. He ordered Murphy to hitch the horse to the hack. He met his son, who brought with him the sheriff and his deputy, at the end of his lane where it adjoined the Hazlett Church Road. He'd watched for their approach from his upstairs lookout with field glasses, hobbled downstairs when he spied them, left the house, got in the hack, and made his way up the lane to the main road.

He drove the hack slowly, but still, he arrived first. One thing he hated more than most was to wait on someone. He fired a cigar, smoking without removing it from his mouth, and watched the three riders approach, springing into view on the rises, disappearing again into the gullies. The land rose and fell before his eyes, much like ocean swells, as far as the eye could see.

"Where'n hell you been, Pleasant?" he said, when the men drew rein before him. His eyes itched as if tortured by an eye malady, and he dug into them one at a time with a huge fist. But when he stopped, the eyes still itched without relief, and he suspected they were as bright as a redbird as they usually were these days. "We got to evict Reyes from my land, and I been waiting out in this damned wind half the day."

The sheriff, Pleasant Rathaus, swept his hat from his head, leaned far back in the saddle, as though to escape the man's wrath, made a commonplace excuse, and continued to allow Rust to demean him, although everyone else in the area feared the sheriff. Rathaus had the reputation of being a crazy man when riled. At length, Rust, having vented his anger, picked up the lines, and let them down onto the back of the horse and made for Felipe Reyes's small house, a half-mile away.

Felipes Reyes's yard, small and neat, was raked-over dirt. No vegetation grew nearby that might be fuel for a runaway fire that could burn down the house. Six skinny cats rushed up to the four men and crowded about their feet as they walked toward the door.

One cat, a black and white tom, tangled in the deputy's feet and threatened to turn him upside down. Bowler Tallman, the deputy, regained his balance, and kicked the creature up against the wall of the small house. The tom bounced off the wall and dashed away, shocked. The rest of its kin followed with equal speed.

"Cut that shit out, Bowler," said Rathaus. "Them creatures ain't hurting nobody."

"I mean to leave this house today with the deed to this here property," said Rust. "You hear that, Pleasant?"

"Yessir."

"Then, by god, see you go along with whatever happens here today."

"I will, Honus. I'll do it."

Rust had thought it over while waiting in the hack of what to do with the boy, Jorod. At first, he'd been of a mind to send him on to the house, but after he weighed the matter for a time, he decided it was best he went with them to the old squatter's shack. Hell, it might teach him a thing or two.

The sheriff raised his fist to knock on the front door. But Rust didn't give him the chance. He shoved Pleasant Rathaus to the side. "This ain't no social call, Pleasant." He poised his enormous bulk and rammed the door until it fell open, sprung upon its hinges, hanging to the side at an angle.

"Reyes," he yelled out. He stepped over the threshold into

the front room of the house without concern or respect. He ducked his head beneath a hemp line strung and bowed in the center with curing tobacco. "Reyes," he called again. No answer. He moved deeper into the house, followed by the tall, lanky sheriff, Jorod next, and the sheriff's round-faced deputy.

The parlor was tiny. Many plants hung from strings; chilies, tobacco, and other plants and herbs like rosemary, sage, and parsley, in the act of drying. The only ones Rust recognized for sure were tobacco, sage and the chilies. The rest, he figured, were plants the witch, Leona, used in her deviltry.

A painting of the Blessed Mother, housed in an ornate, gilded frame, hung from the far wall. He regarded the painting as an act of idolatry the family used somehow in their practice of witchcraft. He was a bit fearful of the face in the frame, and attempted to ignore the eyes of Jesus Christ's mother, which followed him as he penetrated deeper into the house.

The other men entered as well. Rust pushed open a door to an adjoining room, and discovered Leona Reyes seated on a small wooden chair before a tiny religious shrine. The shrine itself was set upon a small, unpainted table covered with scuff-marks, confirming its heavy use over the ages. Leona Reyes sat stiff-backed, her lustrous, long black hair falling down below her shoulders to her breasts. Her hair, Rust figured, had recently been brushed out. It caught the light and deflected it. He watched as she paused in her religious obligations, looked up once, a lit match in hand, turned again to the candle, and directed the flame to the wick.

She lit the candle, blew out the match, placed it in a tray, and slid from the chair onto her knees upon the rough planks of the floor where she knelt and jabbered away, or so it sounded to Rust.

He and the other men stood and watched until she broke off her prayers, as though she'd been unable to concentrate with them watching her.

She rose from her knees. "You could've at least knocked. There was no need to barge in like that. If you've ruined the door, you'll have to pay for its repair."

"I'm looking for the old man," said Rust. He'd regained much of his usual swagger and rough edge, although the image of the Blessed Mother still lingered at the back of his mind.

She said, "He went out to gather the eggs. He'll be right back."

No sooner had she spoke those words than the report of a door banging shut came from somewhere to the rear of the house.

"He's in the kitchen now," Leona said.

Honus Rust left the "witch," pushed aside the men gathered behind him, for they all stood and clogged up the doorway, and stomped out of the room.

"He's sick," Leona said, as she followed the men. "He's an old man . . . and has a bad cold."

"I'm sick too," Rust said. "Sick of y'all squatting in the middle of my land."

The reproachful eyes of the Holy Mother watched him again all the way across the parlor to where he pushed on into the kitchen. Her penetrating eye sent a chill quickly up his spine.

Felipe Reyes placed the eggs in a brown crockery bowl resting on a small stand alongside the wood cook range. He took up a cup of coffee that was sitting alongside the egg bowl, no doubt cold by now and sat in a chair at the kitchen table, and started rolling a smoke.

Rust saw the man jump nervously, temporarily startled at his sudden appearance, and he felt a hot jolt of pleasure that he could frighten a man in this manner.

"What do you want in my home?" Reyes said. He continued the business of rolling his cigarette, diligent and careful, with

the square of an old newspaper upon the table beneath his hands to catch any tobacco he might spill.

"I come for my property, Reyes. I'm damned tired of you squatting on it all these years."

Reyes placed the cigarette between his old, parched lips, picked up the square of paper, poured the few flakes of tobacco he'd spilled back into his tobacco sack, dropped the sack on the tabletop, and stared up at his uninvited guest from eyes that looked as black as the darkest night. "I don't know what you're talking about, Rust."

Reyes had learned the English language in school in Mexico City many years ago, and he told this to Rust every chance he got, which Rust resented. The old man was comfortable using the vernacular of the common man in the area, as well as the Spanish he'd used as a child and young man.

"I'm talking about this here land of mine. You're squatting on it." Rust stood at the old man's boot heels. Reyes's legs were crossed and resting against the ledge of the table.

Reyes struck a match on his thumbnail and fired his cigarette. "And I'm telling you, I have the honest deed to this land from my father, and that you, right now, are standing upon my property." He inhaled, then exhaled slowly, clearly enjoying the pleasure of his cigarette despite Rust's intrusion. "This land came to me through legal paperwork handed down to my father from his father and his father before him, given to him in a grant from Spain."

Rust shifted on his feet, barely able to control himself. "I think you know—but if you don't, I can teach you—them old land grants ain't worth goat shit."

Reyes pulled on his cigarette, his eyes unwavering. "That's your opinion, Rust."

"Well, sir, it's the truth. But to show you where my heart is, and in order to avoid a long, drawn out court battle, I'm still

willing to buy this land from you . . . bad as I hate to buy my own damned land."

Reyes blew smoke, chuckling. "My land ain't for sale. To you nor to anyone."

Rust turned his heavy head. His jowls swung away beneath his chin with accumulated fat, the result of his self-indulgent lifestyle. He looked toward the sheriff, who still stood in the parlor. He said, "Pleasant, arrest this insolent old crow."

Rathaus stuck his head inside the kitchen. "Arrest him? What for, Honus?"

"By god, because I said so, that's what for."

"I'd have to have a reason to do a thing like that, Honus."

Rust stared into the sheriff's face until the man wilted under the pressure. "I guess you know if you don't arrest him, what's going to happen come time for election, don't you?"

Rathaus shrugged. "Give me a reason, Honus. A reason's all it'll take."

"Well, hell now, if that's all it takes, how's about trespassing? Is that reason enough to suit you?"

Pleasant Rathaus was a tall man, without an ounce of spare fat on his entire body, flexible as a wind-blown tree limb. He stepped deeper inside the kitchen, tugged his hat down tighter, and said, "Well, like you said earlier, it'll be a hell of a court battle, but if that there's what you want, I 'spect I'll oblige."

" 'Bout damned time," Rust said. He shook his head in consternation. "I swear it's like pulling teeth to get you to do any damned thing."

The sheriff turned to the small man. "Well, Felipe, I'll have to arrest you for squatting on Mr. Rust's land."

Felipe Reyes sipped his coffee in silence and smoked his cigarette.

Rust stepped up again. "Aww hell, Felipe, you don't want to go to jail over this little old shirttail of land, do you?"

The old man held his silence.

"I'm still willing to buy you out. We can ride into Witness Tree Station, hunt up my lawyer, Smiley. You've heard of him, ain't you, J. Reed Smiley?"

"Sure. Who ain't?"

"He can make out the papers. I'll pass into your hands a fair sum of money and everything'll be wonderful."

"Naw, I ain't going nowheres, I reckon," said Reyes. "I'm too old to move about from place to place. I figure I'll stay right here. You know how it is with folks and their home place."

"Well, then," said Rust, "I reckon a couple of days in jail might change your mind. Arrest him, Pleasant."

Rathaus stepped up. He attempted to latch onto the old man's arm. Felipe Reyes shook off the hand, and shot a look of dire warning toward the sheriff, eyes lit up like an oven fire.

"Keep your hands off, Sheriff. I already told you, I ain't going no place. You ain't welcome in this house."

"Sheriff," said Rust.

"Now, don't try my patience, Felipe," said Rathaus. "Haul your raggedy old ass off that chair and come on. I'll take no more bullheadedness from the likes of you—an old man, and me the sheriff of the county. Now, come on. I done warned you my last time."

Still, the old man sat there, drinking his cold coffee. He stared up at the intruders from his ancient eyes and squinted through the wayward smoke clouds of his cigarette.

Sheriff Rathaus released a long-held breath that sounded like a breeze through the top of a cedar tree. He reached out and took hold of the old man's shoulder again. Reyes shrugged out from under the hand. Rathaus grabbed up the old man, and lifted him out of his chair and clear off the floor. Reyes's feet dangled an inch or so above the wooden planks. Rathaus held him by the front of his denim jumper.

"I ought to beat the dog shit out of you, you crazy old fool."

Leona Reyes watched from the threshold between the parlor and the kitchen. She spoke up in a sharp command, her voice strong as though filled with muscle, remarkable for such a small woman. "Put him down, Sheriff. I'll talk him into going with you. Don't hurt him. He's an old man. He is ill." She then spoke to Felipe in Spanish.

Rathaus eased Reyes's feet back onto the floor, still holding him. His fists were wedged tight in the old man's jumper front.

"Why, Miss Reyes," said Rust. "You sound like you got half-decent sense."

"You'll kill him if he don't go with you. I'm doing this for him, not for you. He's ill."

Rust smiled. "Come on in here, girl." He stood with an arm outstretched to Leona Reyes.

"Come, Father." She stepped deeper inside the kitchen. "These men plan to kill you."

When she stood within Honus Rust's reach, he latched onto her shoulder, spun her around until she stood with her back to his stomach, facing her father.

"Now, I think we can settle this here little matter and not be bothered any rushing off to town and to jail," he said. "How's that sound? Anybody interested?"

After a few minutes, with no reply from the old man, still held in a tight grip by the sheriff, Honus Rust continued, "I want you to hunt up the old man's deed, Leona. I figure you know where he keeps the thing." He placed his hands about her thin neck, and held her with the grip a black snake uses to crush a rat.

"Leona doesn't know where it is, Rust," Reyes said. "If you harm her, you'll be the one goes off to jail."

"Hell," Rust said, "I own the damned jail. Law too, far's that goes."

"I reckon you'll be right at home then. If you hurt Leona, I'll see to it that you end up in one of the cells—your own cell, even if I have to go all the way to the statehouse."

Rust laughed at the absurd image of the ragged old man moving wraithlike through the marble halls of the statehouse, eyes agape, head thrown back to stare at the lofty vaulted ceilings. He applied terrific force upon Leona's neck. Her bones crackled in the instant quiet of the tiny kitchen. She gasped, or attempted to, for Rust had constricted her windpipe. Rust could feel her throat quivering, feeble and bird-like, in his fingers as she struggled for air.

"Now if she don't know where you keep it, by god, shuffle off and return with it. I've had about all this business I can stand. I won't take no more."

Rathaus released Felipe Reyes, and the old man disappeared into a small room off the kitchen.

"Well, by god, Bowler," Rust said. He turned to the deputy, who so far hadn't spoken a word and might as well have been a mute. "Are you going to allow him to go off by hisself like that and return with a blunderbuss to shoot us all dead?"

"Go in there with him, Bowler," the sheriff said.

Tallman scuffed off after the old man.

Minutes later, Reyes returned. Deputy Tallman followed. Reyes walked to the kitchen table, and placed in the center of it a thick set of rolled-up documents of ancient parchment, tied with a frayed bow of dim yellow silk. He said, "Now, take your hands off my child." He sat back down and picked up his cup to finish his coffee.

Honus Rust released the girl, stepped to the table, and snatched up the documents. He tore away the faded ribbon, let it flutter to the tabletop, then scanned the papers. To his distress and anger, he discovered the writing was in Spanish—as he'd expected—but, also, and this he hadn't expected, the ink of the documents, through the ages, had eaten deep into the finely scraped leather paper until it was dim and hard to make out.

"How'n hell you expect a man to make out what's said on these here papers, Reyes? Hell's afire. This might be anything. Might even be a bill of sale for a bull, for all I know. That ink's faded right into the damned paper. Who knows what it says?"

"I do," said the old man. He sat back, and rolled another smoke in his neat hand.

"I doubt you can read English, old man, let alone Spanish."

"Oh, but I do. I know all that is written on those papers." Reyes taunted him with a scornful smile. "You've heard me say often enough that I was given a proper education as a child and young man, which I know you resent." Then along with exhaled smoke, he let roll from his tongue all the ranges, their numbers, the sections, and the full hectares included in the documents, which comprised in its original form the equivalent of thirty-thousand acres.

Rust's eyes bulged in surprise and awe.

"Aww, you're making all this up," he said. "It ain't nobody owns that much land."

"And Spain granted my great-grandfather's brother more land than that, equaling forty-five-thousand acres." The old man smiled in triumph at his tormentor. Smoke rolled out of his nostrils in small puffy clouds. "You see, my European ancestors came early to this land, unlike yourself."

Those words humbled Rust. He felt trivial and insignificant, which was something he disliked above all else.

"These acres were worked by cities of people. Entire families were born on this land, working for my ancestors. They grew to maturity here, married, had families of their own, grew old and died. There are graveyards here that are unknown, even to me. My great-grandfather had so many horses no one could number them. Plus, a greater number of cattle. Sheep, too, and goats.

He owned enormous farms, which grew nothing but vegetables as well as orchards—"

Rust cut him off. "Aww right. Aww right. However, the thing is you're now penniless and useless as well. You couldn't buy an extra goat to save your hide. What's more important, at least for now, is how're you going to prove you own this piece of land you claim you own, and which I claim you're squatting on? Tell me that, *señor.*"

"I'll have to leave that problem to my Savior and God. I didn't tell you all this as a braggart, but as a lesson in how events in life have a way of changing . . . many times for the worst . . . or so has been my own experience. Rust and moths devour everything in the end, so they say. But, I'm sure a man your age knows this already."

Felipe Reyes had conceded. Rust saw this plainly.

"Now, if you please, since you have what you came for, I'd be obliged to you if you'd give me a few days to gather together my belongings. Mere land isn't worth the life of my daughter. If I'm to live in Witness Tree Station, I'll have to have the price of my property in order to do so."

Rust took up the pale yellow silk ribbon, tied up the bundle of documents and thrust them into an inner coat pocket.

"Money? Hell, I already give you the money, Reyes. You took it with you when you went off into that back room there. You've likely got a iron safe back there you put it in for safekeeping, I'd say."

Leona Reyes ran through the parlor into her bedroom. Before any of the intruders were able to make a decision of what to do, she returned. She held in her tiny fists a huge, ancient pistol. Her hands wobbled under the weight of the cumbersome weapon as she pointed it at Rust.

"Go," she ordered in her strong voice. "Leave my father's property. Go home to your fine ranch. Enjoy what you already have. Leave us alone. We want to live our lives in peace, and not have you badger us. Now, go."

Bowler Tallman threw up an arm to knock the weapon out of her hand. He struck the end of the gun barrel, however, and forced it upward. Leona jerked the trigger, and blew a hole in the ceiling. She cocked the weapon again, determined.

Rust's ears rang from the sound of the gunshot. He jumped, startled, fearful she'd shot him. He leaped again, farther backwards, watching plaster snow down from the ceiling. Leona regained command of the gun and swung it straight into Rust's face.

Tallman struck at her once more. His arm swing was wild. He struck her wrist, and the force of his blow caused her to pull the trigger again. The gun boomed cannon-loud inside the small kitchen. Plaster cascaded again from the ceiling in a large dust cloud. The desperate sounds of scuffling feet and harsh breathing struck up in the small kitchen.

Pleasant Rathaus took two quick, spontaneous steps toward Leona, lifting his own pistol as he moved, and still moving rapidly, struck her with an incredibly sharp blow above her left ear, which sounded as if he'd dropped a fat melon onto a hard surface.

The girl didn't even sigh. Her legs crumpled beneath her weight, and she fell straight down instantly.

"Jesus," Tallman said. "Hit her kind of hard, didn't you, boss?"

Rathaus stared dumbly at his deputy. His eyes were about to glaze over. He was gasping for air, in loud squeaks, jerking and shuddering. His chest rose and fell like the pistons of an overworked steam engine. He turned two complete circles, casting about the room, searching for more trouble to subdue.

"What do you expect? She was fixing to kill the whole damn lot of us," he blurted.

"Didn't kill her, did you?" Rust said.

Jorod Rust stood in the doorway, staring round-eyed in amazement at the motionless, facedown girl.

"Leona," the old man whispered. He fell to her side, turned her onto her back, and cradled her head in the crook of an arm as if she were a child.

Rust saw where the blow of Rathaus' pistol had driven the hair of her scalp deep within the indentation created by the blow. He assumed she was dead, her skull crushed. Reyes attempted to lift her, to rise up with her in his arms. But he was far too weak and old to do so, long since passed the time when he could've performed this chore. He gave up, and sat with her head in his lap as if he were too shocked for the moment even to curse her killer.

Tallman shifted on his feet, scuffed a toe on the floorboards. "What now, boss?"

Rathaus regained his wind. He looked at Rust now from steady, but questioning eyes.

Rust realized the sheriff had fallen deeper under his control. "Why, hell, Pleasant. Don't look at me. You're the feller who did it."

"Yeah," Rathaus said, "but at whose bidding?"

Rust shrugged. "I don't see how this here'll be no problem. We warned 'em. They didn't see it our way's all."

Felipe Reyes looked up with dark eyes. "You'll go to jail for this, Rathaus." He swung his gaze to Rust next. "And you . . . you'll suffer too for this. You're the one to blame. You—"

Talking over Reyes as if he weren't in the same room, Rust said, "And anyways, this here's how we found 'em when we come in."

"What'n hell you talking about now, Honus?" Rathaus said.

"Why, sure. We come in here to check on 'em. I hadn't seen 'em in a week or so, and decided something must be wrong. Then me, being the caring neighbor, sent for you, and we come in and found the girl laying there on the floor. The old man was on the back porch, hanging from a rafter, both of 'em dead as a doornail. Must've killed the girl, and then hung hisself. Crazy old loon."

The sheriff swung about, and without mumbling another word, thumped back through the parlor and brushed out through the slanted front door. Seconds later, he returned with a rope in hand. Felipe Reyes had his back to him, still cradling the girl in his lap. Rathaus nodded to Tallman, and the deputy caught the old man by the shoulders in a grip that no two men of Reyes's strength could break.

Before the old man could shout or struggle, Rathaus caught him by the neck in the loop of the rope. Reyes came to life as Rathaus started dragging him across the floor toward the back door. He set his boot heels into the wood planks, and at times, finding a purchase, he reared up swinging, kicking and snarling like a trap-caught wolf. His eyes rolled in fear, snot bursting in a fountain from his nose. The ragged, pathetic old man attempted to scream, but Rathaus tightened the loop, cut off his wind, and all the sound he could make was a weak mewl that might've come from a kitten.

Rust opened the back door, and stepped to the side. Rathaus dragged Reyes outside, across the porch to the two meaty middle posts that held up the rafters and tin roof.

"Hold him there, Bowler, while I tie this rope over this rafter here," he said.

Reyes found a tiny amount of slack in the rope then, sucked in air, and kicked at the sheriff. Tallman caught the old man by the hair of his head, and slammed him hard back onto the porch floor. Blood and snot sprayed across the floor in a wide arc.

"Jesus Christ, Bowler," the sheriff said. "Hold the old bastard down."

Reyes fought with the strength a man sometimes finds when

he stares death in the face. He latched onto one of Tallman's hands with his snagged old teeth, and clung to it with the fierceness of a redbone hound, a raccoon in the death-like grip of its teeth despite enduring a beating by its owner.

Tallman removed his revolver with a free hand, and slapped the barrel hard against Reyes's head. Reyes gasped in pain, but didn't relinquish his hold on the deputy's hand. At length, after three hefty blows from the .45, he sighed deeply, and slumped inward, chin at rest upon his chest.

"Old sonofabitch," Tallman said. He shook his hand, scattering blood across the floor of the porch. "Hope he ain't got rabies." He bent over to nurse his injured hand.

"Ain't probable," said the sheriff. "Somebody help me here."

Honus Rust stepped across the porch and did his part to help hang Reyes. He supervised the operation. He beckoned to his son, Jorod. "Well," he said, "come on over here. Lend a hand."

Jorod Rust stepped forward, caught the old man by the shoulder and seat of the pants and held him aloft until the noose was tight around his skinny neck. The sheriff hung Reyes from the rafter, then nodded, and Jorod turned him loose. Felipe Reyes swung about in slow circles in the relentless rope's snake-like coil. Soon, Reyes squeaked out his final raspy protest.

"Somebody fetch a chair," Honus Rust said. "Got to tend to details, boys."

Jorod went into the kitchen, fetched a chair, took it to the porch and upended it beneath Reyes's body.

When it was all over, Rust stood back and hiked his trousers. "I 'spect you'll have to call in the coroner, Pleasant."

"Well, that's the usual practice in these here cases," Rathaus muttered.

The sheriff was straining to muzzle his full sarcasm. Rust was aware that Rathaus deeply resented him telling him how to handle his job. All of a sudden, the sheriff had lost the fear he'd experienced earlier when he'd acted from anger and killed Leona, but now with Rust's full backing, he'd relocated his confidence.

Bowler Tallman said, "Nope. Not right a-ways, no how. Miller's gone up to Camp Smyth."

Rathaus looked at old man Rust. "That's right. Bill had a funeral to attend up there. He'll be gone several days, I reckon."

"Aww well, hell," Rust said, "that there don't matter. Ain't going to hurt none to leave this old fart hang here a few days, is it? Can't move him, can you? Till the coroner comes out?"

"Not supposed to move anything on a crime scene," said the sheriff.

"This here ain't no crime . . . least not anything that would involve anybody else," said Rust. "It was murder, I figure. Murder and suicide. Financial problems, most likely."

"Well, that's for Miller to decide, I reckon," Rathaus said. "But, that there's how I see it too."

The men stormed out of the house, flushed the cats to the side, mounted up, and left the neat yard of Felipe Reyes in a rush. Rust led the way in his Studebaker hack. The sad house sat there, with its front door sprung open, and the hungry-eyed cats watching them leave.

CHAPTER TWELVE

The four men—Fixx, his two sons, and Batch—approached Felipe Reyes's tiny house at an easy lope. The half-dozen cats were sitting atop its ridgepole, staring down at them. The men discussed this oddity that Batch had brought up. He studied the cats as he followed the other men across the yard toward the front porch. Something was different about the place, he decided, but couldn't quite place it. Could it be the cats? They'd been underfoot on his every visit. He shook off his musings, though, and followed the others onto the porch.

"Whoa," Fixx said. He held up a hand.

Batch watched Fixx stop in his tracks, eyes on the door. The door's bottom hinge was aslant, and the door sat at a crooked pitch upon the floor, open wide enough to allow a man to pass through.

"Something's not right here. Looky here at this door," Fixx said.

"That old man drink, Batch?" said Clive.

"Never hung around here none. Probably drinks about like most men," he said.

"This door's been forced," Redman said. He stepped up and stuck his head inside the front room. Fixx stepped alongside him. He thrust his head inside too and called out in a loud voice, "Anybody home? Reyes? You home, Felipe?"

Batch joined them, calling out as well, "Leona? Leona Reyes, you home?" He stood back with the others at the sprung door.

At length, Clive stood to his fullest height, peered above the heads of the others.

"We better have a look around, don't you think, Pap?" Redman said.

"Wait a minute. Don't go in till I return," the older man warned. "Something's not right here."

Batch swung to the side. Fixx stepped down off the porch, walked across the yard to where the horses stood nosing the ground for grass, finding none in the well-tended yard. Fixx slipped his rifle out of its boot, turned and strode back across the yard. The cats atop the ridgepole, stood erect now, and Batch heard them moving about as they paced back and forth like mountaineers crossing a familiar ridgeline.

A harsh mechanical click struck up as Fixx jacked a shell into the chamber of his rifle. He stepped onto the porch, and strode toward the door. All the men stepped to the side to allow him to pass in ahead of them.

"Anybody home?" Fixx tried once more. When he received no answer, he crossed over the threshold and stood inside the parlor. Batch watched Fixx staring at the drying tobacco swaying now in the breeze that penetrated the house from the open door. "Well, come on in," Fixx said.

The ranch hand stepped deeper inside the room. A horrible sense of unease worked inside his mind. His stomach muscles tensed up, anticipating that Leona or her father would step up at any second, and him with no explanation of why he'd entered without permission.

He followed the men to the first room they came to off the living room, a bedroom. Fixx pushed the door inward an inch or so, warily. Batch could see into the room. A small shrine sat in one corner. He saw where the candle had burnt down to the lip of its holder. Wax had dripped down the sides of the brass candlestick. With caution, Fixx pushed the door all the way back against the inner wall, and entered. Batch followed the others inside.

The bedroom looked as if it belonged to a fastidious woman. Everything sat in place, the floor swept clean, a few small rugs cast upon the floor at various sites, with one at the side of her bed. It looked as if this was Leona's room, and she used the rugs on arising of a morning to prevent placing her bare feet on the cold floorboards. The scent of melted candle wax, and of more drying herbs, which he noticed draped from the low ceiling, loomed in the room. Nothing, save for the spent candle, looked awry or out of place.

Batch turned to the side, and followed the rest back to the parlor. He took note of the small sofa, the two rough, scarred chairs made of walnut, heavy and ancient, or so they appeared to him. Nothing in the parlor looked out of place either, except for the low slant of the front door.

He followed Fixx toward the kitchen, and before he reached the arched doorway that divided the two rooms, Fixx raised an arm to halt them. Redman, though, walked on past his father's warning hand. Now, he too stopped, and held up a hand.

"My Lord," said Clive Fixx. He'd peered past his father and brother to see what'd alarmed them. He sprang back, turned in two quick circles as if to flee, then remembered himself, and calmed down. He kept his eyes turned away from the kitchen, all the same.

From where he stood Batch saw a woman's leg, knee bent, exposed from above that point down to her ankle and a small flash of yellow and red, which was the color scheme of her dress. He knew then what the three men inside the kitchen were staring at, but still couldn't see much more than her one leg, and the flash of her bright dress. He stepped past Clive and placed a hand on the inner boards of the arch, leaning on it a bit, unwilling to strain his stubbed-off leg any more than need be.

Leona Reyes lay dead, Batch saw. He removed his hat and said, "That was a fine woman. About as fine as you'll see, I 'spect. I guess she *is* dead, ain't she, Mr. Fixx?"

Redman turned to him and stared into his face, not realizing that Batch couldn't see what he and his father could. "Well, now, shit, Batch."

"Yeah," said the older man, "she's dead all right. Dead, and them cats been at her face, her soft parts too."

Unable to take the man's word for it, he too stepped the rest of the way into the kitchen. "Jesus Christ in heaven," he said.

He knew for sure then what was different about the place. He heard the cats in a scamper on the roof like rats scurrying about in the attic of a house. "Them damned cats. They're fat as pet dogs."

The cats had eaten off Leona Reyes's nose. Both eyeballs were missing, as well as her cheeks. The ranch hand couldn't bear further investigation. He'd seen too much already, and stepped backward. "What'n hell happened here?" he said from the parlor. His mind filled up with wonder and he was shocked at the horror in the Reyeses' kitchen, growing numb fast.

"Well," said Redman, "I tried to keep you back out of here. You had to see, didn't you?"

Fixx cast a stern eye at his middle son. "Ain't you a fine one to talk?"

The older man bent a knee, scanned the side of the girl's head, the crushed skull, the hair imbedded deep inside the depression, driven in by the blow of some heavy object. Fixx rose up, in time, tugging his handkerchief out of a rear pocket. He blew his nose, and put the handkerchief away. "There lays the gun. Somebody struck her with it. That's what killed her."

Fixx turned to Batch. "You got anybody in mind might of

done this? She have any boyfriends, anything like that?"

"Well, she might've had one. Don't really know. I do know Mr. Rust don't like this bunch. Neither does Jorod. Honus has tried to buy this little scrape of twenty-five acres from Reyes for years."

"Why? The damned place won't even grow decent brush and weeds." Redman removed his hat and scratched an itch atop his head.

"Who knows?" Batch told him. "Mr. Rust sometimes don't need much of a reason for what he does."

Fixx swiped at his brow, and said, "Well, I know Honus is a certified no-account . . . but I ain't yet ready to call him a murderer." He shifted his rifle to the other hand and stepped past the body.

Batch said, "Well, when I first caught on with him, I'd of thought so too. But he changed a few years ago. I think the man went nuts. So help me, I do."

Fixx looked again at Batch, shook his head. It was plain to Batch that Fixx wouldn't think the worst of the man he'd grown up with. As if drawn by an invisible hand, he followed the ranch owner to the back door.

Fixx swung it open. Batch heard a sudden, tremendous rushing sound, like the wings of many birds thrashing the air to escape. He peered over Fixx's shoulder, and watched as a black cloud of birds lifted to the sky. The cloud wheeled off. The strident voices sounded like dogs crying out in surprise and defiance at being disturbed. They were unmistakable, speaking in the one voice that is so familiar to every man on the face of the entire planet.

"Crows," Batch muttered.

He followed their progress as they wheeled high into the sky. They flew off as if to exit the county completely, then swung on wing again, soared higher, turned, and dove toward the tiny shack. The meal they'd been feasting upon still hung there by the remnants of its neck. A scrawny meal at best and with nothing much left for the crows but frayed strings of flesh. They swooped again, and at length fell to earth a hundred feet away from the back porch, and walked about in circles, one foot at a time, with their legs extended forward manlike, fretting aloud their frustration and defeat.

Batch turned away, and this time Fixx himself couldn't look for long at the torn, tattered remnants of Felipe Reyes's pitiful body. The old man removed his handkerchief, and honked into it, with the intent of nothing more than releasing tension, or so Batch supposed.

Fixx put away his handkerchief. "This here ain't nothing for nobody to see."

"Well, Pap," said Redman, "what'll we do now?"

"Ride into Witness Tree Station. Let the sheriff know. The coroner Miller'll have to come out, and take the man down, and carry the bodies into town."

He pushed past Batch and the others, turned back into the kitchen, and as Fixx started toward the parlor, the abrupt, encroaching sound of the sprung front door scraping loudly across the floorboards rang out. Batch hauled up in surprise.

"Who'n hell's in here?" someone called from the door.

Fixx recognized the sheriff's voice, and said, "Steel Fixx, Sheriff. We're in the kitchen."

The sheriff and a shorter man entered the kitchen. The shorter man was stocky and ruddy of face, with an underlying layer of freckles. His sandy hair matched his bushy sideburns and his eyebrows.

"Well, there she is, Miller," Rathaus said. "The way we left her. There's the gun. You boys ain't disturbed nothing in here, have you?"

"No," Fixx said.

Batch learned by this that the sheriff had had prior knowledge of the deaths.

"What're you doing here, Steely?" Rathaus said. "A body ain't supposed to enter a crime scene."

"I come over to thank Leona Reyes for tending my daughter, Molly, when she was dying. Didn't know I'd find a crime scene. Should've put a sign on the door, or nailed it shut. Give a man some warning. This is quite a shock, finding a mess like this."

"Well, you ain't supposed to be here, Steely. Messes like this're better left to the likes of me and Bill here. We're both of us kind of used to it. Looks like them cats got to her."

Bill Miller bent to both knees alongside the girl. He lifted the hair back off the wound, scanned it for a time, then said, "This is the wound that killed her. Crushed skull." He got up, dusted off the knees of his trousers, although there was little of it, for the floor—except for the small spatter of dried blood—was spotless from repeated sweepings.

Miller held the revolver in hand, placed it on the tabletop. "And this is what crushed it." The coroner exhaled, nodded around to all there, and stepped toward the back door. "Say there's another one out here?"

"Yeah," replied Pleasant Rathaus. "Was anyways when we left. It's the girl's father, Felipe."

Batch stepped out of the coroner's way. Miller opened the door, and scuffed on outside. The sheriff brought up the rear. The rest, though, remained inside the kitchen. Batch, Fixx and his sons, though, heard every word spoken by the two men on the porch, could've watched it all if they chose to look. Batch, for one, did.

Miller walked around the body, inspected it from every angle, dropped to a knee where he peered up at the old man from a ground view. He got to his feet after some time of intense scrutiny, took out a medium-sized pad from an inner coat pocket, and started sketching in long looping swirls, using elaborate flourishes to recreate the scene on the back porch, which included the upended chair.

Finished with the sketch of the hung man, he put away the pad, and walked back into the kitchen, the sheriff close behind.

Miller pulled out a chair at the table, took up his pad again to put the final touches on the sketch he'd drawn. Then, satisfied with the porch sketch, he scooted his chair up close to the girl, and sketched her pose as well, from several angles.

"How'd you happen to find 'em, Pleasant?" Fixx said. "I take it was *you* found 'em, wasn't it?"

"Yeah. It was me," answered the sheriff. "Well, me and your cousin, that is—Honus Rust. Honus had some concern for these folks. Said he hadn't seen 'em for some time, and being neighborly, he decided to fetch me. This mess here's what we found."

Batch jumped in his skin, hearing those words. "Since when's Honus Rust ever decided to check on any of his neighbors? He was forever railing against this old man."

Rathaus cut him down cold. "Who asked your opinion on anything, Mister?"

Batch shut his mouth and figured it better to hold his peace.

Miller scooted back up to the table, finished his sketches, and set about writing up a report. He put away the pad, finished, slapped his knees, got to his feet, and said, "Well, I guess we're done here, Sheriff. Save for carrying off the bodies. I'll go out and grab the bags and stretcher." The coroner then left the house.

Batch and all the men stood around and stared at one another with grave discomfort until the coroner returned with a canvas bundle beneath an arm, dragging a stretcher along behind. He dropped the bundle to the floor, placed the stretcher alongside Leona's body, and shook out the bundle, which proved to be two long, wide canvas bags created for bearing off the dead and remnants of the dead.

Miller fanned one of the bags out to its fullest, placed it alongside the girl, then looked to the sheriff. "Want to lend a hand, Pleasant?"

Rathaus helped place the girl inside the canvas bag. Together they set her onto the stretcher, and carried her outside to the coroner's wagon.

Batch stepped forward, keeping his eyes on the front door, awaiting their return. "The sheriff's lying, Mr. Fixx." He withstood Fixx's intense scrutiny for a time. Fixx eventually turned his head from him, and set about rolling a cigarette.

"I know he is," Batch continued. "Honus Rust don't care about nobody but hisself . . . and that Jorod, and little Honus . . . don't even much like Hughie."

By the time Fixx finished rolling his cigarette and fired it to life, the coroner and Rathaus had returned.

They stepped onto the back porch, took down the hung man, doing so with some difficulty, and returned with the ravaged body upon the stretcher.

"Got to shut up this here house, Steely," said the sheriff.

The men followed them outside and watched as the sheriff and the coroner placed Felipe Reyes in the back of the wagon alongside the body of Leona. The two men set the tailgate back in place, and Batch followed Fixx up to the sheriff.

"Who you 'spect done this, Pleasant?" Fixx said. "I guess you probably ain't got no idea, though, do you?"

"We ain't really supposed to say so, but, yeah, I figure I know who done it." He cast an eye toward the coroner as though waiting for his permission to speak.

"Well, sir," said Bill Miller, "it was the old man . . . way it looks to me."

"The old man?"

"Yeah. You won't see a clearer case of murder and suicide in your life. This is off the record, you see," said the coroner. "The old man went crazy, killed his girl, then hung himself.

"That's already down in the report I wrote. Excuse me, Mr. Fixx," he added. He took a hammer and a few nails from a small wooden toolbox beneath the wagon seat, went again and mounted the porch, and walked through the house. Soon, the yard rang out with the sound of the coroner nailing shut the back door. Batch watched as he returned to the front porch. Saw him lift up the front door so that it swung freer, and shut it. He drove nails through the wooden door, toe nailing them at the top, middle and bottom, and managed the entire affair without a missed lick.

"Honus come for you before he found this mess, Pleasant?" Fixx said. "Or did he find it first then come for you?"

"Yeah. Thought I told you that already. He suspicioned something was wrong, so he come for me first thing. That's the way folks is supposed to do. Wish more folks was like him. Things'd go a lot smoother if they was."

The sheriff paused and studied Fixx for a time, then said in a cold voice, but with a smile, "You fixing to write a book, Steely, or what?"

Batch watched Fixx accept the bite of the sheriff's sarcasm without a blink. The old man was strong of mind, he saw.

"I come over here to pay a visit, Pleasant. Like you say Honus did. None of us are seers, I reckon. Not even Honus. But the likes of this here'd make him some kind of major prophet, seems to me. Most of us ain't gifted that a-ways. I, for one, doubt he is either."

"Well, that's how she went, Steely, take 'er or leave 'er."

The coroner returned, put away his hammer, climbed onto the seat of his wagon, and lifted the reins off the backs of the horses. Then he wheeled the wagon about, and left the yard at a decent clip.

The sheriff stood looking at the roof of the shack for a time. The cats were still sitting up there, staring down at the men in the yard. He mounted his horse, grunted under his breath as he stared again at the cats, and then said, "Somebody ought to kill them damn cats. I reckon now they'll run wild, eat up every quail in the county."

"Well," said Fixx, "you're the sheriff. I reckon you're the man to handle a job like that."

"Naw. Never could stand to kill creatures, cats especially. Was hoping you'd do the job." He whipped his mare about in a neat spin, took off, and caught up to the coroner.

Batch followed behind the others and they left the dead man's yard as well.

Curious, he looked back over a shoulder. The cats climbed down off the roof, scampered to the front door of the shack, found it shut, and walked to the edge of the porch. There they sat, on their rumps, six fat balls of fur, staring at the men as they left.

CHAPTER THIRTEEN

Spring turned to summer. The family garden flourished. The tomatoes turned red the past week, and the Fixxes fell to eating their fill of them with each meal, including breakfast, where the boys and the father ate them alongside their biscuits and gravy. Enos went so far as to mix them in with the gravy. His mother frowned at this, but allowed it.

"How can you eat such a dog's breakfast, child," she said.

Olivia and Enos had worked hard in their garden, plowing done right after the ground thawed, then the planting, and when it started flourishing, they fought the weeds, for the weeds too wanted to flourish. It was also work to keep out the crows and rabbits. The sweet corn grew as fast as cluster grass, and the family waited, eager in anticipation of its maturity.

The deaths of Felipe Reyes and his daughter had caused a brief furor in Witness Tree Station and at the Hazlett Baptist Church. Now, though, the talk had died away and seldom fired up more than a few words from the citizens of the area. But Fixx hadn't forgotten. It preyed on his mind in some fashion at every turn of the day. He thought long about it, especially at night. He often wondered if his cousin could've been in some way responsible for the two deaths. Batch had told him of Rust's hatred for Felipe Reyes and of his unnatural hunger for the old man's land. It puzzled Fixx as to what there was about that small piece of land that was so valuable to his cousin. Nothing, at least that he'd yet discovered, could warrant such a desire . . .

and he couldn't see why Honus would go so far as to kill the old man over the land. It wasn't worth it. In fact, Steel Fixx figured that Reyes would've had to run his fastest to even give it to him. The land was useless.

Something else was in play here that plagued him. He recalled Batch's claim that Rust had gone crazy. He also remembered how Honus had looked as he sat in the gazebo that long-ago day, drinking the fancy liqueur, with a monocle—of all pretentious things—dangling down his suit front, and with nothing at all wrong with his eyesight. Murphy had also claimed that Honus had lost his mind.

It was possible Rust *had* lost his mind. There was also the shoddy way he'd treated them—he and Olivia—over the death of Molly. He couldn't conceive of a reason to treat someone in such a callous manner. Honus had traveled with the children up to the house of his sister-in-law despite all that deep snow. He could've come to the Fixx house much easier, if he'd been of a mind to, especially after that first horrible day of snow and wind that had frozen Batch's foot.

He wrestled with the matter every night. Every morning after he'd turned and fretted all night long, or at least the greater part of the night, he found on the arrival of the morning sun that he might as well have been up mending harness . . . at least something productive would've come of his lost sleep. The way it was now, he'd arrived at no conclusion, and faced the prospect of more of the same come bedtime.

His bed was his terrible enemy. His guilt, as well, continued to attack him. He replayed his wife's protests over in his mind— her protests that he should've accepted Molly's pregnancy, and raised Molly's child in his own house. His immense pride had cut him off square, though. He hadn't been man enough to accept what he considered a humiliating defeat.

His caning of Jorod had played its own part in his guilt. All in all, it combined to create a massive bulwark, a roadblock that prevented him from finding the peace he now longed for.

In September, news came from the Rusts that the children had returned, and were now back with their father and grandfather. Batch had overheard a conversation in town, which spoke of their return, and he'd informed the Fixxes of the news.

They were all keen on going over to visit the children, with invitation or without.

"Let's go over there, Pap," Redman had said, at three o'clock one afternoon but with not enough time in the day left to go there, visit, and return.

The following day, though, they all went to see the children— all save Batch. He remained home to do the barn chores, and to keep his eye on the pet bull calf since it would be late when they returned.

The boys, Clive and Redman, rode ahead on horseback, and Fixx, Olivia, and Enos followed them in the wagon. The grass, starting to turn green when Steel and Olivia had visited the grave of their daughter in early spring, had gone over now to the heat and sun, brown and sere. It crackled underfoot as they gathered around the grave.

Molly Rust's grave sat in a sad, sorry hump, sunken in the center, and had failed to accept any growth of vegetation during the spring and summer. It was far too wretched and pitiful a place for them to visit for any length of time. So they rode in silence down the slope, back again to the lane and followed it up to the house where the huge white pillars held up the massive roof of the front porch.

Clive and Redman sat their horses at the foot of the porch steps, and waited for the wagon to arrive with their parents and younger brother. They stepped to the ground after the wagon drove up.

Fixx walked around the wagon to assist Olivia down, but by the time he got there, she'd already stepped down in her eagerness, smoothing out the wrinkles in her dress. They trooped up the steps, mother, father, two older boys, Enos at the rear. Olivia stepped to the side at the door and allowed Fixx to rap out the news of their arrival with an outsized, callused hand upon the grand, imposing door.

He rapped three times before he heard a slight scuffle on the other side of the door, followed by it swinging open, moving in silence on its sturdy hinges.

Sarah Ellen stared up at them from her dark, inquisitive eyes.

"Sarah?" said Olivia, for the girl had grown, changed since the last time she'd seen her. "Sarah Ellen, is that you, girl?"

"Yes, ma'am," replied Sarah Ellen. She recognized her grandmother and her face lit up like a spark of light confronting the darkness. "Grandmam," she said. "Grandmam . . . I thought I'd never see you again."

This was all it took. Fixx watched all the sadness and torture Olivia had kept at bay since the death of her daughter shred to pieces. This small girl was the very replica of the girl his wife had given birth to. He watched as she dropped to her knees, and wrapped her arms about the girl in a tender embrace. Fixx reasoned that Olivia's heart was melting. He shifted on uneasy feet.

"You've grown so. My, but you've grown." Olivia held her against her breast, speaking tender words into the long, rosewood-colored hair that covered Sarah's ears. She repeated those words time after time. It was if she couldn't believe she was holding the child after the lapse of so much time. Not so many months had passed, although with all the tragedy that'd taken place in that time, it might very well have been an eternity.

Beth Ann appeared. She stood behind Sarah Ellen, and stared up at the many people who blocked the doorway. The two other girls, Jolene and Margaret, stood behind her, but being younger and shy, they stood apart, satisfied for the moment to watch and wait.

No grownup appeared, however, so Fixx entered the house, soon followed by the entire family. He stood with hat in hand, in the center of the large parlor, which was nearly as large as Steel's entire house. He said to the girl, "Where's your father and grandfather, Sarah Ellen?"

"Grandpap has gone to Omaha on a buying trip."

"Where's your father and little Honus?"

Sarah Ellen shifted, nervous in his presence. "Father's in bed, sir. Little Honus is in there with him."

"In bed? Why, it's ten o'clock."

"Yes, sir." The other girls stood gathered around their older sister as if she was their sole protection. "He was out late. He said I should watch things while he and little Honus took a nap. Little Honus, though, is restless and wants up. I know Father would be mad, so I make him stay abed."

"Where is Mrs. Murphy? Ain't she here, either?" Fixx said.

Sarah Ellen shook her head. He heard the girl's long dark hair sweep across her shoulders.

"She still does do the cooking for the family, don't she?" he said.

"No, sir."

By the look in her eyes, the way she attempted a brave answer, he saw something was amiss.

Olivia said, "Well, who then? Who does do the cooking, keeps the house?"

Sarah Ellen smiled a timid smile, and said, "Why me. I do the cooking. Grandpap says I'm as grown as his own mam was when she took on that chore."

"But, where's Mrs. Murphy? Did she quit?"

Again, the girl swung her curls across her shoulders. "Mr.

Murphy made her quit. Grandpap says he's on the lookout for a new cook, and a new blacksmith as well. In the meantime, I'll serve to do the cooking."

Fixx peered into the little girl's face, shared a knowing look with his wife, spun about and stormed off, but realizing he didn't know which room Jorod slept in, he stopped. "Where's your father, Sarah Ellen? Which room?"

She rushed to him, took his large hand and led him out of the parlor into a long hall with rooms on each side of it that reminded Fixx of hotel rooms. At the far end of the hall, she stopped in front of the door to her father's room.

"Thank you, Sarah Ellen. You go back in there now, stay with your grandmam."

He watched her walk back up the hallway, and noted once more the strong resemblance between her and her mother. His heart broke. He felt it sever down the middle, and separating into two equal parts as though there had been a perforation created there for that purpose.

His temper flared, and the juices in the pit of his stomach boiled and bubbled over with a new hatred for his cousin's son. The longer he stood there and thought about it, the stronger his desire to kill grew. He decided he needed his boys with him.

"Clive." His voice boomed loudly up the length of the hallway, penetrating into the parlor where his two grown sons stood. "Redman, come here. I need you. Both y'all boys."

When they appeared, he said to them, "Whatever happens in that room," he pointed to the bedroom door, "don't let me kill that Jorod. I beg you."

"Yessir," answered Redman. Clive nodded in agreement.

"I mustn't do that." This fortified his decision. "Not in front of the children . . . your mam and Enos. It wouldn't be right."

Clive reassured him. "We'll be right there with you, Pap."

Fixx turned the brass doorknob. The expensive well-built

125

door slid open silently as if it rode on silver bearings.

Jorod Rust slept with his mouth shut, snoring through his nose, facedown on his stomach, head turned to the side in order to breath. A heavy vapor of alcohol rose from him. Fixx's nose wrinkled in distaste at the fetid reek, the raw, rank residue of the sleeping man's excesses of the night before.

The tyke, Honus, lay there awake, and stared up at the intruders with a mistrustful glow in his bright eyes. For a brief moment, the boy's maternal grandfather felt an instant dislike for him. Fixx saw the same sense of treachery, the look of rank one-sided lack of liberality coming from the eyes of the boy, the same devious eyes that he'd grown over the years to abhor in the older Honus Rust. He managed to banish the thought when he realized it was insanity to hate his own grandson.

"Take him into the parlor, Clive, hand him to Sarah Ellen. He'll be afraid of his grandmam I 'spect . . . for a time yet."

Little Honus didn't whimper or mutter a word of protest when Clive lifted him from bed. His eyes remained on his mother's father until the hallway wall blocked his vison.

Clive returned right away. Fixx shook Jorod by the foot. The sleeper grumbled in a feeble protest, but he didn't awaken. After a considerable time of shaking, Jorod shook his head, growled louder and sat up in bed.

His eyes widened in fright, for Fixx towered above him. Fixx reckoned Jorod was likely recalling how his "uncle" flogged him that day long ago on the Hazlett Church Road. Jorod whirled, and swung his legs abruptly over the edge of the bed.

"If the house had caught fire, I reckon you'd of burned up with it, Jorod," Fixx said.

"Sarah would've waked me, I reckon."

"You place a lot of faith in such a little girl," he said. "She's a child."

"That girl's got a lot of gumption, Uncle Steel."

Jorod had called him by that endearment all his life and, though Fixx had first discouraged it, he'd given in to it, accepting it as fact instead of mere habit, knowing it'd developed by the large amount of years separating the cousins once removed.

"Where's Honus?"

"In Nebraska, I think. That there's where he lit out for when he left the yard anyways."

"Must have him a girlfriend, the amount of time he spends up there."

"Buying horses."

"What's he do with so many horses?"

"Buys 'em up at a bargain . . . sells 'em. Makes a little money. Sometimes, though, he is beat on a deal. He leaves for Nebraska . . . sometimes he winds up in Europe. He's a rover, Pap is."

"How come you didn't come for me, when Molly died, Jo?" Fixx said.

"Hell's fire, Uncle Steel, snow was hub deep. How was I to make it over there in a storm like that?"

"They say you had little trouble going into Witness Tree Station during that time. Your pap carried them children out in the storm all the way up to his sister-in-law's place."

"Yeah," Jorod said. He ran fingers through his hair, tossed it from his face. Fixx saw anger stir to life in Jorod's eyes. "Some folks say a lot of things ain't true."

"Mr. Murphy said it."

"Yeah, well, Murphy's got his ass in a sling with Pap. He's going to find his traps sitting aside the road one of these days."

"Murphy go to him about how he's been feeling up his wife? That what's got his back up?"

"Hell, Uncle Steel, how should I know? He's mad at him for some reason or other. He don't tell me why he does anything."

A red rose of anger bloomed on both sides of Fixx's neck.

"Yeah, well, I can see why he wouldn't want to tell you anything."

"Shit," Jorod said. "What's got you in such a damn froth, anyways?"

Fixx caught Jorod up by the bare flesh of his chest in a sudden explosion of arms and hands. "You know what's got me all in a froth, I reckon . . . goddam you to hell, anyways. The way you allowed Molly to die—"

Clive placed a hand on his father's shoulder. "Pap," he said. "You go easy now, please, sir."

"Jesus, Uncle Steel," Jorod said.

Fixx could plainly see that Jorod was in pain. His harsh fingers dug deeply into the flesh of his chest. "Why'd you not allow that girl, Leona Reyes, to stay with Molly and help her?"

"That woman . . . shit, she didn't know nothing. She done more harm than anything else."

"Batch told me Molly was some better when the Mexican girl was here."

"Batch? Hell, what's he know? A damned orphan the old man took in from pity. And that Mexican woman was a witch. Ask anybody, you don't believe me."

"Well, if nothing else, Leona would've been with her when she died. You weren't here. You have any idea how it might feel to be all alone and dying?"

Clive said, "You ain't helping your cause any, Jo. I was you, I'd learn damn fast to keep my mouth shut."

Redman agreed. "You're right on the edge of having your neck wrung. You better shut up."

They all waited. Fixx heard his own breath, raw in his chest, coming in gasps. He'd forget to breathe, then realize it, and grasp at another breath as if it were a balloon floating out of his reach. He was keenly aware of Clive's hand on his shoulder, felt him lift it, then set it back down in a gentle pat, as if to remind

him all was well, that it was better to do right than to kill Jorod. Redman stood at Fixx's other shoulder. He appeared ready to spring forward to attempt to prevent the murder he likely felt was imminent.

Fixx's fingers lost some of the savage hold on Jorod's chest. In time, his breathing slowed into gentle swells, and he regained much of his composure.

"I want you to listen to me, Jorod . . . and listen close. You hear me?"

Jorod Rust nodded, but couldn't maintain eye contact with the wild-eyed man standing above him like a demon from a nightmare. "Yessir. I hear you."

"We're leaving here."

Jorod's head sprang upward. Fixx saw the light of hope and relief flare in his face with the precious thought that he was now home free. "And when we go, them children are going with us."

Jorod lunged backward, and tried to break free of Fixx. "No. You ain't taking them kids."

"Like hell, I ain't. You managed to kill my daughter. I'll be damned to hell if I allow you to do the same to her babies." He struggled with Jorod there on the bed, his breathing wheezing as loud as a faulty bellows.

"Them kids're mine." Jorod flung himself backward away from those strong arms, those piercing spikelike fingers, but only managed to inflict more harm to his chest.

"Go on," Fixx said. "Keep it up. I'm trying with all the power of my soul to not kill you. Keep on, and I'll do it yet . . . so help me."

"Jorod," Clive said. His voice floated gentle and soothing in the air. "Don't say another word . . . if you want to go on breathing."

Jorod succumbed and fell still, except for the continued spasmodic shaking of his body. "Now, again, I'll say it once

more," Fixx said. "I'm taking Molly's children home with me. Hell, that girl, Sarah Ellen's, the only grownup in the house, way it looks."

Jorod sank then, as if his head and shoulders were too heavy for his chest muscles to hold erect any longer. After a time, he exhaled. "The old man'll kill me."

"Not likely. Not with the way he's spoiled you all your life."

Clive breathed easier, but left his hand in place on top of his father's shoulder, and Redman stood on Fixx's other side, ever alert, as was his nature.

To further ease the tension, Clive said, "Let's go, Pap. Take the youngsters and go on home."

Fixx's face was hard set with the raw hatred that showed beneath the surface.

Jorod's chest sank more inward. He sat in a dejected slump upon the bed, chin at rest on his chest. In a defeated voice, he said, "At least leave the boy, Uncle Steel. Pap'll go crazy if you take little Honus."

"I 'spect Honus had his chance to raise Molly's children. Seems to me he did nothing but make a failure of it. I reckon it's my turn now."

"I guess you know what's coming when Pap finds out what you've done here today?"

Fixx shoved Jorod back onto the bed. "Whatever he does . . . won't be half as bad as what's already been done."

After a lengthy silence, Jorod sat upon the side of the bed. "I wouldn't be too damn sure about that."

"I guess we'll have to wait and see." Fixx spun and barged out of the room.

"I ain't lying," said Jorod to Fixx's back. "When Pap finds this out, there'll be hell to pay."

★　★　★　★　★

Murphy stood blocking the road when Fixx drove the buggy up to the blacksmith's shack on their departure. Fixx pulled to a halt.

"I see you got the youngsters," said the blacksmith.

"Yessir. I'm taking 'em home with me for a time."

"Mr. Fixx," Murphy continued, "I know your place ain't large enough to keep a full-time smith, but I can do other work as well. I can't smith for Mr. Rust no more. Things are right sour here. I was wondering—"

"I can give you work, Adair, if that's what you're fixing to say. None of us cares for farrier work."

"Yessir," Murphy said. "That's what I was fixing to ask you, all right." His face brightened.

Fixx watched the man's face beaming with fresh enthusiasm, his hopes fully realized.

"The other men in the area can use you some too, I reckon. We'll find enough work to keep you busy full-time."

"Appreciate 'er, Mr. Fixx."

"Pack up and come when you're ready."

"Yessir. Got half my earthly trappings in my wagon already."

Chapter Fourteen

Fixx had instructed Enos to build up the fire at four that morning while the rest of the family was at the breakfast table. The bull calf followed Enos at his every turn. It often got in his way, but he remained patient with it.

Fixx returned to the fire after eating, and relieved Enos so he could eat his own breakfast.

"Come on back soon as you're done, Enos."

"Yessir," Enos answered, and hurried off toward the house. The calf trotted behind him, and often stepped on his heels so great was its need to be near the boy.

Fixx chuckled standing at the fire that Enos had built, the cooking pot close at hand. He watched the calf and the boy until Enos entered the house, and the calf, seeing it couldn't go inside with him, ran in a couple of lost circles like a hunting dog on a cold trail.

"That bull calf's dog-like, he's so tame." Fixx had intended to castrate the calf, but hadn't gotten around to it. He doubted Enos would allow it now, so he'd have to take care and keep it segregated when it grew to maturity. He allowed the boy might decide by then—if the bull became too much of a nuisance—to swap it off. There was still time. Everything in its own time, or so Fixx's father had taught him.

By ten o'clock, the air had grown rank with the smell of grain cooking.

Fixx and Enos had their shirtsleeves rolled up past their

forearms, taking turns stirring the batch. The shoats in their pen—weaned and apt to eat anything within reach—were fogging the air with their screams. By noon when an unfamiliar wagon quit the Hazlett Church Road and entered Fixx's lane, the hogs and pigs were in a genuine rage of hunger, maddened by the odor of the grain.

Fixx stopped work, rolled a cigarette, and kept his eyes on the wagon. He watched it disappear into the belly of the land and reappear later, climbing a crest. By the time he struck a match and fired his cigarette, Enos too, had caught sight of the wagon, and still stirring the pot, kept his eyes on its progress.

"Who you think it is, Pap?"

"Don't know," he said, pulling smoke into his lungs, and releasing it with a relaxed sense of pleasure.

He recognized J. B. Maples driving the rig, and said, "Well, now. I really didn't expect that man to drive all the way down here."

"Who is it, Pap?"

"A merchant I met at a store I stopped at in Camp Smyth last time I went up that way for lumber. I 'spect he's come for whiskey."

The nearer the wagon came, the more intently the man and boy watched its progress. It halted in the lane a hundred feet from the springhouse at the base of a limestone bluff, where Enos had set up the cooking pot.

Fixx had built a tiny house of stone over the spring to keep butter and other perishables fresh. The spring was a wonderful source of fresh water. He'd walled off a portion of the outflow in concrete to create a pool, outside the door, to the left of the walkway that led to the springhouse, and with a six-inch cast iron pipe to release the overflow. The overflow entered a small creek, which flowed on down to the Century River, better than a mile away.

Indians had used the spring for untold years before he'd bought this land. Fixx bought it with an eye for a water supply, not only because of household needs but for the making of whiskey as well. Olivia often said the spring was more important to him for whiskey-making than for anything else. He'd been forced to admit she was right. Whiskey making had been important in his family back through the years, until no one living could recall the first Fixx who'd started it all.

The visitor climbed down from his wagon. He flexed his knees to relieve the strain of sitting for so long.

"Nice place, Fixx." He fetched out a handkerchief and wiped his brow.

Fixx watched as Maples scanned the area, the springhouse, the large barn in the distance, and farther off, the house in its two-stories.

"Yessir," the man added, "sure 'nough a nice place."

"Come on down here with us, Maples."

He judged Maples to be in his mid-fifties. But he got about with the ease of a much younger man, lean and fit. Father and son watched as he walked down the path where they stood before the fire.

He nodded to Enos. "Who's your helper, Fixx?" he said, and extended his hand.

After brushing hands, Fixx said, "This here's my master of the distillery, Maples. His name's Enos."

"Good hand, is he?"

"The finest. He knows whiskey-making better'n I do. Got a knack for it the way some have with horses or judging cattle on the hoof. I could leave here right now, and come back later, and he wouldn't even miss me."

Maples laughed. "Sort of makes a man feel unwanted, I'd say."

"I'm happy somebody'll be able to carry on the tradition.

He'll earn a fair living at it, if that's what he decides to do. None of the other boys care a flip for it, except they do take a sip now and again."

"Well," Maples said, "it's sure 'nough great whiskey. I've come for my share of it too, like I told you last year."

"How much are you looking to buy, Maples?"

"Five barrels will do for now, I 'spect."

Fixx whistled sharply in surprise. "Mightn't have that much stuff proper aged. Got plenty of younger whiskey. First of the year, the better stuff'll be ready. Come back then."

"I'll take what you can spare. I can sell all you can make in my store. That's fine whiskey you got here, Fixx."

Fixx directed the merchant to the shade cast by the springhouse, pointed him to a seat on a large slab of limestone, and left Enos at the fire.

When Fixx first settled here, he'd hauled the slab and its twin up from the creek where they'd washed down from the bluff many years ago. Olivia used them now when she came to the springhouse in the heat of the day to snap beans, sew, or to do up other tedious chores. Because of its chill, the spring made an excellent place to sit and talk in summer.

When they were sitting at ease on the slabs in the shade, Fixx reached over and cracked the door of the springhouse. He took down a tin cup that hung from a nail inside on the back of the door, and scooped up a cupful of water from the spring. He passed it to Maples. Steam lifted from the water in a slow curl in the heated outside air. Maples took it and drank it right down, then brushed at his forehead where the cold water must've set it to burning. Fixx handed him another cupful. This time he sipped it slowly, wary of its deep chill.

"I can taste the very center of the earth in this water, Fixx. About as sweet a water as you'll find, I reckon."

"Hard to find good water in this country," Fixx said. "Back

home ever' homestead has a spring like this one."

When Maples handed back the cup, Fixx reached inside the springhouse again, and brought out an earthenware gallon jug. He poured whiskey into his visitor's cup, gave it over to him, and watched the man's eyes glitter as if they were sparks struck from a blacksmith's hammer.

Maples sipped it, and rolled it on his tongue before drinking it down. He wiped his lips, and said, "You don't make me drunk now, Fixx. Shouldn't take advantage of a weary traveler, you know."

Both men, relaxed now, chuckled.

Fixx rolled up a smoke, lit it and settled back against the wall of the springhouse, content for the first time in a long time—shedding his cares, enjoying the flushed feeling as the nicotine invigorated him.

"I can sell all the whiskey you make," Maples said, serious now.

"Transporting it's a problem," Fixx said.

"Yeah, right now it is. But I hear in a few years the railroad's heading your way, be coming right through Witness Tree Station. You'll be able to ship your product by the boxcar load then, if you care to."

"Hadn't heard that."

"Well, it's coming, and that's no lie. I give it another year, two at the most. I'd like a solid promise from you to let me handle your whiskey when it does arrive. We can make a bunch of money, and not no fly-by-the-way deal, neither. I'm talking about a long-term proposition. You supply me with whiskey. I'll bottle it, label it and sell it. I figure we'll both make a pile of money."

"You plan to bottle it?"

"Yessir. Can't sell it by the jug in Kansas City and St. Louis, and them large cities. I'll have to bottle it up for certain."

"You been thinking on this for a time, ain't you?"

"Yessir. I sure have. Right after I first tasted it."

Olivia called them in to dinner.

"Time to eat, Maples. We'll go on up, and come back down when we're through . . . let Enos have his turn. I 'spect 'Livia might like to hear your plan, too."

"Sounds fine," Maples said. He slapped his knees and got to his feet.

Walking up the path, past the barn, Fixx saw the man casting an eye toward the distant hog pen, where the hogs were still screaming as if they were being tortured. Maples said, "Sounds like them hogs might have some coon hound in 'em. Some of 'em's got right pretty mouths on 'em."

Both men laughed at that all the way to the kitchen door.

CHAPTER FIFTEEN

Olivia Fixx's grandchildren fit in perfect harmony in her house. She had tremendous patience, as well as an aptitude to teach, and this is what she did. She found Sarah Ellen easy to work with. The girl knew much of kitchen work already, having had it forced upon her in Rust's house following the death of her mother. Beth Ann, too, was of an age where household chores came to hand with ease and grace. But Jolene and Margaret took a great deal more work. Even allowing them to dry the dishes was a challenge, and she was ever alert, to prevent them from breaking off in the middle of a chore, dash off on a tear having nothing at all to do with their work. They were still childish. Oliva exempted Little Honus from doing household chores, although Olivia felt that even men should know how to find their way about in a kitchen. The men, though, wouldn't hear of it. So the boy was free of these duties, and was allowed the run of the entire place.

For the most part, they handed Honus over to Enos. Olivia caught the child perched on the back of the bull calf on several different occasions. Caught him sitting up there cocky as a jaybird—she claimed—and with a smug smile on his face. She frowned on this behavior, and attempted to put a stop to it. It grew harder to catch the two boys riding the animal, but she knew Enos was masterminding the dangerous deed. She suspected it still went on behind her back and out of her sight. She uttered small prayers, and hoped for the best, giving the safety of the boy into the hands of the Lord.

There was much to like about Honus. When asleep, his face shone with the innocence she'd often witnessed in her only girl, Molly. There were also times—awake—when his lips curled in defiance that reminded her of his paternal grandfather and namesake. When this occurred, she shivered involuntarily. She'd never cared much for Honus Rust, though Steel had told her that when old Honus was a young man he was sometimes likeable. After Molly married Jorod, though, Honus lost whatever pleasant characteristics he might once have possessed, and took on the outward appearance of a typical tyrant. She figured it likely this was caused by the flogging Steel had given Jorod, Honus' pet.

The girls were hers, without a doubt. When they first came to live with her, she'd seen fear written on their faces, and sensed it as well. She went gentle with them and won them over. Now they found themselves at home with her, and of a night, after she helped them say their prayers and put them to bed, it was a rare occasion when at least one of them didn't cling to her neck and whisper that she never wanted to go back to her grandfather's house. That she wanted to live with her forever and ever. When this happened, she had to draw on all her courage to keep from breaking down in tears. It wouldn't be proper she felt, to let them see her—the figure of love, tolerance, of order—crying. She felt it would show that no one anywhere was in control. The children needed order now more than anything except love. So she saw to it that they got plenty of each.

The Murphys had a harder time of adjusting, she noticed. For the first six weeks of their stay, because of the shortage of room, they'd had to live in the house with Olivia's own family. It proved overcrowded with so many people bundled together so close, and the situation became practically unbearable until the men enlarged the small house that had once been for company and for extra hands in haying season. The Murphys moved into it and grew more comfortable, though Olivia figured it must've been much nicer back at the Rusts', where they'd had possession of an entire house with more rooms than they needed for the three of them. Murphy, who, at first seemed uncomfortable as though he was taking charity, soon found the neighboring ranchers coming to him to have their horses shod and their broken equipment welded, which saved them from doing the tedious chores themselves or riding all the way into Witness Tree Station. Now she watched him walking about with a wide smile on his broad, trusting face.

Honus Rust returned from his horse-buying trip to Nebraska and found an empty house. He drove his hack down to visit his elder son, Hugh, who always made out fine in the bunkhouse with the rest of the hands. Rust forgot that he'd fired Joan Murphy as housemaid and cook. His drinking had gotten entirely out of hand by now, and he sometimes had difficulty distinguishing reality from what he made up in his mind.

"Where the hell is everybody, Hughie?" he'd said.

Jorod had gone off to live with his lady-friend in Witness Tree Station and left Hugh to explain everything to their father. Hugh told Honus that Jorod would return when he felt it safe to do so, stating his father wouldn't likely kill him in town in front of witnesses.

Hugh related the tale of the missing children to his father, and Honus Rust flew into a rage. Hugh managed to drag him back to the house after a great deal of persuasion, and sat him down at a table where they shared a bottle of whiskey. The old man fell to the floor drunk alongside his chair. Hugh had covered him with a blanket, and left, going back to the bunk-house.

By the next day, Rust had nearly forgotten his blood vow to

bring back the children no matter the cost. In the light of a new day, along with the return of reason, he decided he needed to plot out a plan, one that would bring back his grandchildren, and do so with the law behind him. He wouldn't mind to lose the girls so much, although they could at times be helpful, but Honus, the boy, he knew he couldn't live without. Fixx would pay for dragging off that boy. He meant to see to it.

Once more, he forgot that the Murphys had fled his house. His gut began to roar with hunger. He yelled for Murphy's jumpy wife, Joan. He received no answer, got to his feet, and made his way down to the house where the blacksmith's family lived. No one answered his knock, so he entered, discovered it bare to the walls, and decided they too had fled, as well as the children. He recalled Murphy's warning, vowing to kill him if he touched his wife once more or even looked at her with anything that resembled lust.

He should've killed the man right then he knew now. He could've done it all right. The man was huge, but he had little fear of him . . . except he'd seen in Murphy's eyes the look of determination that he'd meant every word he'd said. This'd stopped him in more ways than one. He'd refrained from patting her on the butt from that day forth.

Now that the Murphys were gone, he wished he'd gone ahead and killed the smith. He hadn't harmed the woman, he figured. What did she expect, being alone for long stretches of time in the house with a man whose own wife was long dead? There was nothing left to do now but send Hugh into town and hire another cook—and while there, to bring back that boy, that reprobate youngest son of his. Rust knew exactly where he was, and in what house in town he was living—with the widow of that merchant who'd died last year, or maybe it'd been the year before.

He went to the barn, and instructed the wrangler, Archer

Payne, to take a horse and hunt up Hugh. Afterward, he went back to the house, took up a bottle of his green liqueur, a pitcher of cold water, the sugar bowl and perforated flat spoon, and fought his way up to his room on the third floor. He sat, relishing the ritual of preparing the drink with his own hand. He'd given up instructing anyone else to do this for him some time back.

He prized this precious green drink, and now, when it was ready, he sat back, sipped it slowly, savoring it, and plotting out a way to bring his superior-acting cousin crashing to the ground, and with him, his entire family.

He would have to bring the children back with the law favoring him. He had little worry on this score. The sheriff had fallen under his control. He had enough on Rathaus to ship him off to the pen for life, and if he pushed a bit, he could even make the man climb the gallows steps.

"Hell," he said, "didn't I see him kill that Mexican girl? Killed her with one blow of his revolver barrel. Me trying to persuade him to be lenient with her.

"Me and Reyes always got along right fine. Felipe had even been so kind as to leave me that small piece of property he owned, and with the railroad fixing to come straight through the heart of it too. Had given it to me, he did, with no more thought than what a man gives to snapping his fingers. It wasn't nothing but a dirty shame when I saw Rathaus drag that old feller out of his shack by a loop about his neck. Me forced to stand by and watch while Pleasant and his deputy hung him, and left him swaying there. Right there on the poor old man's own porch rafters too."

Rust had no fear that Rathaus wouldn't agree to whatever plan he might hatch up to do away with the Fixx family. Yes, sir. He'd do away with them all—the entire family right down to the least one—the one with the big ears and goofy smile. That

Enos. He'd fix him as well. He was sick and tired of hearing the name Fixx spoken. He'd lived all his life in the shadow of their assumed superiority.

He needed now to find a way, and there were many ways. To select the best one, would be the challenge. He had plenty of time—lots of it. It'd come—the solution. He sipped from his glass, set it on the table, and scooped up the spyglass from the floor alongside his chair. The haze had lifted now. The haze he felt existed in the air was, in truth, in his eyes. With the telescope, he could see all the way to the Hazlett Church Road.

It wouldn't hurt a thing to be cautious. "Steel come before. What's to prevent him from coming again? Me, by god. I'll stop him. I'll stop Steel's stealth and sneaking approach. I'll be able to see him long before he turns off the road and enters my lane."

Rust would be ready. Ready for Fixx, or anyone else who might come skulking around. He could see forever from his third-story lookout, using his scope—a dandy instrument. It would detect any danger, long before it reached him.

To be more prepared, he got up, walked to the gun case, and took down his favorite rifle.

"Now, by god," he said, "let 'em come again. I wish to hell they would."

CHAPTER SIXTEEN

Steel Fixx's grandchildren were comfortable and secure in his house, happier, they said, than they'd been since the death of their mother, and though they didn't have the wonderful Christmas this year that all children dream of, he'd heard Olivia promise them that next year things would be much different. The Murphys, too, were satisfied in their new situation.

The merchant from Camp Smyth returned in December to pick up the remaining barrels of the whiskey order he'd made that summer. He promised to return the following year to pick up another load.

The family had survived another winter. The flowers were up and blooming, and Enos—fifteen now, growing daily—was in the process of breaking up the garden. He had an extra garden to plow this year because of the Murphy family. They weren't satisfied to share one, and had decided they needed a plot of their own. This kept him plenty busy.

He grew stronger by the day, and found at the end of every new one a sweet fulfillment for his hard work. He sat, feeling complete and relaxed with no trace of guilt that he hadn't given it his best effort. No one needed to tell him he was growing up. He went out each day, did his work, and was relaxed in the evening when he curried the bull calf.

On the allotted day, he turned all the full barrels of whiskey. He used the handle end of a log hook and a wedge of wood to turn them. His father had always called for help when he needed to turn them, but Enos felt this was now his job, and had devised this method of turning them, which brought him enormous pride. To him, the aging process felt much like a garden growing. It took much time and plenty of attention.

The tyke, Honus, was more fun to be around each day. Although, there were times when he could become downright disagreeable, and even mean. Enos learned that he couldn't put all his trust in him. Little Honus had a devious streak that Enos couldn't fathom. The boy had full run of the place. He needn't have been underhanded, but he was. Enos decided it was his nature, the same way a mule or a horse or any other creature will sometimes turn on you when you least expect it. He made sure not to turn his back on him for any great length of time.

The girls were a different story, as if written by a different author. They worshiped their uncle Enos, watching him with large eyes. They put all their faith and trust in him, because he was closer to them in age, but still old enough that they regarded him as an authority figure. The older uncles—even with Clive's warm heart—they respected, but as grownups, and they held them in awe as well as esteem, but because of the age difference, were more distant toward them.

The two younger girls, Jolene and Margaret, followed Enos about as if he were the sun in the sky. Sarah Ellen and Beth Ann, being older, were becoming independent, learning this through the daily chores set down for them by their grandmother. So they prized Enos, but not with the blind worship that the two younger girls did.

In early spring, Honus Rust watched the entire Fixx family, including his grandchildren, driving down his lane. The two older boys were horseback in advance of the wagon that carried the rest of the family. He turned his spyglass on his grandchildren—the girls, and then the boy. When he first saw little Honus, he thought the tyke was a different boy. After further examination, he decided the reason he looked unfamiliar was because he'd grown in his absence.

"Aha," he said, "they're bringing 'em back. Too much work raising them kids." He laughed aloud, and felt that fate had sprung a joke on Fixx.

But the boys swung their horses off the lane with the wagon following, heading up toward the orchard where Jorod's wife, Molly, lay buried, and he realized his mistake. He roared in anger, caught up his rifle and threw up the window of his third-story lookout. He balanced the barrel on the windowsill, and took a bead on Fixx's back.

He held him true in his sights, and with his vision clear now after drinking the first glass of what he had taken to calling his "nectar-of-life," he was confident he could hit his cousin. After Fixx, he planned to shoot down the older boys, the old woman, and then that big-eared boy. Gun 'em all down. That's what he'd do. That's what happens to enemies, he reckoned. You gun 'em down. The tyke would be back then, the girls as well. This'd settle the matter of the Fixxes for all time.

He watched them step down from the wagon and the horses, and watched Olivia place a large spray of forsythia upon the grave, the yellow blooms standing out stark against the dun-colored earth. He watched as she turned to the girl, Sarah Ellen, who held another spray of flowers—redbud, he could see. He watched Sarah Ellen walk to the grave and place it upon the mounded dirt of her mother's eternal place of rest.

Going against his baser instincts, he decided he couldn't kill them. Not now. Not here. What excuse could he ever invent to square himself when the news got out? He could think of none. This deficiency of imagination saved Fixx and his family. That, and the fact that Rust knew he shouldn't kill them in front of the children. His stomach fought him and turned sour. He lowered the rifle. Disappointment shredded his soul. He sat down at the table, placed the rifle on the floor, leaned back and sipped his drink. A time of careful scrutiny passed. He felt he'd honestly made the right decision. These abrupt decisions, made in anger, were what got people hung, he decided. He'd leave that kind of action to lesser folks. He was a master of planning, a spider building a web of imposing splendor, crafting it with patience and wonderful skill. His chance would come. He was confident it would. Because it hadn't appeared yet didn't mean it wouldn't.

"Wait," he said to the large room, which he always thought was devoid of the spirit of true ease, though he'd filled it to bulging with comfortable chairs, a large desk, even a soft bed to use when he was too tired to fight his way back downstairs.

"Yessir," he muttered into his glass. "I'll find a way. The proper way. No use to be sent off to the pen or being hung by the neck until my eyes bug out, the way poor old Felipe's had."

He watched the Fixx family step from the grave, board the wagon, mount horses, and leave the orchard gravesite of Molly Rust. At first, he thought they might come up to the house, to visit, or for something else. He couldn't imagine what. But at the lane, they swung toward the road back home. They didn't cast an eye toward the house where he sat poised, at watch from his third-story window seat.

"Steel couldn't bear to look me in the face," he said. He spoke barely above a whisper, with the heaviness of gloom alive in the house, bearing upon his soul. "No, sir. Not after what he did to me, to Jorod. He was always a coward. Always had sneaky ways about him. Even when we was kids. If he couldn't have his way, or beat me at a game, why he devised a underhanded ruse to do so. Yessir, cheating never seemed to bother him—not that old boy. No, sir. But my day's coming. You wait, Honus. You'll win in the end. Your day is in the making. You need to hold on for a while longer."

Honus watched them all the way up the lane, watched them enter the Hazlett Church Road. He continued to watch them until they disappeared into a dip in the ground, and the earth devoured them. At first, he tried to delude himself into believing this was true, but gave it up. It wouldn't be that easy to deal with Fixx. For an instant, rationality returned to the man. He felt a brief urge to weep.

"How'n hell did I put myself in such a fix," he said. "Me'n Steel always fought, but not like this here. Lord, I don't see no way out."

He stifled his emotions and set about building himself a new drink, though the water was now too warm to do so with proper care.

Olivia and Enos's garden had made. They gathered the tomatoes, and dug the potatoes. The hay had made as well, cut and cured, and the men tossed it into the large barn loft. Olivia and Joan Murphy kept busy all this time. They canned many quarts of tomatoes, green beans too. Put up all the vegetables needed to see them through the winter. The boys and Murphy went off to the Century River, and snagged fish by the barrel, carp and sucker. The women put the fish up in jars as well. It'd been hard work, and when the food was all put away, they needed a break, for it was well deserved.

They packed up, all save Batch. He stayed to do the chores. They traveled into Witness Tree Station with the intention of staying in the vacant living quarters of Olivia's sister for three days of rest.

Chapter Seventeen

The first morning after the Fixx family and the Murphys left for Witness Tree Station, Batch arose, dressed, and left the house for the barn to do the chores. The sun was playing peek-a-boo with a few vagrant clouds that set upon the eastern horizon. The birds were busy singing their bright songs in homage to the brand-new day. The cool, early morning air played gentle on his skin. The clean scent of early morning refreshed him. The day would be hot later on, he reckoned, but now he felt a gentle pleasantness wash over him as he walked to the barn. He figured there was little he couldn't accomplish today, no matter what he tackled. It was that kind of day.

He felt pleased that the harvest was all laid-by, and that all the work he needed to do today was the chores. He could always find something useful to do with his time. There was a different feel about work done of necessity as opposed to that performed of a free will. All in all, a wonderful mood of ease and contentment filled him.

He opened the barn door, stepped inside, and froze. The interior was still gloomy with the remnants of nighttime. Something was wrong. God-shivers chased one another up his spine. Goosebumps popped forth on his forearms.

He glanced to his left. Sunlight spilled in through the tiny gaps between the weatherboards of the wall. Thousands on thousands of dust motes danced within the sunbeams. His horse in its stall snuffled in a choked way, unlike its usual greeting.

He saw dust spew out of its nostrils like frost hanging in sunbeams.

He experienced a sudden sense of doom. It struck like a sharp slap.

He crossed the barn to the granary, opened the door, entered and scooped up a measure of oats in the wooden bucket used for feeding. He walked to where his horse stood with its head hanging over the half-wall of its stall. Batch gently pushed it out of his way. Heard it snuffle again in a stiff voice. He dumped the oats into the feed trough and gently slapped the animal on the side of its neck. He turned and took a few steps back toward the granary for another bucket of grain. He stopped so quickly his feet scuffed up dust.

He saw a man standing in a dark shadow a few feet to the east of the granary door. The black shadow was red-rimmed from the sunlight that streamed in through the cracks in the wall behind him. Batch knew exactly who it was, but didn't want to think about it, hoping if he continued to deny the man's existence, this would somehow force him to disappear.

He walked toward the man, figuring he would soon pay for the honorable service he'd done Fixx. He thought once that he should run to the ladder, and scamper into the hayloft. But even if he did make it that far, what then would he do? He saw no way out. He had to face his fate.

When he stood before Rust, he heard the man grunt once. He failed to see the old man throw his punch, but his face and his head exploded with pain. The next thing he knew for sure was he lay stretched out flat on his back, dust boiling above him.

"I took you in, didn't I? Fed you, by god. Made a hand of you. Didn't I, Batch?"

Tears sprang from Batch's eyes. His two front upper teeth had lost their proper anchorage in their sockets. He closed his eyes, hoping to ease the pain.

"Hear me talking, Batch?" said the old man.

Batch didn't want to answer, wanted instead to fall into the peace and deep blackness of unconsciousness. But he had to. "I hear." His own voice sounded strange to him.

"I hate an ingrate worse'n any other kind of bastard. Here I give you a job, fed you, raised you, practically, and this is what happens."

Blood poured into Batch's mouth. He swallowed as much of it as he could stand. It tasted rank, grainy, and salty. Its heavy flow forced him to sit up in order to prevent it from dropping into his lungs. He spat the bitter, brassy liquid to the side. Spat again and again. The blood flow increased for a time then fell off to a seep. He saw a shadowy movement over at the barn door. Two men stood there, rimmed in blood red, as the old man had been when he'd stood in that spot moments earlier. From the floor, Batch didn't recognize either man.

"I reckon I can't do nothing about your treachery. A man can choose his own kind. But one thing I can do, and that's take back the property you stole from me when you turned your coat. That horse you rode off on is mine. I mean to take it home with me."

"That's my gelding, Mr. Rust," Batch gasped and struggled to his feet.

"Your ass, it is."

"You heard Murphy vouch for me. He told you that was my animal. What're you trying to pull here?"

"That animal belongs to me. It's going home with me when I'm through here."

"That gelding's mine, Mr. Rust. That critter's all the property I own in this whole world."

Rust ignored Batch. "I aim to fix Murphy too. First chance I find. You tell him I aim to pay him back for his treacherous and sneaky ways. You hear?"

The two men who'd stood silently by the door moved up alongside Rust. Batch recognized Pleasant Rathaus. The other one he felt was his deputy, but couldn't recall his name.

Rust turned his head to the man Batch couldn't identify. "Find me a lead rope and put it on that gelding, Bowler. I'm taking him home with me."

"No!" Batch cried out. He lunged for Bowler Tallman as the deputy was passing him on his way toward the gelding's stall. The deputy shoved him back against one of the stalls, and when he rebounded, Rust struck him again. He bounced off the wall, and the old man gave him another lick with his huge fist. Batch heard in his head a tolling like a rung dinner bell. He hit the ground hard. The air escaping his lungs sounded like a hog's grunt.

He managed to sit up again, and watched the deputy open the barn door wider and lead the gelding outside. He struggled to his feet, hoping he might do something to regain his property, but had no idea what.

"Come on back when you tie that animal with the others, Tallman," Rust said.

Bowler Tallman grumbled, and led the horse on outside.

Rust turned back to Batch. "Now to show you where my heart is, I don't aim to press charges, as I probably should. I could, as you likely know. For it's again' the law to steal a man's horse. But I'm going to extract payment for your use of the animal all the same."

He struck Batch again. This time, Batch reeled backward, and banged up against the wall, latched onto it, and remained on his feet.

Rust waded in closer, balled his enormous fist, and lashed out again. This time, Batch saw the punch, as Rust swung his large fist. He sidestepped it enough where it struck him on the right shoulder instead of in the face.

"Come over here, Pleasant. Hold this little sneaky bastard while I claim my payment. He's right jumpy afoot for a gimp."

Pleasant Rathaus didn't mumble a word, but stepped up quickly, which was his nature, and before Batch could do little more than hop to the side, Rathaus caught him firmly from behind, leaving his face vulnerable to Rust's sledgehammer blows.

He felt every one of the first five licks, but then his head started spinning. His sense of balance fell apart. He heard the fists striking his head, strange sounding, as if someone else was the recipient of the blows. Rust struck him several more times, and he started fading like the dimming of a table lamp.

Later, he grew aware that Tallman had taken over Rathaus' job, and was now holding him, giving Rathaus a break. Eventually, Rust wore himself out. Batch watched him, through blood-dimmed eyes, stagger over and sit upon the tongue of one of the hay wagons.

"Turn him loose, Bowler. Hell, I'm 'bout wore out. Got to rest."

Batch felt the air rush from his lungs, heard it too, as he struck the hard-packed dirt floor. He lay there glad to be alive, numb to the pain by now. He hoped the men would go off and leave him lying there. He couldn't imagine anything more enjoyable right then than to be left there, to recover or die in peace.

That wasn't the way it turned out, though. Honus Rust regained his lost wind, stood up, and indicated for Tallman to stand Batch up. After that, he beat him until he passed out completely.

Much later, he watched Rust rise from the wagon tongue where he'd likely taken to again when he'd worn himself out once more. He saw him sway like a drunk, crossing toward him.

"Yeah. What now?" Pleasant wanted to know.

"I ain't quite done here. You know what I think I'll do?"

"No, sir. I truly don't," the sheriff said.

"I think I'll burn this barn down. That'll make Fixx sit up and take notice. Make him sorry he took that boy of mine and flogged him. He'd take notice then."

"Yeah. You're right about that," Rathaus said. "Him, and everybody else in the area. You can't burn down this barn, Honus."

"The hell you say. Why?"

"Because the whiskey back there'll create an explosion so loud folks all the way in Witness Tree Station will hear it."

"So?"

The sheriff shook his head. Batch figured it was as if Rathaus were talking to a child. The sheriff dropped his hands to his sides in defeat. "Go ahead, Honus. Burn it down. Do whatever the hell you want to do, but let me and Bowler leave the property first. I don't want to be within a half mile of this place when the fire hits them whiskey barrels."

Batch couldn't tell if this convinced Rust or not, but at least it'd changed his direction for the time.

"Now, Batch," Honus told him, "I want you to realize you ain't free of your debt yet, but that's about all I can do for now, wore-out old man like me."

Rust nudged him with the toe of a boot, and Batch cringed in anticipation of another kick.

"You do hear me don't you, Batch?"

He tried his best to answer, but couldn't. He moved his head and hoped this did the job.

"Good. Now I want you to tell that no-account Murphy for me that his time's coming. You tell him that, hear?"

He nodded again.

"Pleasant," Rust called out.

"Right here, Honus."

154

"Steel's right fond of his barn animals, especially them ox. I think we ought to kill this whole damned bunch of creatures in this here barn."

"I don't like to kill no god damned dumb brutes, Honus." Rathaus was adamant about this, Batch allowed.

Rust stared at Rathaus in disgust. "Well, by god, I mean for you to lend a hand. I think you will too. With what I got on you."

Rust walked past Batch. Dust from his feet boiled upward past Batch's eyes, then slowly sank aground. The mules shuffled about in nervous tension as they hastily swapped ends in their stalls, ears standing upright. Perhaps they possessed some extra sense, Batch thought. One of the riding horses snuffled. The old man shoved on outside. A few minutes passed, and he returned with his rifle held in both hands. The boss-rooster flew up through the cut in the floor into the loft. His hens clucked nervously, and then propelled themselves skyward, following the rooster.

He watched Rust shove Rathaus aside, give him another sneer of disgust, and pass on deeper into the barn and up to the stalls.

The first shot cracked dully inside the barn. Batch's skin crawled. He cringed. He heard an animal fall, and he swiveled his head for a look. Another shot cracked, and the old mule, Pal, crashed to the floor of his stall. The other three mules ran about, panicking. Right away, they started kicking the outer wall. Another mule fell amid a cloud of dust. The two remaining mules barged full out against the wall, attempting to escape. The screeching of boards breaking grated loudly. The chickens in the loft set up a loud, disturbed clucking.

Batch heard the rifle crack again. Two more mules fell heavily to the ground. Dust boiled. The horses screamed in high-pitched unnatural voices. Batch attempted to rise, made it to his knees, then felt a boot crash against his back, and fell on his face. One of the men, Rathaus or Tallman, had kicked him back down, which might have saved his life, for Honus Rust was now in a state of uncontrollable rage.

No!" he yelled, but that was all he could manage.

He gave in then, laying there listening to the horses screaming, the sharp cracking of the rifle, the heavy sounds of their bodies striking the ground, and threw up last night's supper.

The oxen were last to die. He saw them standing there with trust filling their eyes, still waiting for their grain, such placid animals, and faithful. Their large trustful eyes never wavered. Ultimately, the cracks of Rust's rifle closed those eyes. It grew somber-silent in the huge barn. Later, Rust chuckled like a setting hen.

"I knowed damned well Steel was fond to death of them dumb beasts. Thought the world of 'em. He'll likely die when he sees I killed his oxen."

Rathaus and Tallman kept their mouths shut.

Batch sensed their disapproval by the tension in the room, but they mumbled no word of protest. Rathaus took to the wagon tongue, which Rust had sat upon earlier. Batch figured he was waiting out the old man's insane savagery. He'd given up all protest, but Batch could see his repulsion written plainly on his face. Tallman stood by the door and stared outside.

"You boys come and go with me," Rust said.

Batch watched Rust wave for them to follow him outside.

"We still got work to do. So let's do it." He shoved on outside, mumbling and chuckling.

The deputy walked over and stood above Rathaus at rest on the wagon tongue.

"What's the old fool up to now, boss?" Tallman said. He handed him a whiskey bottle with a spider resting on the bottom.

Pleasant Rathaus drank it off, tossed the dead soldier aside, slapped his knees, sighed deeply, and stood up in a rush. "Damned if I know, but we'd better go with him. Whatever he's got in mind ain't going to be pretty. It's best to be with him."

"He's done lost his mind, ain't he?"

Rathaus nodded. "Yep. Nuttier'n a bedbug. If I don't find more to drink soon, I'll be nutty too. I hate like hell to kill dumb brutes. But I'm 'fraid Honus's got more of that kind of deviltry in mind."

They shuffled off toward the door to join Rust. Batch heard Rathaus speak again just before he left the barn. "Sorriest day in my life was when I went with that old man out to Reyes's house. Honus's got me in a jaw grip I don't see no way out of."

Batch lay there for a long time. He'd begun to hope the men had left the property when he heard a rifle crack outside. He sighed. He'd hoped it was all over, but plainly it wasn't.

Another shot rang out. This one followed directly by another. The racket of rolling rifle fire sounded like a raging gun battle outside the barn.

He felt cold. A chill raced up his spine. He knew exactly what the old man, the deputy and the sheriff were doing. He covered his ears to ward off the sounds of the rifle fire, and prayed he was wrong.

Unable to block the rattle of gunfire, he got to his knees, struggled over to the barn door and peered outside, forced to face the devil and the devil's crew that he figured were running amuck in the pasture below the barn.

He saw them riding in the midst of the Fixx cattle, saw the large cloud of dust created by so many hooves tearing up the ground. Dust rose into the air, thick as thunderclouds. He saw the men firing into the cattle, watching their legs crumple beneath their weight and falling on their faces, while others plunged wildly about trying to escape the carnage, and the death, they never knew existed in their quiet world of peaceful grazing and full contentment.

Batch forgot his pain in his shock. He raised upright, stood in the doorway, and watched in disbelief.

"They'll kill 'em all. Ever' damn one of 'em."

He fell into a numbed state. He saw everything that happened, but couldn't quite make himself believe it was real. He tried to tell himself it was a dream. But deep down, he knew it was no dream. It was real, every segment. Too real.

He was a man who'd spent his life attempting to keep cattle alive, spending frigid nights and days feeding them in winter, herding them to grass and water in the summer. Now he stood and watched an event he'd never imagined—the intentional extermination of an entire cattle herd.

Unsteady on his feet, he held onto the side of the outer barn wall, and watched the men eliminate the herd. The cows ran in circles at first, which happened to be the worst thing they possibly could've done because this action presented a better target for the men. Then the herd lit out for the upper pasture in a line, following one old cow.

They were about to reach the ridge, on the far side of which, he knew, lay a gully, filled with draws and a heavy growth of brush that could hide them if they could only reach it. But then, Tallman spurred his mount desperately, and, after a race of a quarter-mile, he forged ahead of them, waving his rain slicker overhead, and turned them in a wide sweep back into the deadly rifle fire.

Nearly paralyzed with disbelief, Batch watched them complete the slaughter. After a time of holding his breath, he realized the deed was complete. Every cow, the bull included, and the calves were massacred, and lay dead, or dying there on the ridge.

On the south side of the barn, he saw the young bull, Star,

dart out from behind a growth of brush, and light out for the ridge. He shouted loudly, urging it on to safety. Star crested the ridge, dropped over the other side, and when he saw it would reach safety, Batch sank to the ground alongside the barn, and passed out.

He came to himself minutes later. The men were riding toward the Hazlett Church Road, leaving the property. He waited until he was sure they were gone, got to his knees, and crawled over to a wagon with the two front wheels removed, blocked-up on stones awaiting repairs. He crawled beneath the wagon bed into the shade, and passed out again.

Some time later he awoke, and felt much better, at least physically, although he was still heartsick from the slaughter he'd witnessed. He sat up beneath the wagon, and got his bearings, then crawled out from under it, found his feet, and stood swaying for a time. Steadier afoot, he took out toward the springhouse. He sat on one of the stone benches to recover from the walk, for the springhouse stood a ways from the barn. When able to, he opened the springhouse door, and feeling the rush of cold air, he figured he would survive after all. He took down the dipper, and dipped up a cold drink.

He sat there in the shade, washed his face trying to bring life back to those muscles that'd been damaged by Honus Rust's fists, and swallowed cup after cup of cold water. His face was numb, swollen and huge beneath his fingertips. He drank a dipperful of whiskey, splashed a handful on his brutalized face and didn't feel its savage burn.

He had to reach Mr. Fixx, tell him what'd happened. With his head pounding in pain with each heartbeat, he decided the only way to accomplish the chore was to light out. There were no horses left. He'd have to walk all the way into Witness Tree Station. In his condition, even riding a horse to town would be chore enough, but to walk—well, he blocked the thought from his mind.

He pushed off with a heavy heart, and with the knowledge that he might not make it to town. But he had to at least try.

He felt somewhat better on the road into town, confident that someone would come along soon and give him a lift. However, an hour's struggle later, his stub started hurting, so he gave up looking behind him to see if a wagon was approaching, and set his mind to walk all the way. The wet-weather spring two miles outside of town was dry, and this made matters worse.

He mumbled a few curses for his bad luck, and sat down on the bank that usually held the run-off water from the spring in a small pool. There was wet mud that hadn't dried up, still fresh and pliable. So he removed the boot from his board foot. The area around the leg, where the foot strapped on, had a red wound there that was about to start bleeding.

He removed the board foot, and eased the stub down into the mud. The mud was cool on his stub despite the heat of the full noon sun.

An hour later, he pulled his leg out of the mud, got clumsily afoot, and hopped over to one of the willow trees that ringed the pool. He stripped leaves from a limb, and, by holding onto the bole of the tree, wiped the mud from his stub. Done, he hopped back to where he'd left his board foot, strapped it back on with tears of pain issuing from his eyes, and put the boot back on. He left the spring more determined than before to reach Witness Tree Station.

A quarter-mile outside the city limits of town, an old man, with a long, biblical-like beard tied down with butcher twine, pulled his wagon up alongside him.

"Want a lift into town, young feller?"

"No. I 'spect not. I'm out walking for my health," Batch said, but climbed in alongside the old prophet all the same, biting his lower lip to keep from screaming out his bum luck.

The old man let Batch off close to the courthouse well pump. He limped lamely toward it like a man about to die.

At the well, he pumped up a stream of water, fell on his knees, and held his head directly under the gushing water.

CHAPTER EIGHTEEN

Fixx sat on a bench beneath a shade tree on the courthouse lawn, along with his sons and Adair Murphy. He looked up once and saw a man stumbling toward the well pump but didn't recognize Batch at first. When he realized who it was, though, he leapt to his feet, and rushed over to him. He saw the ugly bruises upon Batch's bloated face. Purple marks the size of a heavy fist stood out easily visible on his cheeks. The ranch hand's eyes were swollen shut. His nose looked broken.

Batch lay on his back as Fixx stared down at him. The man held his face turned toward where the flow of water had been.

The gush of water had stopped. "Pump up water, boys. Clive, pump water on me. I'm almost dead." Batch's voice sounded harsh and cracked.

"What happened?" Clive said, as he grabbed the handle of the pump and set the water streaming from the spout down onto the beaten, exhausted man.

Batch lingered for some time beneath the stream, but didn't answer Clive. He wallowed in the water the way a hog does. After much time, he sat up and dug at the boot that housed his wooden foot. He pulled it off, and tilted it on end. Blood cascaded from it for a brief time, where his long, taxing walk had rubbed raw the stub end of his foot and set it to bleeding.

Fixx hunkered alongside Batch. Clive had already asked once what'd happened, so he figured the man would answer when he felt able. He could see that what had befallen him hadn't been

162

good. Something bad had happened at home, he feared.

Clive put a tin cup of water into Batch's hand. The ranch hand drank it, and asked for another one.

"Seems I'm always fetching bad news, Mr. Fixx." He downed the second cup in a gulp, stood up, and stared into Fixx's face. "I do believe that Rust bunch killed ever' cow you owned."

"When?"

"This morning. I went down to feed the barn beasts, fed my gelding, turned and started back to the granary to continue feeding, and run smack into Honus."

"He do this to you?"

"Yessir. He must've seen you leaving for town yesterday, because he didn't ask if you were home."

"Jorod with him?"

"No, sir. Nor Hughie. Pleasant Rathaus was there, and that ornery cuss, his deputy. Anyways, he pretty well knocked me senseless with that first lick. Before I could shake it off, he clipped me again. My knees buckled. Later, Pleasant caught me under the arms, and held me up."

Murphy bent alongside Fixx, leaning in close.

"Honus pretty well beat me dumb. After awhile I couldn't feel nothing at all. I guess the thing saved me was Honus wore hisself out. Ever' time he struck me another lick he'd cuss me and tell me how no-account and sorry I was for taking up with y'all.

"He had to sit awhile and rest up. When he could talk again and had some of his strength about him, he jumps up and says, 'Don't relax too damned well, boys . . . we got work to do.'

"I couldn't move. I was beat all to hell. But I could still see a bit, and hear too. At first, Honus had a mind to burn down the barn. Pleasant told him he wouldn't be no party to such as that, but Honus kept after him. Finally, Rathaus told him if he was going to burn it down, to let him and his deputy off the property

163

first. Said when that fire hit them whiskey kegs they'd likely catch and the barn'd go off like a bomb, and create an explosion so loud the folks all the way to Witness Tree Station'd hear it.

"He persuaded Honus it wouldn't be safe to be on the site, because such a fire would bring people out to investigate from all over the area. This brought him around, so he gave up that idea.

"He went to his saddle horse and fetched out his rifle, and Mr. Fixx, I swear to God, I couldn't do nothing about it—but that man killed ever' creature, horse, mule and ox in that barn, 'cept for my gelding. He stole him."

Fixx set his facial muscles rolling in waves. After a time, he relaxed his jaws, and this stopped his facial trembles.

"He didn't kill them ox?" said Redman.

"Yes, he did. He knew how much store y'all set by them creatures. The horses were screaming and rushing around in their stalls. They must've sensed what was up. The mules set about kicking at the sideboards to flee, and would've too, but he shot them down like dogs. Killed them ox last."

Fixx stood up and cast an eye up and down the street. "I'll go fetch Dr. Hance, boys. Carry him upstairs. I'll be along directly."

By the time Fixx set off on his search for Dr. Hance, a crowd milled about the water pump where Batch sat so the boys had plenty of help carrying him upstairs.

Later, inside the Ridenours' apartment, Fixx learned that the horses, mules and oxen weren't the only animals Rust, Rathaus and company killed. Before Rust's thirst for blood abated, he'd killed every cow on the ranch. The lone creature he missed was the bull, Star.

Dr. Hance had already come and gone. Batch's foot rested in a bandage, propped on a footstool.

"Well," Olivia said, "I guess we got the house yet. The barn. They didn't burn anything. We got that to be thankful for, I 'spect. They could've burned down everything we owned. I'm thankful the sheriff talked some sense into Honus's head."

Fixx felt proud every day of his wife, of her steadfastness. Nothing seemed to shake her. Now, as he watched and listened to her relate the dire situation they were in, he felt closer to her than ever before. He bent and kissed her cheek. She pushed him away, and he saw her embarrassment that he'd shown his affection in front of the children and Batch, as well as the Murphy family.

Steel Fixx didn't rely on cattle alone for his means of support. He also sold whiskey, grew corn, and cane to make molasses, which they sold off by the barrel to buyers down from Camp Smyth, who in turn shipped it to Kansas City and St. Louis. Even so, the loss of his herd struck him hard.

"Can we take 'em to court, Pap?" Clive said.

Fixx smiled at his son and weighed his chances in a court of law. He said, "Ever' man involved in that dirty business is going to have an excuse. So when it comes down to a matter of who to believe—and it will, I'm sure—the court will take Rathaus's word over Batch's."

He slapped his shirt pocket, dug out the makings and set about to roll a smoke. When done, he fired a match on the underside of his thigh, and lit up. "And that's where we stand in the matter, boys."

He finished smoking, crushed out the live coal of the cigarette between forefinger and thumb on the thick build-up of callus there, balled-up the remainder of the cigarette, and dropped it inside his shirt pocket to dispose of outside later. He got to his feet, walked to the hat rack, took up his hat and headed toward the door.

"How long you figure them cows been dead, Batch?"

"Just long enough for me to walk to town. The ones nearest the barn longer. The ones scattered farther off a little bit less."

Olivia Fixx got to her feet. "Where are you going, Steel?"

"Up to the butcher's. If he thinks any of that beef'll still be edible, I'll hire him to go out to the ranch and butcher it up."

"I'd like to go too, and we need to talk some. Can I tag along?" She looked to Mrs. Murphy, as if for her permission. The nervous woman nodded her assent.

"Yes, ma'am, you certainly can," Fixx told her. "Be happy for the company."

Olivia hastened to find her bonnet, and with it in hand, she said, "I never much took to summer-killed beef, Steel." She placed the bonnet on her head, ready.

"That's all right," he answered. "I know a couple of needy families in town. I was fixing to give it to them. If they think they can use it."

Olivia exhaled tiredly. "I guess you can always find folks in worse shape if you look, can't you?"

"Ain't that the honest truth?" Steel Fixx said.

CHAPTER NINETEEN

The men were gone for the day to old man Swifford's ranch ten miles south of their place on a buying trip. Swifford had some cows he planned to sell and Fixx wanted to look at them. The only man remaining on the ranch—not counting Enos, who was not yet a man—was Murphy.

Olivia was sitting on the porch. She'd taken to sitting out on the swing, with her eyes trained on the lane ever since Rust slaughtered their cattle. The children were gleefully larking beneath the large bridal's wreath bush on the south side of the house. She smiled, listening to their musical laughter. Enos lingered nearby, and Star—growing larger by the day—romped after him. The noon meal was over, the dishes done up and put away. Olivia sat mending ripped jeans. But she kept most of her attention on the lane and the Hazlett Church Road. As a result, she stuck herself several times with her needle.

She hadn't wanted Steel to go off. Not today. She'd had a feeling about today. A feeling something bad would happen. She hadn't said a word of protest to her husband, though. She knew Steel needed to buy more cows to start a new herd. The sensation of foreboding lingered strongly in her mind, and nothing she'd thought of banished the warning voice in her psyche.

Murphy had his forge fired up. A lazy smoke drifted high in an undeviating line from his shop, for no breeze moved the leaves of the shade trees in the yard. Olivia heard him at work on the anvil, and its steady, bright ring comforted her. At least she was not completely alone. Murphy was an enormous man, and strong, Fixx had said—almost as strong as a mule. But when she recalled Batch's warning to Murphy, that Rust meant to fix him too, she felt intensely uncomfortable. She shuddered as a strong impression of near panic swept through her.

She yelped in brief pain as she stuck herself with the needle again. She repeated the tiny childhood rhyme her mother had taught her as a child, intended to prevent further injuries, and looked up from her work to see riders coming.

Honus Rust, and three riders, came in a trot up the lane toward the house, Rust in a runabout, the others on horseback. She flung the jeans to the floor, leaped to her feet, and burst off down the steps into the yard.

"Enos! Quick, gather the children . . . bring 'em to the barn. Honus is here. Quick now, do as we planned." She saw the boy's eyes widen in surprise and fear.

She ran on as fast as she could toward the blacksmith shop, yelling in a high, excited voice for Murphy as she ran. "Murphy," she cried. "Mr. Murphy. Mr. Murphy."

Murphy stepped out of the shadows, and caught hold of Olivia to halt her mad plunge, for she'd almost surrendered to terror. "What is it, ma'am?" he said. "What's fired you up so?"

"They're here, sir." Her breath came in quick gasps and not just from the exertion of her brief run down from the house. "Honus is coming. You must hide. Remember what Batch told you. Honus vowed to take his revenge on you. Run down by the creek. I'll tell him you went with Steel."

Murphy smiled at her. "Ma'am, what kind of man would I be if I fled to the creek and left you, the kids, my wife and daughter to that man? He's been going crazy for some time. I figure now he's tipped all the way over the edge."

He turned and hurried back into the darkness of his shop. In a minute he returned, shotgun in hand.

"I'll run to your house, and fetch Irene," she told the blacksmith. "She needs to hide with Molly's children."

She struck out toward Murphy's house, hair streaming wildly in the wind.

The two women, Irene and her mother, stood by the gate as she charged up to them.

Olivia stretched out her hands to the girl, Irene. "Come, girl," she said. "Honus Rust is coming up the lane. You got to hide with Molly's children."

Mrs. Murphy shook her head in doubt. "But, Mr. Rust won't harm Irene. Lord, he's known her since she was a young child."

"Irene's sixteen years old, ma'am, and a woman. She has no business being around them men. Now, please. Please, send her with my youngsters. They'll hide out in the barn. We already know, Sheriff Rathaus won't allow Honus to burn the barn, because of the whiskey. Come now, hurry. If the men've been into alcohol this morning, it ain't no telling what they might do if they see this growing young girl."

She grabbed Irene by the hand and tugged her through the gate. When the girl looked to her mother for guidance, Mrs. Murphy nodded her assent, and she fled to where Enos was leading the children toward the barn.

Enos halted to wait. Irene was running full out toward the barn, and when she caught up, they entered together. He led them through the barn, past the long row of stalls on both sides of the aisle to the aging room at the back. Enos had grown up in this room. At times, he'd stayed out here until one of the boys showed up to bring him to the house for supper or to bed. He knew every inch, every nook, every crack in the entire barn, but was acquainted with the aging room more than any other part of the building.

Above the two racks, where the whiskey was in the process of

169

aging, was a tiny room built back into the wall. Enos had knocked the room together when he was nine years old. He'd equipped it with a door that had no knob with which to open it from the outside, and hinges that showed only from the inside. He fitted the door out to look like a part of the wall itself. The room was hidden from all but the most probing eyes. A finger between the slats was the only way to enter the room from the outside. A push of a foot opened it from inside.

This is where he planned to hide them, his nieces and Irene Murphy, and the boy, Honus.

He set the ladder against the top row of whiskey barrels below the door to his hideout, climbed up and swung open the door. Honus sighed in surprise and anticipation at the sight of the wall that opened up like magic to reveal the tiny hidden room. The smaller girls ascended first. Margaret climbed the ladder on shaky legs, fearful she would fall, but Enos encouraged her from the ground. When the girls were all in the room, Enos helped little Honus up the ladder, with the boy striking him with his fists at each rung, wanting to go it alone.

When he handed him inside to Sarah Ellen, the boy caught Enos by the thumb and bit him hard. With great self-control, Enos resisted the urge to slap him, and instead said to the girls, "Make sure he don't make any noise while you're in here. You can hear the least racket all over the barn."

Sarah Ellen looked at him with fear plain in her wide eyes. She nodded. "We will, Uncle Enos." Honus squirmed like a fishing worm in her arms, but she managed to control him.

"I'll tell you a story if you behave yourself," said Irene Murphy, in a no-nonsense tone of voice.

Honus's eyes lit up, and he agreed.

"Now, it'll be a little bit dark in there until your eyes become used to it," said Enos.

He shut the door and enclosed them inside. He heard Irene

say, "But, you'll have to keep quiet. I'll have to speak in a whisper, so keep quiet or you'll not be able to hear me."

"It's spooky in here," Honus said. "Why don't you tell me a story now?"

Enos took down the ladder, and laid it on the floor on edge beneath the whiskey barrels. His thumb throbbed, but he soon forgot it as he raced out of the barn to hide the young bull.

Star had grown more independent and less inclined to follow Enos. But when he burst outside, the growing calf came in a run up to him, and skidded to a stop at his hand. He spoke words of encouragement to it over his shoulder as he dashed back up the incline toward the house.

His mother stood on the bank above the blacksmith shop. He heard her gasp in distress. "Whatever on earth do you intend to do with that pet bull, Enos?"

"Hide him."

"Hide him? Where? It's too late to run over the hill. The men are nearly here."

He passed her without another word. The calf ran at his heel and almost tripped him several times, as it'd done for the greater part of its life.

"Hurry, Enos," his mother called. "They're coming."

He reached the root cellar with the calf butting up against him, nearly knocking him over. He reached down, caught hold of the door—a trapdoor that led down four steps below ground—then plunged on down, confident Star would follow.

Follow him he did. Star shoved him up against the far cellar wall. This caused tears of pain to spring from his eyes. He turned, aware that Star would never abide remaining in the dark cellar alone, so he reached up and pulled the trapdoor down, and stayed inside with him.

At first, in that close, cramped dark space, he feared the calf might panic, tear the cellar apart, and give away their position.

He touched the animal, though, and it settled down, and licked his face with a tongue that'd grown leathery and rough, as the creature grew daily toward full maturity.

Olivia returned to the porch. She picked up her scattered sewing, and placed it on her lap with hands shaking so much she feared doing any more than hold the needle and thread poised above the jeans. Oddly enough, when the runabout that carried Honus Rust pulled to a stop at her gate, her hands fell as calm as a pretty day in May.

There were four of them when she'd first spied them. Now she counted three. One of the intruders was missing. The sheriff, wiry and angular, all arms and legs, stood alongside his horse. Rust was climbing from his vehicle, and her daughter's husband, Jorod, stood at the yard gate waiting. The deputy wasn't with them.

Olivia calmed her soul, and her hands ceased to flutter as well. She felt in command, confident she could easily handle any situation that might arise.

As the unwelcomed visitors entered her yard and when the gate slapped shut in its familiar voice, she renewed her work on the pair of torn jeans in earnest, but with an eye on the men all the while.

The men reached the foot of the porch steps and halted there. She rose from the swing, dropped her sewing on the seat, and walked to the edge of the porch at the head of the steps to bar their way.

"Missus Fixx?" said Pleasant Rathaus.

"Let's settle one thing right now," she announced in a bold voice. "You can come up, Sheriff Rathaus, but them other two with you there ain't welcome here . . . especially Jorod."

"I don't have no intention of climbing them steps, Olivia," Rust said, his eyes bright red, shining in his huge face. He dug into a shirt pocket and produced a fat cigar.

She watched as he lit it, shook out the match, and said in protest, "I'll not have you scattering your trash in my neat yard, Honus Rust, if you don't mind."

He glared at the gentle woman for a time, but reluctantly gave in. He allowed the match head to cool, and placed it in a coat pocket.

She turned her full attention to the sheriff. "Now, Sheriff Rathaus, what business is it brings you to the Fixx place today?"

"We come for my kids," Jorod said.

"I already told you, Jorod Rust, you ain't welcome here. Not after killing my Molly. Please refrain from even speaking within my hearing. You just standing in my yard is enough to make me sick."

"Them kids are mine. I reckon I got a reason to stand in your yard, and . . ."

Olivia cut him off. "You ain't no fitting father, Mister, and a rank drunkard, besides."

"Well, that there's your opinion. It ain't what them kids of mine think, I'll bet."

She turned to Rathaus. "Sheriff Rathaus, I'll not be a part of any discussion until this scoundrel shuts his mouth."

Rathaus cast an eye to Jorod to indicate his displeasure. Jorod shuffled his feet under the man's gaze. His lips worked to speak again, but the elder Rust raised his hand, and Jorod clamped down on his words.

"I'm 'fraid Jorod's right, Missus Fixx. We have come for the children," said Rathaus. He removed his hat. A heavy line of beaded sweat stood upon his forehead.

"They ain't here," said Olivia. "Besides, I don't see them children going anywheres with the likes of Jorod . . . nor Honus. Those children met with neglect in Honus's house. I don't intend to let 'em go back over there. Besides that, my man ain't here.

None of the men are. If you want to pursue this any further, come back when Steel's home. I figure he's better able to contend with y'all than me."

The sheriff wiped sweat from his forehead with a wide, blue handkerchief. Afterward, he wiped down the sweatband of his beaver hat as if this act required his full concentration.

The bull calf was in a playful mood. It continued to lick Enos in the face, and butted him in a gentle nudge. It swapped ends in the closed, tight space inside the cellar. Every time Star swapped ends, he banged up against one of the shelves that lined the walls, rattled vegetable jars, and created a minor racket.

Enos whispered to the creature to calm it, but the bull remained bent on playfulness, cutting shines and didoes in the cellar. Enos shuddered with each noise the bull made until he worked up a sweat, for fear he'd be discovered at any second, though he knew that if the men were on the porch with his mother there was no way they could hear the calf's commotion. He whispered softly to the animal, scratched it behind the ears, and hoped for the best.

"We ain't waiting around till Steel comes home," said Rust. "We mean to take them kids home with us today. Now stop your nonsense, and bring 'em out from wherever you got 'em hid."

"I told you already. My grandchildren ain't home. They went with their grandfather."

"Yeah, and where did he go?" Rust said.

"To town."

"Ma'am," said Rathaus, "we just come from town. We didn't see 'em there. Nor did we meet 'em on the road."

"Yes, well . . . I suppose they was upstairs in my sister's apartment."

Rust laughed at this, removed his cigar, studied the ash on its tip for a time, then took a step forward. He placed a heavy foot upon the bottom step. "That there's a pretty fair lie, Olivia." He smiled a sly smile, and stared hard from reddened eyes. "It's still a blamed lie, though. Ain't nobody ever told you you'll go to hell as quick for lying as you will for stealing?"

"You just accused me of being a liar, Honus Rust. Now get your foot off my steps."

He didn't answer, but stood there, puffed his cigar with his huge chest thrust forward, his shoulders thrown back, and stared at her with his foot still on the step.

"If my man was home, I doubt you'd accuse me of such a thing," she said. She felt her temper rising.

Rathaus looked to Rust. "I 'spect if the kids ain't here, Honus, why, we better come on back when they are."

Rust shook his huge head. "They're here," he said. "Olivia hasn't told many lies in her time . . . man can see she ain't good at it. Them kids is here, Sheriff. Damn me if they ain't."

"She's got 'em hid," Jorod said. "In the barn loft . . . be my guess."

"We'll just have to search about until we find 'em," said the rancher.

"You'll do no such of a thing . . . not with Steel gone, you won't. I won't allow y'all to roam about this place, kicking open every door you come to . . . looking under every basket. I won't allow it, Sheriff Rathaus."

"You ain't got no say in the matter, Aunt Olivia," said Jorod.

"This property belongs to Steel Fixx, Sheriff, boughten and paid for. He ain't here to protect it. I see you can go on and do Honus's bidding, but there'll come the time when Steel *is* here . . . and anyways, what'll you have to say for yourself when I spread the word you been going around bullying women?"

"We got a paper for them kids," said Jorod. "Show her that

paper, Pleasant."

Sheriff Rathaus fumbled at his vest, and produced a sheet of paper from an inner pocket. "It's true, Missus Fixx. Here's the paper. It's a—"

Olivia had taken all she could. "I see it, Sheriff, and you might as well put it back in your pocket. Come back when the men are here if you want to pursue the matter further."

She was pleased that so far Rathaus had remained calm. She'd heard he was seldom in such an easy-going mood, and lived by the flaring of his temper, relying on the law to back him when things got rough. She feared what would happen if this changed.

Rathaus straightened to his full height, shook the paper in the air above his head as if this act might have the power to conjure up the soul and character of the law to swoop down upon this woman, and bring her to her senses. In a shrill voice of one offended, he said, "Missus Fixx, if them kids are here, I want you to bring 'em out of wherever it is you got 'em hid, and hand 'em over to their father—their grandfather."

"And I'm telling you, Sheriff Pleasant Rathaus, they ain't here, and even if they were, I sure wouldn't hand 'em over to the likes of this bunch. They ain't fitting to rear children."

"The law ain't got no say about who's fit and who ain't, Missus Fixx. All the law says in this case is that you must surrender them children. I'm fast losing my tolerance with you, ma'am. If I was you, I'd see that they're brought out here to their father." He lowered the paper from above his head, tapped it a time or two on the flat of his opposite hand. "This here's a court order. It says you must relinquish the children to their true and legal father, Jorod Rust." He paused for a breath.

She saw his eyes grow colder.

Again, he spoke, "If you don't produce the children, I'll have to take it upon myself to conduct a search of the place. I hoped to avoid that, but you leave me no choice. I'll ask you once more to bring 'em out. Will you do that for me, please, ma'am?"

She folded her arms across her breast. "I told you, they ain't here."

She watched Rathaus exhale as if he'd been digging up stumps all day long. But she allowed that his tiredness instead had probably arrived from a long, fierce bout with the bottle last night.

He slipped the court order back into his vest pocket, cast a glance once more at her, then swung about, and walked swiftly out of the yard. Both men followed him.

Olivia stood on watch from the porch for a time, but seeing they weren't going to mount up and ride off, she ran down the steps and chased after them.

Running full out, she caught up to the sheriff and grabbed his sleeve. "You know what Steel'll think about this, don't you, Sheriff? It ain't proper going about another man's place like you're fixing to do."

"Ma'am, I done give you your chance. You passed it by. So now, I'll find them kids myself. Step back, please, and let me do my duty."

Their progress took them nearer and nearer the barn. The blacksmith's shop stood between the house and the barn. They would have to pass the shop to reach it.

"They're in that barn, Pleasant, sure as Jesus died," Jorod said. "Look how she's acting. My kids are in there." He started to run past the sheriff, but Rathaus reached out, and caught him by the arm and stopped him.

"This here's my job, Jorod. You'll have to face that fact, or else go on home. Wait till I find 'em and bring 'em to you.

"You might not think I'm much to look at, but, by god, I'm the old boy you're going to have to look to for authority around here. Now you calm down and find your place."

Jorod stood there red of face, fully chastened. He fell behind Olivia at the rear of the procession. She could feel the heat of his hatred for her as she pressed on after the other two men.

She continued clutching the sheriff's sleeve, trotting alongside him to keep pace. In front of the blacksmith's shop, she caught hold of his forearm with both hands.

Rathaus shoved her with all his strength. She hurtled through the air for a short space, and then felt the ground jar her beyond all justification to her short flight. This knocked the wind from her lungs. Fixx had long ago spread the driveway leading up to the blacksmith's shop with creek gravel, because it once had been a place of perpetual damp, mucky for horses and buggies to traverse. The gravel tore at her palms. In her fall, she scraped both hands and her arms halfway to the elbows. She leaped up again and chased after Rathaus. Blood trickled down both arms and hands, and ran from her fingertips to the ground.

Sheriff Rathaus saw her coming on. He stopped, turned to face her. "Lady, don't dare touch me again. I'm warning you, and I seldom give a second one."

Murphy stepped from the shadows of the blacksmith's shop, holding his shotgun. He said, "Now ain't this here a pretty out, treating a woman that a-ways? Have you lost what little common sense you once possessed, Rathaus?"

Honus Rust flung his cigar to the gravel. He stepped forward. Olivia heard gravel crunch beneath his heavy tread. "By god," he said, "so you found you a place to hide out after all, did you?"

The blacksmith said, "I warned you I was leaving." Murphy's voice still bore remnants of respect for his former, long-time employer. "Anyways, I put in my time at that ranch."

"Yep," Rust laughed. "And I paid you plenty to put in your time too, didn't I?"

"You paid me for work done. I worked hard for my pay. I'd

still be there if you hadn't changed for the worse, Honus." He turned his attention to Olivia. "Come over here, Olivia . . . by me. You got blood dripping down your arms. You need to go to my house and let Joan wrap 'em up for you."

"I've come out here to settle a matter of family, Murphy," Rathaus said. "It's the worst kind of duty a lawman can tangle hisself up in . . . the lord knows. I hate it worse'n any other duty. But I've got a court order to gather up them kids of Jorod's, and to hand 'em over to him. What's more, I reckon you know better'n to go about with a shotgun in your hands . . . me on the place. Unless you're fixing to go rabbit hunting."

Murphy said, "You know rabbits ain't fit to eat this time a-year, Pleasant. I got this shotgun here for protection, and I'll use it, if I must. I figure y'all boys should leave on out of here. You know very well Mr. Fixx ain't home. Come back when he is. You'll be better served that a-way."

Olivia stepped backward, away from Rathaus as he spoke. "This here court order I got in my pocket don't say nothing about who should be home when I carry out the orders written down on it. It says to fetch this man's children to him. I mean to do that very thing, Murphy. So I'd appreciate it if you'd hand me that shotgun as a precautionary measure."

Murphy shook his head.

"Wait till I finish my duties here. I'll give 'er back to you when I leave."

"Yeah, well, how'd I go about protecting my boss's property then . . . you holding my gun?"

"Hell, sir," the sheriff said. "I'm the law in this county. You think I'd do anything to harm one of the citizens I swore to protect?"

"I think you've grown blind, Pleasant, like a snake in dog days. You act like you don't know right from wrong, anymore. This is sad, because when I first voted for you, I felt you was an honest, upright man." Murphy stepped out of the shadows of his shop into the full sun, hoisting the gun as he stepped forward. "I don't know whether the missus here told you this already or not," he continued, "but in case she didn't, I'll say it myself, haul your sorry asses off this property, boys, and step nimble as you go."

"You're interfering with a man of the law, Murphy. I'm carrying out the legal duties of my office."

"Ain't the way I see it, Pleasant. I figure I'm preventing that good lady there from being bullied. Now, when Steel Fixx returns, I reckon y'all can come back and take your business up with him."

Murphy mounted the shotgun to his shoulder. The cocking of the hammer clicked loud. The three men took several backward steps fearfully, warned off by the malicious, harsh click of the hammer.

The blacksmith turned to Olivia. "Mrs. Fixx, please go on up to the house with Joan until this thing's done. She can tend your scratches for you."

Olivia felt relieved, and walked in brisk strides toward the blacksmith's house. She could see Joan Murphy leaning from the doorway of her house, watching.

She reached the gate leading to the Murphys' yard, hand poised above the latch. She stopped, hearing the woman in the doorway moaning low from despair. She heard a sharp cracking explosion erupt from behind her in the direction of Murphy's shop and turned to see who'd fired the rifle.

She was familiar with the sound of shotguns and rifles, and could differentiate the report of each. This one hadn't come from Murphy's shotgun. Mrs. Murphy fell in a heap on the doorstep, and Olivia ran to her.

CHAPTER TWENTY

Olivia looked to see who had fired the shot. She saw Bowler Tallman step from the shadowed side of the blacksmith's shop. The deputy still held his rifle high. Smoke from the barrel curled upward in a gray cloud, and the blacksmith lay humped up on the gravel. His shotgun was several feet from him, where he'd flung it after Tallman back-shot him.

Rust's brash voice roared out, "It's about time, Bowler. Hell, I thought that sonofabitch was going to run us off like a pack of whipped hounds. Where'n hell you been?"

"Jesus Christ," the deputy said. "I thought you'd be right proud I saved your hide for you. But all you want to do is grumble. You're one of them fellers who'd bitch if you was hung with a brand-new rope, ain't you?"

They left the blacksmith's body prostrate upon the ground. Olivia saw them enter the barn. She chased after the men, with Joan Murphy in a swoon upon the ground.

Rathaus had finished making a search of the barn loft when she burst into the barn.

"Well, where'n hell are they?" Honus cried out in his booming voice. "Where's them kids? That little one, Honus?"

"Calm down some, Honus," the sheriff said. "This here's dirty business and no gain for me anywheres I can see. A thankless, sorry mess. I knew it wouldn't be as easy as Jorod thought. You go on as many of these chases as I have you have a feel for how difficult they can be. You'll have to have patience, I 'spect.

If you know what that means . . . that is."

"Well, sir, I reckon I do know the meaning of patience. Ain't I been patient ever since Fixx stole them kids from my house? Now, step down off your high horse. If you know how to . . . that is?" Honus was losing control. Olivia shuddered, and felt a chill despite the day's heat.

She followed the men as they searched the stalls. Rathaus lagged back, a black look of offense on his face, sulking, she noticed.

Inside the hideout, Irene Murphy heard the men crashing through the barn, opening and shutting stall doors, searching for them. Honus, the child, had behaved himself so far. She'd pacified him with stories she'd whispered to him. But, on their ending, he struggled for freedom from his sister's arms. Then his father's voice—his grandfather's voice rang out, and he attempted to call out to them. Irene clamped a hand over his mouth, but the boy bit her, and she released him, much to his bad luck. She grabbed him up and pulled him close to her face. "Listen to me, you little horror, you keep your mouth shut. Don't you dare utter a sound. If you cause us to be found out, I'll cut a keen peach tree switch and give you the whipping of your life." She slammed him down hard on his bottom. This jarred him enough that he shut his mouth. "Do you hear me now, Honus?"

"Yes, ma'am," he said timidly. He hung his head and kept quiet.

Irene heard the search of the barn continue. They were all afraid to breathe, Irene figured, save for Honus, who sat and blew sighs from boredom, but he was still under the influence of the red-headed girl's stern voice, so he tried to hold himself as still as possible. Every time he heard his father speak, she expected him to cry out.

She heard the men approaching. They grew closer and closer to the aging room door. She was sweating and soon the palms of her hands were damp from her anxiety. Sweat rolled down her back. Her clothes clung to her body like a second skin, and this made her miserable. Still, she held Honus, her hands on each side of his face, in a most uncomfortable position for them both, but she dared not release him. She knew the difficulty children have holding still for any great length of time. She kept her hands there as a caution, where, if she felt him about to call out, she could cut off his shout.

She'd heard the earlier shot from outside. This'd worried her, for she too was familiar with the varied sounds of firearms, and realized her father possessed only a shotgun. This sound, she could tell, didn't come from a shotgun. She worried for his safety, although she remained steadfast in her duty to the children. She'd keep them safe, even if it meant she had to sit atop little Honus.

The door to the aging room swung inward, and banged off the inner wall. She felt the children jump. She clamped down on little Honus's mouth. The men were nearby now.

Their footsteps struck loud upon the hardwood planks. Honus Rust called out in his loud, bullying voice, and she jumped, startled, as did the children.

"Honus," Rust called out to his grandson. "You in here, boy?"

Irene Murphy felt the boy's vocal cords at work beneath her fingers. She clamped down on his face tighter, determined to prevent him from replying.

"Why, Pap," Jorod said, "they ain't nobody here. Hell, you can see every nook and cranny in the place with one glance. They ain't nowheres for 'em to hide. Besides, my kids would ring out if they heard my voice. I'm sure of it."

Irene heard one of the littler girls, perhaps, Jolene, maybe Margaret—they were so much alike she was hard-pressed at times to tell them apart in the darkness—snuffling now. She was afraid the girl was about to cry out. She chanced a soft shush of her lips, and kept her hands clamped over the boy's mouth all the while. The soft, soothing sound she made turned the trick, for the girl didn't utter another sound the rest of the time of their confinement.

Olivia Fixx said, "I told you they weren't out here. Now will you believe me?" There was no answer from any of the men.

Honus, the child, took this time to bite down hard on the palm of Irene Murphy's hand. She bore the shock and pain with little more than a flinch of surprise. She placed her mouth against the boy's ear, and already having tried threats, decided to use the promise of another story to pacify him. "Stop biting me, Honus. If you do, I'll tell you a story as soon as they're gone."

This worked, or maybe, the boy disliked the taste of sweat from her hand, for he released her. She removed one hand, took the chance, and patted the top of his head, as if he were a pet. She placed her hand again close to his mouth. His teeth were frightfully sharp, his jaws strong, she knew from experience.

After an interminable length of time, the men and Olivia Fixx left the barn. Their voices fell dimmer into the distance. Irene released a long-held breath, and all inside with her did the same, including the boy.

"But, we'll still have to keep still," she told them. "They could come back for another look."

"You promised me another story," little Honus said.

And so, Irene Murphy, huddling in the dim, cramped quarters of Enos Fixx's hideout, set about to tell them all a story.

★ ★ ★ ★ ★

"I thought I was in a dream," Joan Murphy said.

Olivia had returned to her side as Joan was rising from her swoon.

Joan looked again to the graveled approach leading to her husband's shop where Murphy lay. Olivia helped her to her feet. Joan said, "I have to go down there, Olivia. He might need me. He *cannot* be dead. I know he's not."

"Then I'll go with you."

They left the yard, and crunched through the gravel down toward Adair Murphy, lying with his face still in the gravel. His hair lifted and fell beneath the gentle tug of the breeze.

"Adair always says I'm too flighty," the nervous woman said. "He had me drink whiskey, ma'am, that day when your Molly died. I'd never tasted it before. But I knew for sure I had to clean that poor girl up. I could've never lived with myself, if I'd allowed a man to do it."

Adair Murphy was still alive, Olivia saw. Bowler Tallman had shot him through one lung, and with each exhalation of breath he expelled, she saw blood bubble forth in a pink froth. Together they turned his head to the side. Joan cleaned out the dirt and small gravel that'd accumulated in his mouth in his efforts to breathe.

He whispered inaudibly. Joan placed her head upon the side of his face in order to be able to hear him better. Olivia watched tears stream down Joan's cheeks but she wasn't sobbing or making any other sounds of distress. "What is it, 'Dair? What do you want?"

This time his words were stronger, "I want to look at the sky."

The women rolled the heavy man onto his back with as much gentleness as possible. He said, "I want a drink—a drink of water."

185

Olivia got to her feet and ran toward the spring. As she ran, she heard the sheriff and the other men conversing in loud voices before they entered her house to continue their search. She reached the springhouse, which was built in the cantilevered style common in springhouses, and flung open the door, took down the tin cup from its hook and scooped it full of water. The cold water from the inner pool steamed cloud-like in her face as the heated outside air rushed in through the open door and merged with it. She closed the door, and ran as fast as she could go. Her skirt tails rose above her ankles with the move-ment of each leg, dust lifted from her feet.

She dropped to her knees alongside Joan and the blacksmith. They lifted his head and fed him the water. He downed it in a gulp and smiled at his wife. "I reckon that there's the best cup of water I ever tasted. Is there any chance I could have another?"

Olivia charged to the springhouse with her tin cup, filled it, and lit out in a run back to the dying man. Murphy this time turned his face from the water. He lay there distracted, Olivia thought, and stared at the cloudless blue sky.

Eventually he spoke, "I always loved you for your helpless-ness, Joan. You were some flighty woman. But that there was how you charmed me like you did. When I'm gone, I want you to allow Irene to take care of you till she leaves home. She's a good, strong girl. You let her handle them things you have trouble doing. I hate to leave you like this . . ." He paused and attempted a chuckle, but it fell short when a coughing spasm claimed him. He tamed the cough. "I ain't got no say in the matter, looks like. But Irene . . . now, she's a strong girl. Lean on her a little . . . anyways till she finds a good man, then you'll have to turn her loose. Don't cling too long to where she won't have no chance at a good marriage."

"But, Adair," Joan protested as she bit back tears, "you'll be all right. You just need to rest. You'll be up and around in a few days."

He chuckled, and said, "Why, sure I will, honey. Sure I will." He strained to lift his hand, but couldn't quite do so. Joan placed her own hands upon his, and the contrast was remarkable to Olivia. His were wide, the fingers short, thick and powerful; the backs of them were singed free of hair from the heat of thousands of forge fires, and the pores were clogged with black soot. Joan's hands lay across his, tiny, delicately built, and pale as a pink rose.

"You do what I told you about that girl, rely on her while you can, but don't keep her home till it's too late . . . you hear me?"

Her voice answered in the squeaks of a rusty hinge, "Yes, sir. I hear you, and I'll do all you say, but—"

"I think maybe I might be able to take me a drink of that water now."

They lifted his head again, but when the cup brushed his lips, he turned away from it. It was as if what a few minutes earlier had been most wonderful to him had turned sour and foul, and he couldn't drink. "That sky . . ." He said this in a moment of wide-eyed clarity. "Lord, but won't you just look at that blue sky!"

He fell limp all over. Olivia figured the blacksmith was dead. She got to her feet, wishing Enos were here to help her. She rushed to the woodpile, caught up the handles of the barrow that Enos used to haul wood in, and wheeled it back to where Murphy lay dead. Joan sat there in the gravel, and brushed flies from his face.

Olivia placed a hand upon the woman's shoulder, patted her a few times, aching for a gentle way to provide the relief she needed. She didn't find one.

"Adair's dead, ma'am. I do believe it," she said.

Joan nodded in agreement, but didn't stand up. Her lower lip fell in a flutter like the busy tail of a wren in search of a proper site in which to build a nest.

"We must get him up in this barrow. Will you help?"

Joan sat there, a solid block of human anguish, nodding her head in agreement. She didn't even know for sure what she'd just agreed to, Olivia thought, or if the matter at hand involved her at all.

"We have to take him inside the house," Olivia said. "Let's not leave him out here in the hot sun with the flies."

Still Joan made no move to help.

"Oh, you poor, dear thing," Olivia said and bent to the shocked woman. She wrapped her arms about her and held her for a time.

By and by, Joan shook off the lack of energy that'd descended upon her when her husband ceased speaking. She looked about, as if she'd just awakened to find herself outside, kneeling above her dead husband who was lying upon the gravel in front of his shop.

"Can you help me load him in the wheelbarrow, Joan?" Olivia saw that a spark of life had return to her eyes.

Joan Murphy got to her feet and helped Olivia load Adair into the wheelbarrow. This was no easy chore because of his weight. But after much hard effort, they completed the task. Taking a handle each, they wheeled him up to the front door of his house. It took them twenty minutes, between periods of rest, to tug and lug the heavy man inside the house. Then, again after a rest, they dragged him into the kitchen. They were unable to lift him upon the wide, sturdy table made of oak. They stepped back outside, neither of them able at that time to clean him up.

CHAPTER TWENTY-ONE

Olivia and Joan sat upon the porch, holding hands. The intruders, as Olivia had come to think of them, charged out of the house, and went off in a search of the outbuildings, beginning with the summer kitchen—where, in the heat of summer, Olivia cooked the noonday meals, and where she and Joan Murphy too went to do their canning to prevent overheating the house.

After a time, the men had searched all the outbuildings. Only one place on the entire ranch remained to be examined—the root cellar.

A huge knotted fist of fear for Enos gripped her heart and attempted to squeeze it dry. She flung herself to her feet, left the distraught Joan Murphy upon her porch, and hurried up to the sheriff.

"It's awfully hot for y'all to be working so hard, Sheriff Rathaus," she said. "Don't you think you might need a cool drink from the springhouse? There's a nice bench down there, and it stays shady all the day. The water is so cold it smokes and is sweet as honey."

She said this as a diversion to lure them out of sight of the house where, in their absence, she could call the boy and the bull out of the root cellar and send them off over the hillside far away from the house.

The sheriff peered intently into her face. His eyes were wide with suspicion. But the rest, Jorod especially, thought it a wonderful idea to sit awhile in the shade, to drink cold water.

"Come on, Pleasant," said Jorod. "Uncle Steel keeps a jug down there. A little refreshment sounds good to me about now . . . how's about you?"

The sheriff's ridged face was still dark with suspicion. He held his ground.

"I don't know about Pleasant," said Tallman, "but, it sounds like a right fine and a pregnant idea to me. I'll go with you, Jorod, if nobody else will."

"Let me fetch my liquor from the buggy," Rust said. "If I recall, the water from that spring is icy cold. It'll work for me to build me a drink. I ain't yet had my morning tonic."

Olivia breathed easier when they started down the slope toward the distant springhouse. But the sheriff lingered, and her heart started pumping blood so fast she heard its thrumming passage roaring through the blood chambers in her temples, screaming like flames shooting up a faulty chimney.

She dared not breathe. What would she do, she wondered, if Rathaus didn't go with them, but stayed to search the root cellar? What would she do if he found the boy? Would he harm Enos? He wouldn't, surely. No one would be so cruel, she prayed.

His repellent eyes settled cruelly upon her, studying her face. He glared at her, as if a mere stare might wring the truth from her. Rust called out a second invitation. He turned, and with great reluctance, ambled off to catch up with the others.

Then two loud sounds "kerwhumped" inside the root cellar. Olivia froze. Her eyes widened. Her mouth rounded. Star had broken jars of canning inside the root cellar, and they'd exploded as loud as gunshots. That was what had happened, she'd bet on it.

On the slope down toward the springhouse, the men heard the racket. They stopped, slowly turned, and cast their mistrustful eyes back toward the source of the racket.

"The root cellar," said Tallman. "Hell's fire, them kids is in the damn root cellar."

Back they all ran up the slope. They huffed and puffed up the steep bank, reached the flat area between the house and the cellar, and ran faster.

The rest of the men were standing, hands on hips, staring down at the trapdoor by the time Honus arrived, huffing and blowing like a much older man.

"Let me do it," he said. His voice grated in Olivia's ears. "Let me do it."

He bent, clasped the handle of the trapdoor, and in a sweep of his arm slung it open. A large swirl of dust, heavy and dark, briefly hid them all as the lid struck the ground in a loud, flat whoosh.

As if Honus Rust had rolled back the consecrated rock, which blocks the entrance to hell itself, a red monster, white of face, bearing a grayish star between its eyes, leapt from the cellar. Star gave a great roll. He bucked and plunged, kicked at the air with his hind legs, and managed to knock down all four men. He would've upended Olivia as well had she not been standing farther back out of the way, biting her lip, fearful her boy was about to be discovered.

Before the men could react, the calf, released from its bondage, hoisted its tail over its back in a half loop, lit out for the hillside and the far pasture beyond. Enos ran up the steps of the cellar in time to see his pet disappear over the ridge. Olivia heard him sigh with the relief that Star had reached safety. Her son turned then to face the men.

"Who was doing all the shooting out here?" he said.

"Them children down there in that cellar with you, boy?" Rust said. He looked up from where he'd fallen on the seat of his pants. He was clutching his chest. His face looked chalky white. He got to his feet, determined to find his grandchildren.

"Answer me, boy. Them grandkids of mine down there?"

The deputy and Jorod Rust had already descended into the cellar. Soon, their heads emerged. The two men tromped the rest of the way up the steps, and stood before Rust.

"Well, by god, did you find 'em?"

"They ain't down there, Pap."

"Jesus," he said. "Where'n the bully-hell are they?"

Olivia noticed his face appeared drained of life as if a large weight was sitting upon his chest, restricting his blood flow.

Rathaus whirled and strode off, walking swiftly. He headed straight toward the front yard where the horses stood steadily switching their tails at the horde of flies that pestered them with greedy determination.

"Where'n hell's name have you got them kids hid out, you little shit?" Rust said. He thrust out a huge hand and caught the boy. He dragged him up tight, close to his face. "I mean for you to tell me where they are . . . and do it quick. I've about had my fill of this old business. If you know what's good for you, you'll call 'em out." He turned to Olivia, and added, "Olivia, you'd better tell me where you and this here boy's hid them kids. I mean what I say."

"Leave him be, Honus," she said. Her voice sounded high and flinty.

"I don't know where they are," Enos said. "I was in the cellar with my pet all the time. I was afraid you'd kill him like you did the rest of our herd."

The big man slapped Enos's face. The fingers of his opposite hand were entangled in the cloth of his shirt.

Olivia caught at Rust's arm when he drew back for a second blow.

"Get the hell away from me, woman," he said, and flung off the small woman in the same easy manner with which he might remove his coat.

Rathaus returned, and slipped a rope around Enos's neck. He jerked him away from Rust and off his feet, dragged him toward the pecan tree in the backyard beyond the summer kitchen.

Olivia saw the rope choking Enos. The boy clutched the rough hemp rope in both hands. He skidded over the ground like an improperly weighted garden disk, Rathaus dragging him along. Olivia screamed. A second voice erupted in a higher scream. Mrs. Murphy had run up the hill.

Rust cried out in glee to urge Rathaus on, "That's it. Hang him. Hang him until Olivia's glad to talk. Her or him. Don't make a shit which."

Oliva watched from frightened eyes. Enos was fighting the rope, trying to find slack enough to admit air. Once, he fought upward enough that his heels dragged deep into the dirt, and plowed up earth in two thin furrows. Dust shot upward from each heel.

The sheriff yanked hard on the rope. Enos fell back down onto the ground, but continued to fight for enough slack to allow his fingers to dig in between his neck and the rough fibers of the rope. The tighter the rope clamped down on his neck, the fiercer he fought.

When Rathaus dragged the boy up to the tree, he stood him up beneath one of the lower limbs. He coiled the rope in his right hand and tossed it upward. The rope struck the under part of the limb, and crumpled back to the ground. When Rathaus stooped to retrieve it for another attempt, Enos loosened the rope, and caught a breath.

Rathaus concentrated on the second throw, and this time it sailed high over the intended limb and fell to earth on the other side. When he bent to retrieve the end of it, Rust grabbed up the boy.

"We'll allow you to catch your wind, and then we're going to hang you . . . unless your mam tells me where my grandkids are," he said.

The frightened boy stood there sobbing. Huge tears fell onto his cheeks as he stood and cried out his fright. Olivia saw him shake his head. "Mam don't know where they're at."

Olivia wasn't fully convinced the men really would hang her son.

Both women fought the men with the full force of the base strength and dedication women possess in the defense and preservation of the young. But the deputy and Jorod forced them back with their fists and the backs of their hands.

A dust storm arose from the feet of the people in their frantic scuffling endeavors. A loud string of curses and screams too, lifted skyward in the backyard beneath the pecan tree, where the rope still hung limp. All birdsong had ceased. The chickens stopped scratching the dirt, and stared dumbly up the hill at the pecan tree, alerted to danger by the loud, frantic commotion.

Enos lurched against Rust and tried to break his grip. He wasn't strong enough, though. All he managed to do was waste his strength and air.

Olivia and Joan were forced to retreat several yards. The deputy and Jorod stopped beating at them and allowed them to step back. It grew silent in the yard. Olivia heard a dove moan far off in the north pasture, where she'd seen the snow-rollers that bad winter. The cooing of doves had always been a sad sound to her, and now it was even more downhearted. Her heart nearly broke from despondency.

Her eyes filled with tears. She watched as Adair Murphy's wife turned away, and retreated, head hung low as she trod slowly back down the slope. It looked to Olivia as if Joan had given up . . . defeated beyond all hope.

The sheriff took up the slack in the rope. It tightened around the neck of Olivia's child, and she recoiled. The fibers that composed the rope were rough, and she figured they chaffed his neck like wire. Still she thought they were bluffing.

"Hold it right like that," Rust said. He leaned in close to the boy. Rust's red eyes filled with malevolent intent. They grew wider and wilder from the hatred in his soul. He said, "Now, boy, I 'spect you'll want your mam to tell me whereabouts them kids is hid, won't you?"

Enos was part man, part boy. Olivia could see his feeble attempts to shore up his courage, and that he was nearly in a panic. He sobbed once more—had never stopped, but had slackened a bit. He continued to shake his head in denial. Fear bugged his eyes as he looked to her for help. Her heart toughened against his situation.

He cried harder. "Mam don't know, I tell you."

"That's it, son," said the rancher. "Go on and cry. I know you know damned well where the kids are. Now, it won't hurt a bit to tell me. You'll save your life." He allowed his words to take hold in the boy's stricken mind—although Enos was too far gone, Olivia felt. Likely he couldn't make sense of what Rust had said.

"Son," Rust said as if he were truly concerned for the boy's safety, "when you choke to death on this here rope, they'll take you down and put you in the ground. Worms'll eat you when you rot down enough. You've seen dead cows, I'm sure. Seen what happens to 'em when they rot. The maggots attack 'em, and eat their flesh. That's how they reproduce. Flies don't care what flesh they feed on. They'll eat yours as soon as cattle flesh. Matter of fact, they might prefer to eat yours."

He paused to give his words time to work strong in the boy's mind.

After a few minutes, with the man peering into Enos's eyes, he said, "I know you want to go on living. I'll ask you again, where'd you and your mam hide my grandkids? I'm serious, boy."

Olivia said, "Be strong, Enos. He's trying to scare you. They won't hang you. Not a child, they won't. It'd soon be out and then what'd they say?" She hadn't yet realized fully the sorry limits these men had fallen to.

Enos continued shaking his head in denial.

Rust roared out in the bellowing voice of a stricken, wild creature, "By god, hang the little bastard. Make 'em both see we mean business. I've had all this bullheadedness I can stand."

Rathaus had gone far past his stopping point, Olivia suspected. Nothing could stop him now, except death. He hauled up on the rope and lifted the boy several feet off the ground, then stood below while the youth lashed out with his feet. He kicked out at everything. He struck emptiness.

Olivia tried her best to maintain command of her emotions. She realized that if she gave in, and revealed that the children were in the barn—she was unaware of the secret hideout, of course—Rust would then have them. Not only this, she had no guarantee he would go off with them and leave the boy and the ranch unmolested. As crazy as Honus was now, he might kill them all. Rathaus looked as if he was nearly as crazy as Rust, perhaps more so.

Enos had swung in the air more than a minute, thrashing wildly, falling weaker. Now Rust stepped up. He lifted a hand, and said, "That there's enough for a time. Let's see does either one of 'em want to say something useful now."

He caught up the boy, lifted him above the restraint of the rope, and allowed him to catch his breath. Enos gulped air in loud gasps. Rust said, "How's about it now, Enos? You ready to talk?"

"Don't you tell him, Enos. Don't you dare."

Enos stared at Olivia uncertainly and then shook his head.

Honus Rust released him, stepped back, and brushed his hands against his outer thighs. "Give him some more. He ain't quite ready yet."

Rathaus lifted Enos by his neck again above the ground.

The next time they lowered him to the ground, he couldn't stand alone. Rust held him erect. When they hauled him off the ground again, his mother said, "You'll pay for this, Honus Rust, and you too, Pleasant Rathaus. You'll pay for this act. When Steel finds out what you've done, you'll both wish you'd blown your brains out when you had the chance."

On his sixth return to earth, Enos had passed out, and the deputy, Tallman, walked to the springhouse for a cup of water, returned, and flung it in the boy's face to awaken him. Rust asked again if it might be time to give up the children, but Olivia doubted Enos heard the man.

CHAPTER TWENTY-TWO

Joan Murphy entered the blacksmith's shop and felt instant relief from the sun's heat. She walked straight to the shelf where her husband kept his whiskey jug. She lugged down the heavy gallon jug made of plain earthenware, fought with the stopper until it gave way beneath both up-thrust thumbs. It popped with a loud hollow thump, and fell to the floor. She cast about, spied a tin cup hanging on a two-by-four from a nail driven partway into the wood. She poured the cup full. This had been the same amount she'd forced down that long ago day when she washed the body of Molly Rust. This same amount, she felt, would be required now to accomplish the chore that was facing her.

She stepped to the long bench against the south wall. Men would often sit and converse with Adair Murphy as they waited for him to repair their broken equipment, plowshares, wagon tongues, or to shoe their animals. This was a job they could do, were often forced to do, but a job that was onerous to them, and one he performed daily and did far better. She knew he'd taken much pride in his craft.

The instant her bottom touched the rough boards of the bench she dropped her head and cried. Her hands shook. Later she watched the dark reddish whiskey slosh up against the sides of the cup, until fearful she might spill it, she stood back up. Her hands ceased shaking. Her tears stopped flowing. She went to the rear of the shop, forced her body into the far corner,

back in the deepest shadows as if she might be able to hide—
even from God. She upended an empty nail keg, sat on it, and
stared awhile at the bright sunlight outside the wide doorway.
She felt safe now—safe to drink the foul red liquid, which she
felt might be more dangerous than fire itself.

Joan took a small sip, swallowed, and right off sprang from
her seat. The whiskey burned the lining of her throat like lye.
Tears streamed freely down her face. She bent over, grabbed
her chest with one hand, coughing, spitting, and gasping for air.
She sat back down to rest. She figured, though, if she waited
too long she'd back out . . . and then what? Minutes later, she
sipped again, before she lost her nerve. This burned as well, but
less than the first one. The poisonous properties of the alcohol
attacked her brain. She experienced a sudden, giddy sense of
safety, of confidence. She sipped a larger drink. It soon became
easier to tolerate the liquid fire now. Before the cup was half-
empty, the alcohol-demon had invaded her body and mind,
spreading fantastic soothing warmth throughout her soul. Her
mind rolled in waves of pleasure, of tremendous command, and
unbending tenacity.

Along with the giddy sense of confidence, she felt one of
outrage, a realization of what she'd lost in her man, and soon,
she experienced a feeling of safety as well. Along with this, a
longing for retribution hit her, seared her brain.

She started wondering what she'd do next. How would she
survive? She and her daughter? How would they earn their
keep? She knew she would wear out her welcome here at the
Fixxes in time, although she supposed the missus, the mister as
well, would insist they stay. But she hated to be a burden—to
the Fixx family or to anyone. Not even to her cousin living in
Winfrey.

How, though, could she dare worry now about her livelihood
with her husband lying in her kitchen, still foul with his day's

work still on him, as well as the tainted odor of death.

"I'll tackle my duty to Adair," she said, "before worrying about what might lay in the future."

She sipped the whiskey, and relived her life with Adair Murphy. What a pair. Had there ever been such a contrast in mates? Adair was huge and rough. She was as small and dainty as the petal of a flower. How had it come about that they married? She journeyed back through their courtship, their early struggles, being out of work for long intervals of time, but catching on at the Rust ranch, where afterwards they were well fixed. They'd had a nice house, were secure in their employment. There'd been a sense of safety at the Rust ranch. A sensation much like whiskey provides, she now discovered.

"How did it all change? When did it change?" she muttered absently. She knew . . . without even asking that question . . . asking anyway, because she needed to feel justified for telling her man that Honus Rust was taking liberties with her.

She figured it would've taken a weak, weak woman to risk all she and her family owned, just because her boss was taking advantage of her? This, she thought, had been their downfall.

"I shouldn't have told Adair," she said. Tears streamed heavily down her face. "It was my fault . . . all because I couldn't stand for any other man to lay his hands on me. My body belonged to Adair alone." Her voice was muffled and weak now as she beat herself up.

She'd told Adair, and, of course, he went to Rust and warned him. Still Rust persisted. She knew enough about men that this should've forewarned her. She was capable of knowing, should've realized what the result would've been. But she hadn't been strong enough. Could she have resisted Honus Rust's advances forever? Was that the reason she'd told . . . the real reason? Did she feel that one day Rust would go further than a mere slap on the butt? Then after this, what would've happened? She didn't know. Now, with the whiskey pushing her, defending her against self-recrimination, she didn't want to know. Tomorrow perhaps, when the whiskey wore off, she might then, but now she didn't.

The struggle that was taking place beneath the pecan trees in the backyard broke through into her outer mind. She could hear the loud voices—hear the curses of the men, the racket, and a sudden sense of guilt struck her down. She owed the Fixxes. They'd taken in her family. More than this, she owed it to the boy, for children are in need of protection until they are capable of protecting themselves. This, she allowed, was natural in all normal women—in every sane woman.

She tipped the cup, downed all the remaining whiskey, pushed up from the nail keg, and walked toward the front of the shop. She was so light and airy she might be able to fly if she really tried. The very air she breathed felt marvelous, the light touch of it on her skin, and most of all, the person living inside her, the guiding force of her life, the decision-maker, had stirred to life. She felt this force yearning to emerge, to take charge. She hung the empty cup back on its nail, walked to the doorway, and stood watching and listening. She saw them, the men, the huge monsters—those who ran things in this world— and she opposed all she witnessed.

"How can they treat a child in this manner, brag, and still call themselves men?" she said.

She left the shade of the shop, walked out into the sun, heard and felt the gravel crunch beneath her feet.

The last time they hoisted Enos, he swung there for nearly two minutes. He ceased thrashing about and kicking. Olivia grew ashamed of the dark stain on the front of his trousers where he'd released his water. When they let him back down, he could scarcely breathe.

"Let him be," she called out. She could no longer bear to see the boy lifted up again. He'd soon be dead if she didn't intervene. She could tell them that the children were indeed in the barn, but she couldn't tell them exactly *where* in the barn—only Enos knew that. "Let him come to. I'll have him tell you where the children are. You'll kill him."

They freed Enos, let him slump to the ground. She went to him. They allowed her to kneel in the dust beside him.

"Now you're acting sensible, Olivia. Why'n the world didn't you do this before? The boy could've died being hung like that!"

This was too much to bear. She looked into Honus's face, witnessed the sorry state he'd descended to, saw those porcine, hate-filled, red eyes. She felt much of what her husband must've felt when he'd taken Jorod out, flogged him, gave him the ultimatum that resulted in his marriage to Molly. She'd condemned Steel for his act, felt he'd made matters worse. But that was before she learned to hate. She now knew how, and she realized if she had the means, the power to do so, she would kill this obese man. Kill Rathaus and Jorod as well. Instead of doing too much that time, she now decided that Steel hadn't done enough. Her sincere rage threatened to tear her apart.

"You're accusing me of being responsible for hanging my son?" she said. "Aren't you?"

"Why, of course, Olivia. It is your fault. You should've told where them children are . . . or had the boy do it. Surely, it is your fault."

She saw the man was serious, without question. She sprang from the ground, lunged for his eyes. A flashing mental picture of Rust's eyeballs dangling on his cheekbones lit up her mind. He swerved aside to protect them, and spoiled her aim. Her fingernails ripped down the side of his face. This felt good, though she'd missed his eyes. She saw a large channel of blood flowing down his cheek, bright against his pasty repulsive face, and felt somewhat vindicated.

He tossed her off, but she didn't fall to the ground, and maintained her footing. She whirled and assaulted him again or attempted to.

Rust doubled a huge fist, and struck her full in the face as she came on. Olivia crumpled at his feet.

In a mist that swirled madly and dimly, she heard him say, "Hang him again. We'll make him talk."

"Hell, Honus," said Tallman, "that lady meant to talk. Give her a chance."

Rust whirled on the deputy as if he were a traitor. "By god, whose side you on, anyways? You'd better watch yourself, I reckon, if you know what I mean . . . and I think you do."

"You might have something on Rathaus, Rust. But you ain't got a damned thing on me I can't fight out of."

"I beg to differ with you. Were you with us out at the Reyes ranch or not?" Rust's voice was harsh, and rasping from overuse.

"Sure, I was, but I damned sure wasn't the instigator of that shit storm," Tallman said.

Sheriff Rathaus ignored them both, and hauled on the rope. Enos swung free of the ground again.

"Hang him. We'll teach 'em all. By god, if we can't make him talk, we'll, by god, hang 'em both." He took a step toward the sheriff and stood alongside him.

It grew quiet for a brief time. Then—

"Booom!"

The leaves of the pecan tree quivered. They quaked like a rain-soaked dog. The doves rose from the ground. They flew off in their tight spiraling pattern toward the pasture, frightened by the loud shotgun blast. The chickens in the yard scattered dust as they scurried toward shelter as if a bolt of lightning was set to strike them down.

The blast knocked Sheriff Rathaus and Rust as well off their feet. The child, freed from the hand of the hangman, crashed to the ground, unconscious.

Rust sat up and dug at his boot top. He hauled up his trousers leg. When he lifted it up far enough, Olivia saw low mounds of blue flesh where the blast of the shotgun had peppered his leg with more than a dozen pellets. "Damn," he cursed, still holding his trouser leg off his pellet-riddled leg. The entry points of the pellets swelled quickly. Blood trickled down his bony, ridged shin.

The shot caught Rathaus in both legs. Olivia saw blood seep through the fabric of each pants leg. He didn't bother to check. Likely, he was an old-head at this game. He seemed to know what the wounds looked like, as well as the length of time that pain was involved before they healed. He was still too stunned to retaliate, however, and Olivia felt this was much to her advantage.

She turned toward the tiny Murphy woman, who stood with Adair's shotgun in hand. Smoke lifted in a thin, dispersing trail from the right barrel.

"You all right, Olivia?" Joan Murphy said.

Olivia watched her step closer, keeping an eye on the men as she approached, as if they were a special type of monster, which these men were, she realized. She placed no faith in them or the chances they might have to ever find redemption, aware of their craft, their cunning, their lies. She wondered why women down through the ages hadn't thought it necessary to hide their fresh-born from these savage creatures.

Plaits of Joan Murphy's hair hung like snakes down her shoulders and back. Her eyes were glowing with fierce intentions, glinting in bright fiery sparks. Her face was blank, Olivia noticed, ready for molding by whatever needs that arose before her. She'd become the avenging angel arrived upon earth.

Tallman and Jorod Rust stood far back, unable to chance a

shot at Joan, for fear she would fire the other barrel at them.

"If I let off this left barrel, I won't aim low," she said in a loud, determined voice. "I want you to know that. Get up." She pointed the shotgun straight at Rust. "Get up, Honus. Get off this property. You already killed Adair. The next one to die'll be you."

Rust got to his feet and by the time he found himself upright on wobbly knees, the sheriff was standing as well. Olivia saw him eye the wild woman who stood in charge before them all. The sheriff smirked as if he was yet unbowed. Joan raised the gun until it stood firm upon his midsection. Both men stood in the range of her shotgun.

"Turn your cunning eyes to the ground, Pleasant Rathaus. Don't never raise them again in my presence. I should kill you all for what you did to my man. I'll do it too, if you don't get off this property. Now move."

Jorod and Bowler Tallman turned to leave. Rust followed them, hobbling along like a cripple.

"I ain't never been cowed by no woman," said the sheriff. "And, I ain't now—"

Joan Murphy stirred in her shoes, took two forward steps, stopped, and planted her feet in the earth as if she were about to chop down a tree.

"One more word, Pleasant . . . one more mousey squeak and I'll blow your head right off your accursed shoulders. Go on and say something, anything. My finger's taken up the slack on this trigger. Don't even breathe too heavy for it might go off. Now get your sad and sorry hide out of here, like those other dogs fleeing yonder."

Rathaus scooped up his hat, slapped it on his head, and struck out in a limp toward the horses tied in the front yard.

When Olivia saw them ride off up the lane toward the Haz-lett Church Road, she watched Joan Murphy kneel to the boy.

He was still breathing. She turned to Olivia, stirring now, her face a blood-smeared mess where Rust's fist had broken her nose. Both lips were cut, and trickling blood into her mouth.

"Olivia?" Mrs. Murphy said, "can you stand up?"

Olivia stirred more to life. She crawled on her knees to Enos, lifted up his head, and cradled it in her lap.

"Thank you," Olivia told her. "Sometimes men can be so fearsome."

"Those creatures aren't men, Olivia. Men don't act like that. Men don't look like they do, talk like they do . . . men don't war on women and children. I ain't got no name for any such creatures."

When he reached the Hazlett Church Road, Honus Rust reined to a stop with Jorod riding alongside.

"You go on home, Jorod," he said. "I'm going into Witness Tree Station. Dr. Hance's going to have to remove these damned pellets."

He could see the sheriff and Tallman farther up the road riding toward town. Dust rose in slow puffs from beneath the hooves of their animals.

"All right, Pap," said Jorod. He swung his horse in the opposite direction, and rode off toward home.

Rust watched him ride out of sight, and thought it odd the boy didn't bother to ask after his condition. He shook his head and felt sorry for himself. He lifted the lines to drop onto the back of his horse, but before he managed to prod the animal into motion, a tremendous blow struck him in the center of the chest. He crumpled like a wadded piece of cast-off butcher paper, and fell across the seat onto his right side. He tried to catch his breath, but at the same time, feared if he did so, the heavy crush of weight atop his chest might grow greater, and kill him.

Sweat broke out all over his body. His clothes shrunk up on him, clutching him in a fearsome grip. He clawed at the collar of his shirt, popped the button at his neck, cast away the collar, and removed his coat. Still far too uncomfortable, he tore his shirt off, and tossed it to the ground. The ghost-like flutter of the falling shirt frightened the horse. It shied. Honus caught up the reins, and halted it before it broke into a run.

"Hold still, you noggin-headed fool. Stand."

It stood.

He lay sprawled out on the seat until the nausea passed, his proper breathing returned, the sweating stopped, the mountain toppled from his chest. He then sat up to evaluate. He felt cold. He shivered and shook. He heard and felt his teeth chattering, and he had enough sense to catch up his coat, put it on over his naked upper body, felt in a pocket, located a match and cigar and lit up.

"Now, what the hell you suppose that was?" he said aloud, after the worst of the attack passed. He got up the horse, swung back onto the road, and headed toward Witness Tree Station. He'd ask Dr. Hance about it, while he was digging the shot out of his leg.

CHAPTER TWENTY-THREE

Fixx, his boys and Batch drove the herd of fifty cows onto his range. Calves ran alongside some of the cows. Others soon would calve. They drove them down into the steep-sided ravine carved out by the runoff from the spring.

The animals smelled water in the creek, and then took off at a trot, bawling frantically, as if they'd invented the sound. They were content they'd reached water, which was all they required right now. The herd, although not as large as Fixx had hoped for, was a start. It would take several years for it to grow to the size of the one his cousin had destroyed . . . but it was enough for now. He felt thankful to Mr. Swifford for this new start-up herd.

"I'm going on in, Pap," said Clive. He swung his horse toward the barn. Redman chased after him.

The old man sat his horse and watched the cows drink with Batch at his side. Batch was the finest horseman and the best cattleman he'd ever run across. Hugh Rust had taught him well. The young man had been born to the vocation, the same as his sons had, while he, Fixx, had been born a hillside, dirt farmer. Batch sensed things about cattle that Fixx had to witness with his eyes, and often several times over before he fully learned for sure what he was studying. Batch was patient and listened when he needed to, spoke when he needed to and watched with his mind instead of merely using his eyes.

Both men sat, smoked, and watched the cattle.

By and by, Fixx said, "Did we make a sufficient buy, you reckon?"

"Passable. There's a few superior cows in the bunch," Batch said. "Should throw a right first-rate herd. It'll take time, though."

"Have to hunt up a bull." Fixx exhaled smoke to the sky.

"You already got one, Mr. Fixx. That Star bull'll make a fine one."

"He's still young, ain't he?"

"He'll be dabbing them cows later in the season, Mr. Fixx," Batch said.

They smoked and talked on. Both men liked to talk cattle and did so fervently.

"Pap!"

Fixx turned his head toward the sound of his son's excited voice. He saw Redman, who'd already put away his mount, come in a run toward them as fast as his long legs would carry him.

"Pap, come quick. Pap," he was screaming.

Both riders turned their horses and set them in a trot toward Redman. Fixx tried to imagine what crisis had arisen for him to be so excited. He knew Redman was level-headed, and wouldn't go about shouting to the skies for his own amusement.

Fixx's horse shied broadside, spooked by the noise and the flying legs and flailing arms of the boy. Redman didn't pause in his stride, but leapt toward the horse with the abandon that comes from full confidence, and caught on behind his father.

"They been here again, Pap," Redman said into the older man's ear. "Get to the house. They killed poor old Adair, damn nigh killed Enos, and beat Mam to a bloody sight."

Fixx's mount humped its back, hopped a few times to show its displeasure at riding double, but Redman lashed its flank with his hat and it sprang forward like a racehorse, ripping

divots from the ground and flinging them high into the air to
the rear.

That night, at bedtime, Olivia Fixx turned her puffed and
discolored face from Fixx. "I owe you an apology, Steel."

Every time he looked at her battered face, he longed to kill
his cousin. Settle matters now and forever. "Why do think you
owe me an apology, 'Livia? You ain't never done nothing to me
that I'd deserve one."

She lay abed, with Fixx sitting beside her, readying for bed
himself. She reached out and took hold of his hand. She kissed
the huge pads of accumulated calluses on his palm, calluses that
grew so great he had to trim them back a few times a year in
order to be able to close his hands around small objects such as
pitchfork handles, and even to roll cigarettes. Her lips felt cold.

"I was mad when you flogged Jorod that time. I felt we
could've raised Molly's child ourselves. I thought you were being willful, cruel, and had your pride hurt. I felt you'd done it
because of your pride."

"You're right, Olivia. My pride was hurt. But, I thought it
had to be done . . . at the time, I did."

"Well, I see now I was wrong," she said. "I wish you'd done
more."

" 'Livia?" he said. He scarcely believed she'd uttered those
words. Olivia had been too forgiving, or so he'd always felt.

"It's true, Steel," she added. "I never knew how to hate . . .
not really. What I thought was hatred before, turned out to be
mere displeasure . . . today I learned what hatred really is. I see
now what makes men go so wild with hatred. Why one man
kills another."

He bent to her, nuzzling her cheek. She was upset, he knew.
Tomorrow she would be her old self again.

"I ain't a bit proud of it," she continued, "but it's the truth. I hate those men. I wish they were dead. I wish I could kill 'em. All of 'em."

She closed her eyes. A flutter of nerves passed through her. Tears ran from her eyes. Fixx experienced a pain—one he'd never felt before. He took her into his arms and held her close to his chest until all her tears ceased.

Later on, she mastered her emotions, pushed out of his arms, and sat up with her head at rest against the headboard. "What'll we do now, Steel?"

"I ain't quite figured that out," he said. "What I'd like to do is go over there and take that man out and hang him. Hang him like he did Enos." He paused, expecting since she'd had her cry of protest, to attempt to talk him out of any such vengeful action. But when she didn't, and continued to rest against the headboard, eyes slanted in a way that he knew she expected him to say more, he continued, "The man's gone crazy, Olivia. He needs to be put away someplace."

Again, she spoke, and he'd never heard such fire, such hatred in her voice before, "You're right, he needs to be put *away*."

He knew the place she meant.

"You should've seen them hang that boy," her voice broke and she cried. She recovered, and continued. "You should've been here . . . seen Adair out there in the sun trying to die, find peace and a way to go about dying with ease, knowing he was leaving Joan behind, and that girl, Irene, nobody left to protect 'em."

"I should've left one of the boys," Fixx said. "Should've left Redman."

"They'd have found a way. They would've got him too. They dropped that deputy off, and later on, when Adair had 'em whipped, with his shotgun on 'em, and them ready to leave, Tallman slipped up from out of nowhere and shot him in the back.

"And Joan had to become drunk before she found the nerve to pick up the shotgun, rush to the pecan tree, and run them men off. But she did it. A finer job couldn't a-been done, and if whiskey's what it took then, I say, thank God for whiskey."

He saw the epiphanic change in Olivia, and while he reckoned the ordeal she'd gone through had been a harrowing one, he now saw it had also changed her outlook on life. He was not sure which way to go now.

Two days following the hanging incident at the Fixx ranch, Rust sat at a table in his third-story room. He watched out across the yard, up the lane, watched to see if Fixx and his boys—perhaps, even that turncoat, Batch—would ride to the house. A short time later, he heard Hugh enter the house from the front door. He knew it was Hugh by the way he had of always banging the door shut. He struggled up from his chair. He felt the pucker marks where the pellet wounds were healing, stretching tight.

Dr. Hance had dug twelve pellets from his right leg, and one, Honus hadn't been aware of, from his left thigh. Thirteen in all. Now he had greater cause to hate his cousin.

When he reached the head of the stairs, he bawled out in his booming voice, "Hughie. Hughie Rust, haul your dog-ass up here. I want to speak to you."

"Coming, Pap."

Honus heard his elder son cross over to the sideboard to the liquor. He heard him yell up the stairwell, "Keep your britches on. I'll be there."

Soon, Hugh appeared bearing a coffee cup of whiskey in hand. He sipped it as he climbed upward.

"Why on earth do you want to hide out up here on the top floor of the house, Pap?" he said, at the top of the stairs. "Hell, it's a mean chore for me to climb up here, so I know damned well how rough it must be for you. The maid has to carry your food to you, and every damned thing. This another part of an old man's craziness? Hope I ain't got that to look forward to."

Honus stood with hands on hips and was in the appropriate mood to dress Hugh down.

"What's got you so riled up, Pap?" Hugh said. "I thought you'd be in bed. You ain't been drinking that fancy liquor already today, have you? That stuff'll shrivel your pecker and rot your brain."

Once, Rust had heard Hugh and Jorod discussing his odd behavior. Jorod attempted to blame it all on the green liqueur, but Hugh disagreed. He'd said his father had been acting crazy even before he went off to Europe and hauled the stuff back with him. Hugh had said it wasn't the liqueur alone, anyway. It went deeper than that.

Before Hugh had the chance to say more, Honus jumped him.

"Where'n hell you been all morning? I been yelling my head off . . . no damn kind of answer. Sometimes I feel like I live in a nuthouse of some sort."

"I told you last night, Pap," Hugh said, "I had to go over to Staley first thing this morning. Hell, somebody has to keep this ranch from going under. You don't seem to take no kind of interest in it anymore."

Honus waved his hands in front of him as if he were shooing flies. "That don't matter a tub of shit, Hughie. What I'd like to know is how come you didn't go with me and Jorod over to the Fixx place. You part of this family, or not?"

Hugh sipped his whiskey, and answered, "I told you and Jorod both, Pap. I'll tell you again. If you want to wage some kind of damned war on your own cousin, by god, you go right ahead on and do it. But leave me out of it. I ain't got no quarrel with Steel Fixx."

"I ought to fire your ass. Do you know that?"

A stunned look spread across Hugh Rust's face. He said, "Now, if that ain't the goddamdest thing I ever heard in my life. Fire me? Hell, Pap, I'm your goddam son. Shit, I ain't the hired help. Fire me, your ass."

Rust studied him. He'd always favored Jorod over Hugh. He supposed this was what had prevented them from growing closer than they had. But he now knew the answer. Hugh Rust was more of a Fixx than he was a Rust. No wonder he'd always felt closer to Jorod. He'd always felt in his heart that Jorod was a true and genuine Rust and had pampered him beyond even his own belief.

Hugh tossed off his drink and stood waiting for his father to continue his attack. But when he took too long, he attacked first. "I think maybe Jo might be right. That green whiskey, liquor or whatever it is, has rotted your brain, Pap. You need to toss it out."

"I don't need for you to tell me what to do . . . that's all I need from you along about right now. I'm going off to Kansas City, Hughie. That's one thing I wanted to talk to you about.

"I been having heart troubles . . . according to Doc Hance. They got some kind of doctor up there that is some fine peaches at doctoring such problems as this. I 'spect it won't hurt any to go talk to the man."

"What do you reckon he'll tell you that Doc Hance didn't?" Hugh said.

"Hell, Hughie, how should I know? I'm telling you this so you'll know where I'm at. But if you ain't interested, well, I 'spect you can pack your haversack, and hit the damned road. I'm not too happy with your conduct here lately nohow."

Hugh Rust started back down the steps. "All right, then," he said over his shoulder, "I'll do that, right now." But when his feet struck the boarding of the second-floor landing, his father stopped him.

"Where do you think you're going, Hughie Rust?"

"You told me to hit the road, and that's what I mean to do," Hugh said.

"Why, shit fire, son, who do you figure'd run this place, and you gone? Bring your ass back up here. I ain't through talking to you."

Hugh climbed back up the steps.

"Pap, you need to take it easy," Hugh said. "Hell, you're getting up there in age. You need to rest up, recover your health. What other man your age goes out, gets his legs filled with shot, and has a heart attack on the same damn day? Go to bed for a time. Recover your health, toss out that green liquor, and maybe you'll feel better."

"I ain't in no mood to listen to you sermonizing, Hughie. I want to tell you what I need done in case of my death."

Hugh Rust set his whiskey glass on the flat newel post at the top of the stairs, and started rolling a cigarette, eyes on his father all the while.

This was the first time Honus recalled ever speaking to Hughie with such frankness. He hoped he'd stand still long enough to hear him out. He watched the boy touch the tip of his tongue to the cigarette paper, roll the paper and tobacco into a firm tube between thumbs and fingers, then seal it, drag a match along his hiked lower thigh, and light up all in one continuous, pretty motion. He'd often watched Steel Fixx do the very same thing, and this strengthened his conviction that his son took more after the Fixxes than he did the Rust side.

"All right then, what is it you want to say, Pap?" Hugh said, blowing smoke toward the ceiling.

Honus hobbled back to the table before the window and sat down. The skin covering his pellet wounds was stretching every time he took a step, ripping and hurting.

"You know that boy ain't worth shit . . . that Jo. I doubt he even knows how to wipe his ass. He damn sure ain't no rancher. The only thing I figure he's worth shit at is dabbing the womenfolk. And they ain't no kind of future in that . . . not and do it with a profit."

He sat down in his swivel chair, brushed a hand through his mop of gray hair, and said, speaking fast, as if he might lose his nerve and back out, "You'll be in charge of the ranch. I got it set up that a-way with my lawyer Smiley. Don't want you to allow Jo to have no say about what goes on concerning the ranch. He ain't smart enough to run a ranch. Shit fire, he'd put it aground within five years of my death if you allowed him to tamper in the business end of things.

"So I guess you'll have to assign him the title of family-whoremaster or something like that. If I didn't love the boy so damn much, I reckon I'd a knocked him in the head a long time ago." He paused, looked at the ceiling, exhaled with a sadness that was about to fill the room, and added, "But, he reminds me of myself when I was a young man . . . except, of course, I had business sense, and Jo, well, he ain't got no sense a-tall.

"I love the boy, Hughie. Always have. Always favored him over you and still do. I reckon you probably noticed that over the years."

Hugh flinched as if he'd been slapped, but the surprise and hurt fled his face, and he settled into his usual strong poker stare. "Got that impression a time or two."

"Well, what you probably don't know is that there are times—like right now—when I can't stand the sight of you. You're so damned much like the Fixxes I want to strangle you. Right now, you standing there like that, you look like that goddam Steel Fixx did when he was your age, and I feel my guts turn over looking at you."

Hugh sucked on his cigarette as if trying to ignore what he'd just heard, but Honus figured it was a difficult, hurtful thing to have to hear . . . but at least he'd spoken from the heart. He figured Hugh would respect this from his old man.

"Well, now you know, and I 'spect I've said my piece. So you can go and run the ranch. Remember when you start looking for me, I'll be up in Kansas City."

When he reached the head of the stairs, Rust's bullish voice compelled him to stop. "You're one hell of fine rancher, Hughie Rust. It ain't nobody can say you ain't. You're the best I ever seen . . . and I reckon I've seen most of 'em. Too bad you ain't a Rust . . . more of one, anyways."

CHAPTER TWENTY-FOUR

Fixx wrestled daily with the problem of how to retaliate against his cousin. He felt at times he'd grown too old. When he was a young man, he wouldn't have allowed this to become a problem. He would've already made his move. But in all truth, he *was* growing old. He was also tired. Tired of the wrangling, tired of what'd turned into a vendetta with his cousin. He wouldn't admit to himself what had started it. He couldn't believe the truth. It was too absurd for belief. That a childhood enmity between himself and his cousin had simply gotten too far out of hand. He'd found no way to stop and start anew. He recalled back when the two families had been close. Nothing like this should've happened, but it had, and now—well, there didn't seem to be a way out. Not now. Not after what Honus Rust had done to his son. Not after what Rust had done to his wife. Not after what Honus had done to Adair Murphy.

Each evening after the day's work, he took to his chair on the porch with a glass of whiskey, sat in the shade there, where the lazy hum of wasps in their rafter nests attempted to lull him to sleep. But as his head was about to nod off, his angry thoughts would intervene, and instead of dropping off, he'd jerk awake. His mind would fill up with hateful thoughts . . . thoughts of retribution.

The summer turned. Still, he sat with his thoughts, and his glass of whiskey. He didn't allow Olivia to enter into these loathsome thoughts. He'd heard rumors that his cousin was in poor health. Heard he'd started visiting a doctor in Kansas City on a regular basis, and that he was dying. It seemed now Fixx was doing nothing more than sitting back, waiting for Honus to die. Do it the easy way. So far, however, Honus hadn't died.

Summer turned to fall. Fall turned to early winter. He still hadn't found the proper way to go. Cold weather chased him inside by the fireplace, where he stared with solemn eyes into the flames as they licked upward, and struck snake-like at everything, but hit only emptiness.

He realized everyone in his family was watching him, felt eyes on him, unable to bring themselves to move in on his thoughts. He figured they were all wondering when or if he'd ever return the latest blow Rust had dealt his family. He read the collective mind of his family. The law? Rathaus was the law. Would still be the law through the winter, through the coming summer, into the fall election. There would be no help from the law. Fixx had already given up that notion, had never really considered it with a serious mind. At any rate, he felt the obligation to strike back at Rust. His need would prod him eventually to make his move. He was sick to death of the torment of his own thoughts.

He recalled the Reyeses' death. How the old man had hung himself. He thought of how Rathaus had hung his son, Enos. He put the two events together, and decided he knew what really had occurred at the Reyes place. Rust and the sheriff had done the murders.

Honus himself, he thought, killed the girl—likely, his blood grew hot for some no-account reason. But Rathaus also had a fearsome temper, was famous for it.

One thing left his mind yet unsettled. That old man hadn't hung himself. If Felipe wanted to kill himself, he wouldn't have taken that route. The gun had been there alongside the girl. Why wouldn't he've shot himself after fracturing Leona's skull with the thing? That bunch had committed those murders.

Reyes and his daughter were deeply religious. He doubted the old man would've braved Hell's fire by killing his daughter and then himself.

One day, after such a long wait, Fixx made up his mind. He downed his whiskey, set the glass on the floor alongside his chair, got up, went to the closet, took down his jumper, struggled into it, and drew out his rifle.

Standing there stuffing his pockets full of shells, he said to the boys seated around the fire, "I'm going over to Honus Rust's ranch. Anybody wants to come along, feel free to do so, but if not, I won't think the worst of you. It ain't going to be pretty what I'm fixing to do."

Redman jumped up on nimble legs. Clive too seemed eager to join in. Batch also got to his feet, and hobbled after his coat.

"You can't go, Batch," Fixx told him. "You ain't family, and this here's a family affair. Even if you was kin, somebody has to stay with the women. You're the old boy elected, I reckon."

Fixx walked to the kitchen. The girls sat clustered around Olivia like baby chicks around an old mother hen. The oldest girl, Sarah Ellen, reminded Fixx so much of his daughter Molly that he turned his head to prevent looking at her, for fear he might break down. All the girls were happy in his house. Christmas was nigh and evenings by the fireplace had become a rallying point for the girls and their grandmother, a place for them to create gifts and craft fresh ornaments for the tree they planned to set up in the parlor. He felt a warm touch of pleasure they were in his house, pleased they were enjoying themselves in anticipation of the coming holiday. For an instant, he fell stricken by guilt. He thought perhaps that what he planned to do now might waylay their plans. The children, he reckoned, had never had a proper Christmas, and if he were the cause of more disappointment, it would be bad for them. He considered it a shame he'd arrived at his decision when he had. Why hadn't he made it earlier, or later, for that matter?

He saw by the fire in Olivia's eyes that his decision—as he stood before her, wearing his jumper, with the rifle in the crook of an arm—pleased her. He allowed that her heart was likely leaping in her chest from joy. She smiled, raised her face to him. He kissed her lips. The children snickered behind their hands, save for Sarah Ellen. For being older, he felt she was aware something terrible might be afoot. He watched her divert her head and concentrate on pinching out biscuits for the noon meal, a chore her grandmother had by this time given over to her.

"We won't be in at noon," he told her. "Should be back for supper, though."

Olivia's face split wider with her smile. Fixx watched it grow in pride. "I'll have y'all a fine supper waiting."

Fixx allowed Redman to saddle his horse for him while he went in a search of Enos. The boy walked around spiritless all day long since Honus Rust had hung him. He'd grown standoffish, elusive. He wouldn't mingle with the rest of the family, which was peculiar, because before that day he seemed to be bursting at the seams to be grown-up, unable to wait until he reached the size when the others would accept him into their inner circle.

Fixx found him in the aging room. The boy was busy grading staves, laying them out side by side, sizing them up by eye before fitting them into the bottom of the barrel and hooping them with iron. The steel cable lay in a snake-like coil at his feet waiting for him to attach it to the barrel in order to cinch down the staves and properly seal the barrel. Enos was so busy, so intrigued by his work he didn't look up as his father entered the room.

Fixx watched him work, watched his fine, capable hands,

long supple fingers involved in a job they were adept at, and felt his pleasure at seeing someone so caught up in a job he enjoyed. He placed a broad hand on Enos's shoulder.

"We're going now," Fixx told him. "You help Batch with the chores. He's sometimes unsteady afoot."

Enos nodded indifferently, and continued his work.

"We should be back by supper."

Enos nodded again. This hurt Fixx. He realized what the act of the hanging had done to Enos, saw how it'd crippled him. Enos was not the boy he'd once been, and perhaps now, he'd never reach the potential Fixx had read in his future. It was no minor sin, what Rust had done to him. It'd take time, he figured, for the boy to regain all he'd lost. At least, he hoped Enos would find a way to return and take his place with the men. If not, the boy would have to learn to live with it. They all would find a means to live with his affliction, and there was no doubt Enos suffered intense hurt from the crime committed against him. He wondered if his youngest son possessed the mental toughness to fight his way back from the trauma of such an experience.

Staring death in the face could never be thought of as something ever to be forgotten, and being snatched from the hands of death at the final moment might scar a person so much there'd be no way to return, no matter how tough he'd once been.

Ultimately, he left him there with his work. He caught up his horse, and he and his older sons left the barn at a trot. Fixx reached the lane then kicked up his horse into a fast trot. He looked back once. He saw the young bull, Star, busy at its work in the upper pasture, imprinted visibly, bull and cow, on the bright horizon. He smiled. Batch had known exactly what he'd been talking about.

Chapter Twenty-Five

At the steps that led up to the broad porch of the house of his cousin, Fixx pulled up, and dismounted.

"Stay here, boys. I'll see if Honus is home."

Clive and Redman sat their horses, watched their father mount the steps to the porch and cross to the door on quick feet, as if he were in a hurry. As he rapped against the large door with the butt of his rifle, ignoring the brass knocker, he felt their eyes watching his every move. The horses snuffled, heads hanging toward the ground, blowing dust in minor clouds. The boys were nervous, he decided, for their saddles squeaked repeatedly beneath their rumps as they shifted about in anticipation of the unknown.

After several minutes of loud rapping, the door swung open. A short, round-faced old Mexican woman stood there, drying her hands on her yellow apron. She frowned up at Fixx, frowning or squinting, he couldn't say which. This then was the new maid Rust had hired to replace Joan Murphy.

"Jorod say tell you he ain't home," said the old woman.

Fixx flashed a brief smile, unable to refrain. "Bully for him. Well, is the old man in?"

This confused her. The term "the old man" was lost on her. Her face screwed up in complete puzzlement.

"Is Honus Rust in?"

Recognition lit up her face, when she heard the name of her employer spoken. "No. He went away, to doctor."

"Well, all right," Fixx said. "Thank you, ma'am."

He tipped his hat, and went back to his horse, mounted, swung it around, and set his heels against its sides. The boys followed him, but didn't bother to question their father.

When they reached the Hazlett Church Road, they turned toward Witness Tree Station, and when they reached the post oak tree where, years before, Fixx had caned Jorod, they drew rein. Fixx swung his right leg over the saddle horn, dug out papers and tobacco, and rolled one up. He struck a match on his saddle horn and fired the cigarette. "Jorod'll be going into Witness Tree Station before too long. 'Less he's sick. We'll wait for him. Wasn't no use in frightening that old woman, barging in the way we'd had to do . . . bad 'nough as 'tis, her having to work for that bunch."

They sat there, smoking, joking about how the old woman had made the slip-up the way she had, with a look of innocence on her face. She hadn't realized what she'd given up.

"What about Honus, Pap?" said Clive. "Reckon he's really gone off to the doctor?"

He said, "Hear he's pretty bad off. Been traveling all the way up to Kansas City to see a doctor. I guess they ain't no limits to what a man'll do to try and save himself when he's got the money."

They moved off the road to allow their mounts to forage in the grass beneath the post oak tree. Fixx and Clive sat, leaning back against the tree. The old man sat there paring the build-up of callus from his palms and fingertips with a pocketknife, slicing the toughened skin from the pads of his palm into thin slivers that curled tightly like wood shavings. Redman, ever the nervous one, stepped back to the road, and knelt there on one knee in the dust as he waited for sight of Jorod.

"You know what I aim to do to Jorod, Clive?"

"I think so," Clive said.

"How do you feel about it?"

"I don't like it, Pap," he said.

"Me, neither."

"But, I reckon something's got to be done," Clive said.

"You're right, son. Honus forced us to do something about this here."

Two hours later Redman rose to his feet in the road. "I see him. He's coming, Pap." He crushed out his cigarette, and hurried down off the road into the ditch brush. "Jorod's coming, Pap," he said again and settled in beside his father.

Fixx exhaled. He stood up and stretched the kinks from his lean body, still agile after sixty-four years of eternal work, freezing winters, and torrid drought-stricken summers. He walked to his horse, and took down his rope.

"You boys mount up. Allow him to pass, then catch his ass up and bring him back here. And by god don't you dare let him get away. Remember all through this afternoon what Honus did to Enos, and remember what Jorod did to Molly. We'll show him the same mercy he showed her and Enos. I've thought it over for a long time, and decided this is the only way I can go, and still call myself a man. Now go on with it. And don't lose your nerve, even if he is kin."

At length, Jorod passed by. The soft *plop plop plop* of hooves in the deep dust sounded dull to Fixx. Jorod kept to a lope, eyes on the road ahead. Fixx gave him a few moments, then nodded. The two brothers lay their heels into the sides of their horses, and the hooves of the horses yanked up large divots of sod as they leaped ahead abruptly, leaving the old man dodging clods of dirt.

Jorod was riding one of his father's favorite horses. Honus had grown so obese he seldom rode these days, but he still loved horses, Fixx knew well. This one was a splendid creature and had raced and beaten the better horses in the county. Fixx's boys rode fine animals as well, but they couldn't match the steel blue with the small, regal head perched proudly on its long, graceful neck.

Fixx watched his sons catch up to Jorod. Jorod turned in the saddle, stopped, and whirled broadside in the road. This, Fixx figured—other than leaving the house—was the sorriest mistake Jorod Rust had made all day long. By the time Jorod recognized Clive and Redman, swung the horse back toward town and dug heels into its sides, his cousins were nearly upon him. At that, the boys pursued him for twenty more yards before they caught him. Five more yards and the regal blue horse would've left them breathing his dust.

Fixx watched Clive reach out with a long arm and latch onto the blue's halter. Saw him throw his weight backward, putting his shoulders into it, as if he were setting the hook in a fish. Clive's mount squatted. Its hindquarters slid so close to the ground its tail, with its full weight upon it, dragged through the dust. Redman had reached out for the animal's headstall too, but a second later than had his brother and he about fell onto the neck of his own mount when he missed his grab.

Even with Clive's hold on the blue, the spooked animal still attempted to flee, rearing up at the same time, frightened by an event it likely had never run up against before. This made it difficult for Redman to catch it on the off side, but he managed to latch onto the blue's headstall as well. It was all over except for the hellish cloud of dust they created.

The large wall of dust hid Fixx's boys and Jorod for a short time, but Fixx breathed easy. He was sure they'd nabbed him. But as he thought this, he watched with anxious eyes as Jorod leaped from his saddle and set out in a desperate run toward the heavy ditch brush, seeking shelter, or maybe thinking the brush might be too dense to allow the Fixx brothers' horses to enter.

Clive lashed the side of his mount, urging it onward in a full-out run. He guided the animal alongside his cousin, set a foot against Jorod's back, and kicked him hard. Jorod spun head over appetite, then sat upright and stared about him in an apparent daze, gasping for air.

Jorod got to his feet still cursing. It was likely the boy had guessed that what lay in store for him might be worse this time than it had been the time Fixx had flogged him. Fixx sighed. What the boy didn't know for sure was a blessing, he reckoned. Clive and Redman hazed him back up to the road, with a horse on each side. They forced him back to the post oak tree, where Fixx stood waiting for him with rope in hand.

"What're you going to do with that rope, Uncle Steel?" Jorod said. The urgent fear of what lay in store for him caused his eyes to jiggle violently up and down in their sockets.

Fixx hadn't bothered to craft a proper hangman's noose. Didn't know how to build one. He placed the loop over the boy's head, and yanked it until it was snug around his neck.

"What the hell, Uncle Steel? What're you doing?"

Fixx pointed toward the fine, grayish-blue horse that stood alongside the road. "Fetch his horse, Redman." He tossed the loose end of the rope over one of the lower tree limbs.

Redman brought up the horse. Jorod continued his jaybird chattering, asking what was going to happen to him, although it was plain to see. Wondering aloud why they were treating him this way . . . since they were kin.

"Don't say no more, Jorod. I can't hear you." The leathery old man figured this'd be the hardest job he'd tackled in his life.

Clive and Redman wrestled him to the ground, bound his arms behind him, and set him in his saddle. All three were drenched with sweat by the time they'd finished the task. Jorod continued to fight them. He kicked heels deep into the flanks of his animal. The creature screamed in fright, flung its head about with so much violence it came close to butting heads with its rider. Still he kicked the animal, despite the rope around his neck, which had he succeeded, would've caused him to hang himself.

Jorod slumped over in the saddle, worn out from his struggles. The horse trembled beneath him, and attempted to blow away its fright. Jorod fought for his breath as if the rope had already cut off his air. He reclaimed his wind after a bit, raised his head, and peered into Fixx's eyes. "Why are you doing this, Uncle Steel? Pap's the one done the hanging. He hung that boy, Enos. Wasn't me. It was Pap and Pleasant. Pleasant did the actual hanging. Me and Tallman just watched."

"Should've stopped him, Jo," said Redman. His eyes were afire, sweat stood heavy upon his forehead from setting Jorod in the saddle. "How could you let them do that to a kid—to Mam . . . her a woman and old at that? How was it you had to shoot poor old Adair in the back . . . and him the kindest-hearted sort of man you'd ever want to meet?"

"That's enough, Redman," said Fixx. "Don't speak no more to him." He figured if he allowed Jorod to ramble on long enough, the boy would talk them into turning him loose.

The other end of the rope lay across the limb above the boy and his horse. All that remained was to lead the horse out from under him—gravity would accomplish the rest.

"Ride on off up the road there, boys. I'll be along afterward. You don't want to see this."

When his boys were gone from sight, Fixx raised Jorod's head. He said, "You're the blame for this, Jo. You know that, don't you?"

Jorod sobbed, attempted to find his air and sob at the same time. All he accomplished, though, was to make a loud, sorrowful chuffing sound deep in his chest. It became nearly too much for a man to bear. Fixx felt of a mind to turn him loose, but he dared not. The complete collapse of control, of the grief he'd witnessed in his wife's eyes wouldn't allow any such thing. Not after he'd witnessed the horror and hatred in the depths of her soul. If he backed down now he might as well go ahead, sell out and hit the road. His daughter's memory, though, his son's loss, and his wife's grief propelled him on. He'd gone too far now. He wouldn't back-step.

"Why didn't you let that Reyes girl tend to Molly? What would it've hurt—even if it didn't help any? Molly might've found some comfort from it."

"I didn't think, Uncle Steel," Jorod said. "I'm sorry I did that to Molly. I wish I had it to do over."

"I wish you did too, Jo. Believe me, I do. Damn my soul, but I wish it were so."

"I was drunk, Uncle Steel," he said. "Ain't you never been drunk?"

"Yessir, I have. But I damn sure didn't kill my wife as a result."

"Please, Uncle Steel. Give me a break."

Fixx recalled all the pain the boy had caused. The grief. Thought too of the way he'd gone about it. The arrogance he'd shown.

"What happened to the Reyeses, Jo? Y'all killed them, didn't you? Honus wanted that old man's skinny-assed couple of acres. He killed 'em. Then called it a murder and suicide didn't he?"

"That was Pleasant, Uncle Steel. He did that. He's the one to blame for that."

"You there?"

"Yessir. I saw Pleasant kill that girl . . . hit her too hard with his pistol barrel. Then hung the old man. That's all on Rathaus."

"Your pap was there, wasn't he?"

"Yessir, but . . ."

"*But,* your ass. Pleasant did what Honus wanted done. Didn't he? Why'n hell did he want with that sorry piece of ground?"

Jorod started crying again. "I don't know, Uncle Steel. Hell's fire, I don't know. Don't hang me, Uncle Steel. You won't hang me . . . will you?"

"It's out of my hands now, Jo. Ask Jesus for forgiveness. Go on now, son, while you still got the chance."

The boy's sobbing wrenched Fixx's heart. He longed as he'd longed for nothing else in his life to cut him down and turn him loose. But he couldn't. The fear of going to hell for eternity couldn't change his mind. He was on the far side of that now. He caught up the blue's reins, stood in front of it. He was ready now to lead it forward, leave the boy strangling to death, kicking away his life.

"Please, Uncle Steel. Please, sir. Don't hang me. Don't you do it!"

"I'll fry in hell with you, Jo, but I can't turn my back on all you've done. I ain't anywheres near that much of a man."

He stepped backward, watching the boy's eyes grow wide, and the urgent threat of death staring back at him.

"Uncle Steel!" These were Jorod Rust's last words.

Fixx led the animal out from under him, spun, and walked off fast, as if it were possible to outrun his cousin's voice pleading for mercy.

"I ain't your uncle, Jo. I ain't your goddam uncle." He felt as lowdown as a man ever feels. Jorod Rust's begging voice would haunt him for the rest of his life. He was struck down by regret, and knew if he had it to do over, he'd turn him loose. When he reached the road, and learned his own horse was following him, he stopped and waited. He wiped sweat from his brow on the sleeve of his jumper, vaulted onto his horse's back, and raced off up the road where his two sons waited. They were watching him come, but were unable to see from where they stood how long and how much Jorod would suffer before death eased his misery.

Fixx let Jorod hang there for more than thirty minutes. He didn't know for sure how long it took a man to strangle to death. He wanted to make sure. At length, they rode back to the post oak, cut Jorod down, draped him over the back of Honus Rust's nervous horse, led it back onto the road, and rode toward the Rust ranch.

No one answered the door when he rapped, so the three men rode down to the bunkhouse. Archer Payne, the junior ranch hand, and as such, was still doing duty as horse-wrangler, met them. He stood in the shade of the bunkhouse and stared at them as he leaned against a puny tree that grew in the tiny, miserable yard of hard-packed earth.

The men reined up in front of the bunkhouse leading Honus Rust's blue horse. Archer pushed off from the tree, and walked out to the small wooden gate. The ranch hand stopped abruptly. He stared with a gaping flytrap-mouth. One hand rested atop the gatepost.

"I knocked at the house," said Fixx.

"Mr. Rust's gone, sir. He's in Kansas City." The horse wrangler became all eyes, as he tried to determine for sure who lay draped over the horse's saddle. "That old woman he hired don't speak much English. She's from down south. She don't always like to come to the door."

Archer pushed through the gate and entered the roadway. He stood there and stared bug-eyed. Both knees were out of his jeans, which revealed his knobby knees. Archer was studying the man draped over the saddle, watching from covert eyes, as if he feared Fixx would accuse him of being nosy.

"Sir, is that there Jo?" he said. "Jorod, you got there?" He'd lost his battle with proper decorum.

"Yeah. It's him. Hughie here?"

"No, sir," Archer said. "Hughie went up to Staley this morning. Ain't made it back yet."

"Will he be back today, you figure?"

"Oh, yessir," he said. "He'll be back some time later in the day, I'd say."

Fixx raised the blue horse's reins, offered them to the young man. "I reckon you ought to take Jo down and put him inside someplace out of the sun. We can do it for you, if you prefer."

But Archer didn't offer to take the reins. Fixx swiveled in the saddle. "Take him down, boys. Lug him into the bunkhouse. Spread him out on the floor, so none of them working boys'll have to sleep where a dead man's been a-laying. I know I wouldn't want to, was it me."

Clive and Redman carried Jorod inside, returned, and then mounted up.

Fixx said, "You tell Hughie to send for us . . . if he wants us for anything. Honus's mam and my pap were brother and sister. Me and him are own-cousins."

The wrangler came out of his daze. He reached out and caught up the reins the lean-faced old man held out to him. "But, sir, I saw him a while ago leaving for town. Shit fire, sir, Jorod can't be dead."

"He is, though." Fixx whirled to go.

"Well, sir, what happened?" Archer said. "What killed him, you reckon?" He trotted after the old man's horse.

Fixx hauled back on the reins, and turned the horse to the boy. The animal snorted, tossing its head as if frustrated, raising dust.

Fixx leaned toward the young man. "I hung him, son."

He whirled the horse again. Steel Fixx was now tired of it all.

The three men set heels into the sides of their mounts, and fled the Rust ranch. The last time Fixx looked back, Archer

Payne stood staring after them, still wide-eyed, mouth bowed in befuddlement.

CHAPTER TWENTY-SIX

The Fixx household grew extra busy. The closer to Christmas, the busier the house grew. The girls and even little Honus were in a constant blur of excited activity. Every chance they found, they set about finishing the gifts they were creating for all the occupants of the ranch. Sarah Ellen was determined to present a gift to everyone, including the hand, Batch, and to Mrs. Murphy and her daughter, Irene. Sarah Ellen and Irene were now fast friends, despite the age difference. Irene enjoyed having Sarah Ellen at her elbow, and Sarah Ellen thought of Irene as an older sister.

Olivia Fixx invited the Murphys to eat their meals with them following Adair's murder. For the most part—except for breakfast—they did so. Olivia Fixx and Mrs. Murphy formed a close bond through the ordeal they'd shared that day, a bond that was strong and long-lasting, and much like the girls, Sarah Ellen and Irene, Olivia thought of Joan Murphy as sort of a sister—although, in this case, she was the older one.

Enos had been coming out of his dull state of mind. So much so, that Sarah Ellen had talked him into allowing her to go with him in search of a small cedar tree to set up in the parlor. They'd set the tree search for the upcoming Saturday.

But the long-awaited, much-anticipated event didn't take place. On Saturday, Olivia Fixx's brother-in-law, Henry Ridenour, stood tapping on the Fixxes' front door. Sarah Ellen allowed him to enter. Henry was a man of pale skin because his job required him to remain indoors for days on end, running his store. He stood tall and thin, built much like Sarah Ellen's maternal grandfather, bundled up in a heavy coat, the collar of which he'd upturned to encase his neck, and he peered out from it like a turtle from its shell. He stepped inside, shut the door behind him, removed his gloves, bent his collar down, and beamed at the small girl.

"Why, my word, Sarah? Is that you? Sarah Ellen?" He pronounced her name, *Saree.*

"Yes, sir," she said. She discovered then who the man was. She soon was at ease with him, because of his familiar build, happy face, and radiant eyes.

"I scarce recognized you, girl, you've grown so much," Ridenour said. "Is your grandmam in?"

"Yes, sir," Sarah said. She whirled. "I'll fetch her, sir."

The Ridenours' youngest daughter, Bridget, was about to bear her first child. Since Bridget was having a difficult pregnancy, Olivia's sister, Bernadette, felt she should be with her. Bernadette planned to leave right away for Staley where Bridget and her husband lived—she, and the mister as well. They expected—nothing disastrous happening—to stay for only a week. The Ridenours needed Olivia in Witness Tree Station to tend the store in their absence.

This proved one more disappointment for Sarah Ellen, and for them all, except for little Honus. One place seemed as alike as any other to him at this stage of his life. The children had counted on the cedar tree, the Christmas celebration, wishing it to be here at home. For this house was where they felt safest, and welcome, for the first time in their lives.

Fixx stepped to Olivia's side as she stood packing for town. He saw she looked disturbed about leaving.

"What's wrong, 'Livia? What's grieving you?"

She sat down on the side of the bed, hands in her lap, and in a dark mood. "It's these children, Steel. They ain't never had a decent Christmas in their lives. Sarah Ellen, above all. Lord, she's been so busy around here. She and Enos were going out to hunt up a tree for the parlor. Them kids, Steel. You know how rough an old row they've had."

"Yes," Fixx said, "I do know. What I don't know, though, is why it's got you so upset? You didn't think I'd let you go off and leave us all alone for Christmas, did you?"

He felt Olivia's eyes on him when she realized his intent. Tears tumbled from her eyes, and she cried harder than she had when Molly died. By and by, she sat on the bed, and he sat beside her. He placed an arm about her and pulled her close.

"Sarah Ellen wanted to put up a tree, Steel," Olivia said.

He stroked her hair lightly. "That ought to be easy enough to arrange. The ditch alongside the Hazlett Church Road is full of Christmas trees. We'll stop and cut one down, take it along with us. We're all going with you to your sister's, 'Livia. With Mrs. Murphy and Irene going to her cousin's place in Winfrey, that'll leave us all to spend Christmas in town."

She smiled at him, a huge sunny smile. "Steel Fixx, if you ain't the best-hearted man—I reckon there ain't one nowhere." She laughed from a heart filled with joy, and rested her head against his chest.

"Didn't even get to attend the funeral," Honus Rust mumbled with his head down, sitting there in despair.

"Didn't know just when you'd come home, Pap," said Hugh. "It was best not to leave him lying around too long. The weather had moderated some. He was souring already so we went on ahead and buried him."

Rust raised his head, took up his glass and sipped. The redness in his eyes had passed on by now. His vision was always excellent when they cleared. At times, he felt his boys had been right all along. This stuff, he decided—he held aloft the glass containing his fancy liqueur and studied its contents—was the cause of his failing eyesight. This was his third drink of the morning. He found when he consumed only this much of it, the redeye he suffered from disappeared. Although, he realized that before he'd taken to this particular drink, he hadn't been bothered any by poor vision. This occurred only a few years after he'd taken to the drink he now referred to as "this stuff."

He could see the orchard from his window. All the way up to the new grave—the grave that contained Jorod's body, his life's blood and favorite child. The grave lay in a sad hump, red earth piled high in a mound of a shape unmistakable the world over. It was always a sad thing, looking on a grave, he reckoned. Something was gone for all time from the living. A thing much missed. But, in this case, with Jo, his favorite child, so young, so full of dash and zest, it hurt worse. Jorod had been a child in a world of men, one to carouse, to whore-about, to raise hell. His death was too much for the old man to accept.

He had a sudden impulse to rush out, locate a shovel and pick, dig into the grave, and open it up to see for sure if what Hugh had said was true. It wasn't possible. Was it? The boy— gone? So soon? This put him in mind of an old adage. He forgot he wasn't alone, and mumbled, "Only the best of 'em die young, I 'spect."

"What'd you say, Pap?" Hugh said.

Rust spun his swivel chair about with Hugh standing there, and said, "Aww, hell, Hughie, it ain't nothing. Talking nonsense."

Honus Rust was of a mood to ruminate on the past as he gazed out the window at his son's grave in the orchard. The grave alongside his mother's.

"At least you had the decency to bury him by his mam. If you'd buried him alongside that Fixx girl, I'd of had the boys dig him up and rebury him. That was good thinking on your part, Hughie."

"I knew you didn't care much for Molly," Hugh said. "Figured you'd raise three different colors of hell. I didn't want to have to dig him back up to rebury him."

Rust sipped his drink, unable to decide if the foreign liqueur was sinister, blameless, or somewhere in between. At length, he decided it had to be sinister or blameless, for it damn sure wasn't in between. He said, "They'll be hell now, Hughie. I guess you're in, ain't you, son? Got to be a payback. We can't allow this to happen . . . not do no damned thing about it. You know that, I reckon."

"I don't know how you and Steel ever got yourselves in such a jackpot, Pap," Hugh said, spreading his hands. "Hell, this is dumb, and you know it. Where will it all end?" He dropped his cigarette stub to the floor and ground it beneath his foot. He was a man accustomed to the outdoors, and far from his true realm while indoors, except while in the rough-built bunkhouse.

"By god, now. You watch it there. You'll mar that wood, and it cost me a-plenty."

Hugh Rust laughed at that. "Jesus, here you are drowning in wet shit and you're worrying about a few sticks of wood. That's a dandy one, Pap.

"And while I'm at it, I want to tell you how stupid you're acting. You're a man who made more money from his land than anyone else in the entire county. You ought to be a pillar of the community, ought to be looked up to, well thought of, but you don't give a damn about any of that. Hell's fire, all you want to do now is war on your cousin.

"And you could be a help to people who're in a bad way. But you'd rather beat some old man out of his few acres than to help him out any." He dug out a book of papers and his tobacco sack and started building another smoke, more to allow his temper to die than to appease his nicotine demon.

Rust removed his cigar and held it between his huge fingers, allowing the smoke to curl upward in the light streaming in through the window. The liqueur was working fine by now. He felt relaxed and in total control, content to sit and watch the cigar smoke change patterns in the bright sunlight, and in the end, when he spoke, he felt as if he were in a dream world, speaking without malice. "Wasn't nobody helped me none. Besides, that Reyes land is going to be damned valuable soon. And this deal between Steel and me'll end in death. He's going to have to die . . . or me, one or the other. That's the only way out I can see, Hughie."

Hugh Rust snorted in disgust, and fired up his cigarette.

Rust sat there in his relaxed and dreamy condition, thinking on his youth. Then he said, "When Steel and me was growing up back in Cave's Cove he had a feist dog. My word, but that little bitch was one fine squirrel dog. Her name was Tuffy. That Tuffy dog never hunted like most ever' other dog around there. She worked at it by what you might call 'sense.' She didn't need to follow her nose, but had something extra. We gave it that name, 'sense.' She hunted by sensing or by sight or some god-dam way or other.

"All of them larger dogs would chase around, follow their noses wherever they led 'em. And when they did manage to tree, it'd be halfway up the mountain, and by the time you got up there, most of the time, the squirrel would've already jumped the tree. This would force you to follow again. The next time they treed, it'd like as not be back down under the mountain or on the other side of the steep-assed thing.

"That Tuffy dog now, she didn't work your ass off in order to fetch a mess of squirrels. I wanted that Tuffy dog. Don't ask me why. Steel and me was thick then, and when I wanted to use Tuffy all I had to do was ask. But for some reason or the other—

still ain't figured it out, not yet, not to this day—I took it in my head I had to have Tuffy. I saved my money. Worked all summer long on Grandpap Fixx's farm up on Little Pigeon and went to Steel. But when I showed him the money, and said I wanted to buy Tuffy, he looked at me like I was the craziest bit of news to come along all summer. He wouldn't sell her. So, what'd I do? I shot her. Shot that dog on the sly.

"Steel didn't for the world think it was me did such a thing, and I didn't disabuse his opinion. But his old man—my uncle, was part devil, and could see clear through a person. He caught on right away what happened to Tuffy. Then Steel found it out. Don't know if his pap told him or not, but he knew it. And, well, we've been fighting ever since that day."

"A dog? That's what this is all about?" Hugh said. "You killed his goddam dog? All this started from that? That what you're telling me?"

"Yep."

"Jesus Christ." Hugh Rust stood shaking his head. "I ought to lock your ass up in the smokehouse, Pap, until you regain your right mind. This old business has got to stop sometime or another. I give up, Pap. I'm leaving. You want to, you can leave the ranch to Jorod's children. I'll fend for myself."

Rust reared back and laughed. When he asked again, if Hugh would throw in with him, the son failed to answer, but turned and fled back down to the ground floor and slammed the door leaving, almost taking it off by the hinges. Honus Rust kept to his hideout loft, drinking in peace, and from time to time laughing loudly. At length, he stepped to the window to see what Hughie was doing.

He watched him enter the barn and soon reappear with his two mules hitched to the wagon and drive from his sight. He ran to a back window, watched him pull up to the bunkhouse. Watched him load his entire outfit aboard the wagon. Honus continued watching, by now having returned to his chair in front of the window where he'd first started spying on Hugh, which had entailed a feverish journey around the entire room, staring from every window. He saw him fetch from the corral his four saddle horses, bought with his own money, he knew. He watched as he tied them on behind the wagon, mounted to the seat, and got up the mules.

As his son struck off up the lane toward the Hazlett Church Road, the old man pushed his head out of the window and screamed for him to return. Hugh ignored him, though, and continued striking out, leaving the ranch forever or so it looked to Rust.

As they rode in the wagon toward the road to Witness Tree Station, the children saw their uncle Hugh sitting on his wagon seat at the head of the Fixx lane. The girls jumped up and down, clapped their hands and called out his name before they reached him. Hugh Rust sat erect and alert on the wagon, smoking, waiting for them to reach him. All his gear, his clothes, saddles, extra tack, his entire outfit, lay hidden beneath a tarp to keep off the rain and sleet that had set in at a slow fall. He sat and waited to talk to Fixx, and to see the children again.

He heard the girls call out his name and this made him feel proud. He smiled and waved to them. Their wagon pulled to a stop. He stepped down and walked over to them. The eldest girl, Sarah Ellen, caught him around the neck, calling his name time after time.

"Uncle Hughie," she said. "Why didn't you come see us?"

He squeezed the little girl tight to his chest. "I'm here, Sarah Ellen. I reckon I'm here now, ain't I?" His voice bubbled out his joy at seeing them all again.

The other girls took their turn hugging his neck. The boy hung back. Hugh said, "What about you, Honus . . . you got a big hug for me as well?"

The tyke hung back as though Hugh had asked him to give up his favorite toy, but at length he stepped into Hugh's arms. "Where's my pap? Where's my grandpap, Uncle Hughie?"

Hugh Rust looked into the face of Olivia Fixx. Something in her eyes warned him off. "Why, they're home, I 'spect."

He figured Steel and Olivia Fixx had put off telling them of their father's death. What sort of people would it take to reveal that their grandfather had killed the children's father? Likely it'd be best if they never mentioned it at all. He was glad the job wasn't his.

"When are they going to come see me?" little Honus said.

"Someday you'll see 'em again, I guess." He nodded to Fixx, to indicate he wanted a word with him in private. The older man climbed down from the wagon. Clive and Redman sat watching nearby, on horseback.

"What is it, Hughie?" Steel said.

"Well, sir, it's about this war between you and Pap." He paused to see what reaction this would bring. When Fixx's face remained impassive and calm, he added, "Pap told me about your dog. How he killed it back when you both were boys. Is that how this god-awful mess got started?"

Fixx weighed matters for a time. "I 'spect so. It's odd, Hughie, but you know I still dream of that dog from time to time. That Tuffy dog was quite some she-dog."

"I can't believe something like a dog could lead you to hang a man like you did Jo. I can't see it." He kicked at the frozen sod.

"Honus didn't leave me no wiggle room," Steel said. "You heard how him and Pleasant Rathaus, and Jo and that deputy, Bowler Tallman, come to my place, killed Adair Murphy, hung my boy till he was damn near dead and beat up Olivia. You heard all that, didn't you? Hell, Hughie, he killed off my entire herd!"

"I'm leaving home, Steel. Right now, I doubt I'll ever be back. You and Pap have run me off. Pap expected me to take up his case. I didn't give him no answer. But he found out soon as he saw me leaving. I'm not joining in on this raggedy-assed deal. This has got to be the dumbest thing I ever heard in my life."

"Did Honus tell you how him, and Pleasant and Bowler Tallman, went over there to the Reyes place and killed the old man and his daughter?" Steel said.

"Knew something happened over there. Didn't know the whole story. How'd you find this out?" He leaned in closer.

Fixx spread his hands appealing for understanding. "Jorod told me. Pleasant killed the girl with his gun barrel. Hit her too hard. They hung the old man so it'd look like he'd killed his daughter, and then hung hisself. They got the county coroner to come out and make the thing official. I'd say Bill Miller really believes the tale hisself. Must've looked to him exactly like what happened."

Hugh Rust exhaled a long tired sigh. His breath fogged large in front of his face. He felt yanked about on every side, standing there with the rain and sleet falling on his shoulders.

Fixx dug out the makings, hunched over at the waist to protect it from the dampness, and when he poured his cigarette paper full, he passed the sack to his cousin once-removed. This gave them both enough time to set their thoughts a'right. They smoked in silence for a time. At length Hugh said, "Looky here at me, Steel. I got something . . . a favor to ask of you."

"What's the favor, Hughie?" Steel said.

"I want you to try and make up with Pap." Fixx's face clouded over, but Hugh continued his pursuit. "In fact, I'm begging you. It's got to stop . . . and stop now, while y'all are both still alive. If not, I reckon this is the last I'll see of you."

"I reckon things have gone too far for that, Hughie. Much as I want to, I can't forget it. Anyways, I'm sure your pap wouldn't agree to any such a thing."

"I'd work on him, Steel. There's times when he's his old self. I could work on him then."

Steel said, "I'd love nothing better than that, Hughie, honest to god. But I can't. This is something a man has to do—and still live with himself . . . three o'clock in the morning."

Fixx was as bull-headed as his father, Hugh figured and walked back to the Fixx wagon, hugged all the kids, save for little Honus who would have no more of it, and when he passed Fixx by, striding for his wagon, he nodded to him. "Be seeing you, Steel."

"Come around and visit us when you find a chance, Hughie," Steel said. "You're always welcome in my house."

Hugh saw the man's breath steaming skyward in the chill. He swung up onto the seat, picked up the reins. Fixx walked up alongside and placed a hand on the sideboard of his wagon.

"Don't want to lose your friendship, Hughie, hear me?" Fixx said.

"Yessir, I hear. I 'spect we'll still be friends, no matter what. I ain't never killed nobody's dog." He lifted the reins over the backs of the mules, and let them drop in a gentle slap. The creatures got up and on their way. He looked back at the family. He saw them huddled in the wagon as he was climbing over a low ridge. His heart pumped fire of pure regret. He realized he'd just suffered a most painful loss.

The sleet had hardened, replacing what little rain there'd been mixed in with it earlier. It drummed somberly off his hat. Old Moe Hardesty over in Staley had been after him for years to run his ranch for him at half shares in the profits. He headed the team in that direction now. He reckoned he would go there and learn if Hardesty was really serious about his offer.

CHAPTER TWENTY-SEVEN

The Fixx family set up a Christmas tree in the parlor of the upstairs apartment over the Ridenour General Store. The tangy scent of the freshly cut cedar tree tugged at the nostrils of all there, creating a cheerful mood in the room. The tree was thickly branched, rounded, and cut right to fit the room, tall enough to impress the children, yet not so tall the branches bent over at the ceiling. It was a flawless tree for that particular room. The children and Olivia hung silver and red imitation silk bows upon the heavy limbs as well as popcorn strings. Olivia climbed up on a chair and placed her special white angel on top. The children "oohed" and "aahed," staring wide-eyed at the shining baubles and beads. The tree thrilled the children so much they sometimes merely stood and stared at it without speaking. There had been little in the way of Christmas celebration in the home of Honus Rust.

On Christmas Eve, Olivia permitted the children to stay up later than their usual bedtime. She read to them from her large book of Christmas tales and poems. They ate popcorn and drank hot apple juice, spiced with cinnamon and clove. The children were nearly overwhelmed by the expectations of Christmas Day, of the tense wait that made their expectations even dearer.

Olivia attempted to persuade Enos to join in on the festivities, but he shrugged when she suggested he read a few tales to the children. His refusal disturbed her without end. In her mind, he was still a child even for all he'd undergone, the changes that'd occurred in him over the summer, the way he'd leaped ahead in growth, taller now than she, higher than his father's shoulders. He would be a large man, she figured.

Enos still often sat with the men at the fireplace, but now in their midst, Clive, Redman, and Fixx, he held back, and didn't attempt to join the conversation.

The family had been living in the apartment for only two days, but already Redman had grown eager to return home. He extended his feet closer to the fireplace. "How much longer, Pap, you expect?"

Fixx laughed at Redman's impatient nature and said, "Well, I guess we hired on for the duration, son. So that depends on the baby that's fixing to be born. You wouldn't want to try to rush nature any. The baby'll be along when it feels ready. We'll go home when we've been relieved of our duties and not before. Batch has everything under control at home. The Murphys likely'll return from Winfrey before Henry and Bernadette do. Relax, while you got the chance. Enjoy Christmas, son."

Olivia looked up from her book of tales and poems. She spoke to Redman in a snappish voice, "Redman Fixx, I swear if you ain't the most unsettled boy I ever saw. You put down that whiskey glass right now. Come over here and read some to these babies. My voice is 'bout worn out."

Clive sat in a cheerful mood, due in part to the whiskey he'd consumed, but also because of Christmas Eve. He snickered behind his glass, reached out and gave Redman a playful shove. "Go on over there, Red. Give Mam a break. You ain't too good for that, I reckon. Anyways, that job'll fall to you someday when you're married and have chaps and gals of your own."

Redman downed his whiskey, leaned forward, placed the glass on the stone hearth, and got to his feet, unable to deny his mother's demand. "Yeah, you're right," he said. He slapped Clive on the shoulder in return, passing by him. "You're the voice of experience, ain't you? How come you ain't got married yet?"

"I will when I find a woman cooks half as fine as Mam."

"Yeah, you're a real authority in that area," Redman said. He loosened up now as he crossed the floor to his mother to take over the chores as the official reader of Christmas tales and rhyming poems.

"Spoken more from the voice of excellent Fixx whiskey," said Fixx. The men laughed heartily.

Clive grew more extroverted than usual, and he was one given to reveal his emotions freely to start with, unlike Redman. He reached over and took hold of Enos, who sat between father and brother, in a glum funk. He left his arm there for a time in his natural way, then drew the boy's head to his shoulder and held him like that for a time.

"This here's my old buddy, ain't you, Enos? You wouldn't sell him to me, would you, Pap?"

Fixx assumed a serious face, as if he were considering the proposition. "No, I can't in clear conscience see my way to do that. 'Sides that, if I was to sell him, I reckon it'd take a slug of money. More'n what you've got, Clive. More'n what you could scrape together in the entire town of Witness Tree Station. Sorry, but I can't do it."

Without a word, Enos broke loose from his brother's embrace, got to his feet, stalked off into the bedroom, and shut his family out of his life when he banged the door shut. Clive and Fixx exchanged surprised and hurt looks.

"Leave him be, Steel," warned Olivia. "That boy's still hurt. Sometimes I wonder if he'll ever find a way over it. Surely, I do."

Fixx sat there with his whiskey. "Wonder what would've happened to me if I'd walked out on my pap, like Enos just did me." He said it without expecting an answer.

Olivia said, "There ain't no way to know that, Steel. How can you judge the situation unless you have been treated the same way Enos was?"

The warm feeling of cheer jumped up and departed when the boy fled the room.

Christmas Day was but one more day to Honus Rust. He entered the sheriff's office in Witness Tree Station.

Bowler Tallman held a glass of whiskey aloft, and dipped it in Rust's direction as he approached the desk. "Well, looky here now," said the deputy. He wore a wide smile. He'd fallen under the hex of whiskey, sitting in the sheriff's chair.

Rust pulled a chair out from the desk, and sat down. "Having a little celebration, Bowler?"

"Why, sure," Tallman said, smiling widely. "It's Christmas. A grand day for a celebration, I 'spect."

"Where's Pleasant?"

Tallman sipped his whiskey. "Went off to Big Boy Hines's back door to buy a bottle. It was his turn. I went last time."

"How'n hell long you two been at it?"

"Started last night," Tallman said. "Ain't stopped yet."

"You'll be out like the dead before noon then. Won't be worth shit for nothing."

"You don't know me and Rathaus." He leaned forward in his chair. "Me and that silly sonofabitch stayed drunk for a week once. I got a feeling this'n will outlast that'n. I'd offer you a sip, but this is got to hold me till Pleasant comes back."

"That's all right," said Rust. "I don't want to be drunk for what we're going to do today."

Rust witnessed a dubious expression spread across the face of the deputy. But Tallman, he knew, was a man born to tangle with the fates hidden in everyday life. He trod the very rim of hell daily and likely felt it a fair day's outing, more so when primed with drink. Tallman smiled a wolfish smile. His eyes were bright. His teeth were bared and yellow. "What's on your mind today, Honus?"

The door burst inward, bounced off the back wall and back into the face of Pleasant Rathaus. The sheriff had enough time to halt it with a foot before it could smack him in the face, but it'd been close.

Tallman threw back his head and laughed boisterously as if this was the funniest incident he'd ever witnessed.

"That's right," said the sheriff, "laugh on, you wormy little bastard.

"What'n hell're you up to this morning, Honus? Come to town to celebrate Christmas, did you?"

The sheriff slammed the door, strode with heavy feet across the floor, placed two quarts of whiskey on the desk, and shoved Tallman out of his chair.

"Yessir," said Rust. "I did, by god. I did come to celebrate. Today's a day of celebration, ain't it?"

"Yessir," said the deputy. "Today's a day for a fine celebration." He dragged up a chair and sat down with those of his own breed.

CHAPTER TWENTY-EIGHT

The Fixxes finished their breakfast early so the children could celebrate. Now the gift exchange was over. The children had settled down in the upstairs apartment, free now to play with their new toys, and to enjoy the presents they'd received. All were busy at play, on the floor and in the chairs. Sarah Ellen sat by the window reading her new book by the grudging gray light that crept in through the window. Outside, the snow fell in tiny flakes, half sleet. A strong wind pushed it along, at times horizontally. The other girls were busy on the floor, drawing pictures on a new drawing pad Saint Nick had brought them. The boy, Honus, had fallen asleep immediately after he opened his presents, lying at peace now on the sofa in Enos's arms.

The adults were grouped together downstairs in the kitchen. Olivia set about in a stir, busily preparing the Christmas meal for later in the day. The men were at the table, talking cattle and ranching, sipping coffee and smoking, as the room filled with the wonderful scents from a large beef roast, spices from several different types of pies, pudding, biscuits, and a spice cake.

"Stopped in the tavern for a time last night," said Clive. "And—"

Olivia stopped her work, hands on hips, head cocked. "You were in the tavern? I was worried about you. I'd hoped you'd found a nice girl, but no such luck."

"Aww, Mam," Clive said, "you'll not rid yourself of me that easy."

"I want some more babies to tend." She was at him more and more these days, encouraging him to find a decent girl and marry her.

"Ain't you got enough now to keep you hopping, Mam?" Redman said.

"Watch your tongue, Redman Fixx. It's high time you started looking for a girl as well."

Clive took up the thread of his aborted conversation, and offered the others the bits of information he'd learned last night. "There's talk of the railroad coming to Witness Tree Station," he said.

Fixx exhaled a stream of smoke toward the ceiling. "That merchant, Maples, that comes down from Camp Smyth for whiskey, said something about that a couple years ago. Must be true, after all."

"This'll be good for the town," Redman said.

"Yep," Clive said. "Won't have to drive our cows all the way to Winfrey to ship 'em."

"It'll be a worthy thing for the entire community," Fixx said. "A thing like this'll be outstanding for the area. I'm in favor of it."

Olivia turned back to her work. "Will wonders never cease?" she mumbled under her breath.

"Why, ma'am, listen to you," said Clive. "Ain't you the one always been for progress?"

"Go on with you." She shooed him with her apron tail.

They'd locked the doors of the store in honor of Christ's birthday. The family was ready to settle in for a peaceful day.

Later, someone pounded on the front door. The windowpanes rattled loudly in their framework.

Fixx turned toward the sound, and called out, "Store's closed today. Come back tomorrow."

The heavy hand pounded again upon the door. The windowpanes rattled to the point of breaking. He got to his feet, left the kitchen, and passed on into the store. He flung open the front door, and his jaw dropped in surprise. His cousin, Honus Rust, stood there, staring at Fixx, hand aloft, ready to rap again.

"What is it, Honus, to bother a man on Christmas Day?"

Rust smiled broadly. "The sheriff's fixing to come over soon, Steel. Has a warrant for your arrest."

"My arrest? For what?"

"For the murder of my son, Jorod," Rust said. "Thought I'd better tell you. You'll need to prepare yourself."

Sheriff Rathaus emerged from his office across the street, followed by the deputy. The deputy spun on his toes at the sidewalk and hurried off in the opposite direction.

"What kind of trap you laid this time, Honus?" He watched Rathaus's energetic approach from hooded eyes.

"Why, just what I said," Rust said, still smiling. "I 'spect you're going to stand trial for murder . . . them boys of yours as well. Might want to tell them too while you're at it."

"You know they ain't nothing to this, Honus. Where's the witnesses?"

Rust's eyeballs jiggled wildly in their sockets. "Nothing to it, my ass. Killing Jo was nothing? I'll let the sheriff speak to you about that."

Fixx stepped out onto the sidewalk. He shut the door behind him, blocking the view of his wife and sons.

Fixx watched as a crooked smile filled with stealth and pure deceitful deviltry broke out on Rust's broad face. "Got you now, Steel. Took a long time, but I did it. I mean to see you hung. Your boys as well. I reckon you won't have to worry that your hair'll get any grayer, Steel. I doubt that's any kind of great consolation to you, though."

The sheriff sprang up onto the sidewalk on nimble feet.

Fixx allowed Rathaus was at a stage in his inebriation that he made his every move with the suppleness and dignity he lacked in his normal state. He knew his trait for strong drink, knew him to be a man to hold his own with it. He saw that Rathaus was now in a state from which murders are committed with no thought at all to repercussions.

"I have a warrant for your arrest, Steely Fixx." He stepped closer to Fixx and thrust his bony face forward.

"I don't see 'ary a warrant, Pleasant."

Rathaus smiled. "It's coming, Steely."

Fixx turned to go back inside. "Come back when you find it, Pleasant."

"Might as well stay where you are," Rathaus said. "Bowler's gone for it now. The judge had it signed already. All it needed was for me to pick it up. Bowler'll be along directly."

"Come back when he lays hands on it. Till then, I'm going inside with my family, enjoy my Christmas meal."

Fixx opened the door and entered the store. His sons met him. His wife peered up at him, looking for answers, standing between her two grown sons.

"What is it, Pap?" said Redman, he placed an arm about his mother and drew her close.

"Claim they got a warrant for my arrest."

"Oh, Lord," Olivia said.

"For you and Clive too. I 'spect Rathaus got Judge Craft drunk so he'd sign the thing."

"The boys as well?" Olivia said. "Not the boys too."

He turned to Olivia and nodded. "I'm afraid we're in for trouble, 'Livia. I have no idea how this'll turn out, but it won't be good whatever 'tis. Better prepare yourself for the worst. Tell Enos to stay with the children. Hand him Henry's twenty-two rifle. Tell him to guard the children."

"You think it's that bad?" she said. Her eyes grew wider with each revelation.

"Looks like it to me. They've been drinking. Well Rathaus has. Honus hasn't. But he's plenty belligerent."

Olivia stepped closer to Fixx, looking up at him. "Whatever happens, you did the right thing. I was wrong once when I thought you should forget it. I'm convinced now you did right."

"Right or wrong," Fixx said, "won't matter none now. We've got to expect the worst." He turned to his sons.

"We going to fight, Pap?" Redman said.

"We ain't got no other choice, son. You boys fetch your rifles. Load up. This here ain't going to be no day off. I'm sorry I got you into this jackpot, but I can't change things, and you both know what to do.

"If you see me fall, don't hesitate, keep on shooting. Won't be time for me to come to you if I see y'all fall. Keep this in mind. Protect yourself. I demand that of you."

"I'll be there, Steel," said Olivia. "I'll be there with you."

"I know, and I wish you were a hundred miles from here. Go now . . . tell Enos."

She nodded and rushed off. He called out to her as she passed into the kitchen. "Henry's rifle's in the closet at the foot of the stairs. Try not to let the children hear what you tell Enos."

Olivia caught up the rifle. She slammed the closet door, opened the door to the upstairs hallway, and lunged upward.

Enos met her at the head of the stairs. She decided he'd heard her running up the steps, and stepped out in the stairwell to see what was wrong. "Where's the youngsters?"

Enos jerked his head backward, indicating inside the room. "Playing. It's old Honus again, ain't it?"

She nodded.

"I still feel my guts crawl," he said, "thinking about that time . . . when he hung me. I can't forget it."

She set down the rifle and caught hold of him, a thing he'd

avoided with deliberate emphasis since the hanging. She allowed he equated his ordeal with her ruthless determination for him not to reveal where he'd hidden the children. But he allowed her to hold him for a time. She felt his resistance crumble. "They've come for your Pap."

"The sheriff?" he said.

She nodded. "Your brothers as well. Judge Craft signed a warrant. Now they'll have to go to jail . . . or—"

Enos shook his head. "Pap won't go to no jail, Mam. You know that better'n I do."

She nodded, lowered her head and started crying. But this fleeting run of emotion soon passed, and she raised her head to him. "Listen, son, and listen close. If something happens to the rest of us, your father wants you to protect the children. No matter what happens, he wants you to keep Honus from dragging them off home with him. Hear me?"

He nodded.

She handed him the twenty-two rifle along with a fistful of shells. "Take it inside with you. If he comes . . . do what you have to do to prevent him from taking 'em, even if you have to shoot him."

"Yes, Mam. I'll do it."

"And whatever you do . . . don't expect no mercy from him. You know this already, but don't you dare fall into the trap of ever thinking so. If you have to . . . you shoot that man right between the eyes. Hear me, Enos Fixx?"

"Yes, Mam," he said.

She reached up, took his face in her hands. "It'll be hard for 'em to get past Pap and the boys. I doubt it'll go that far, but you must be ready if it does. I wish Batch was here with you.

"I'm so sorry for what I did to you that day, Enos. I need to hear your forgiveness. What I did was heartless."

"It wasn't nothing, Mam," he said.

"I've felt 'twas . . . in my heart.
from your lips. I won't leave without
me right away."

She watched Enos struggling to speak.
time in coming, but after awhile he nodde
ease your mind, I forgive you."

She bit her lip. The boy had grown so
overnight, it seemed—taller than she was. "Th
love you, son."

She felt Enos's eyes on her all the way down
stumbled once, almost fell, recovered, and then hur
haste grew so great it was as if she was bearing a pa
to douse on a parlor fire. When she turned at the bott
steps, she lifted her hand to him.

"I love you too, Mam," he said.

This brought a wide smile to her face. A bright and lea
joy burst from her heart. She passed on through the doorw
and entered the main part of the downstairs apartment.

The three men stood at the door, ready. They wore their
heavy coats, for the cold was fearsome. The snow and sleet
pounded loud against the windowpanes, driven by a strong
wind. She noted that her husband wore his Christmas gift, a
new coat, one with wide checkerboard designs in red and white.
She started to tell him to remove it, so he wouldn't make such a
broad target because of its bold colors, but she didn't have the
chance.

The sheriff or Honus beat on the door. He pounded away
like a piston at work.

Fixx smiled at her, took her hand, bent and kissed her cheek.
"Pray for us, 'Livia."

She nodded, and saw him in a wavering mist through heavy
tear-filled eyes. Fixx swung to the boys. She heard him instruct
them to remain inside unless he called for them or if they saw

257

fall into deep trouble, then come out the door in a
iring.

pened the door. He stood face to face with Sheriff
us. The man held the arrest warrant in hand.

got a warrant here," Rathaus said, waving the paper under
s nose, "signed by Judge Craft, by god. It's for your arrest
to the immediate relinquishment of the children you have
our care. The children of the man you murdered. Your sons,
ve and Redman, are also named in the paper as accessories
the unlawful hanging of Jorod Rust."

Well, here it was, the way he'd always feared the bad-blood
dispute would end. It surprised him it'd taken this long. Today
was the day. He saw no way around it. The huge swinish face of
his cousin loomed in his vision alongside the sheriff. The deputy,
Bowler Tallman, stood off to Honus's right.

Fixx cleared his throat. "Mind if I see your paper, Pleasant?"

"Why?" said the sheriff. "You ain't no lawyer."

"No, sir, I ain't, but I *can* read."

Rathaus wasn't about to hand him the paper until Rust
nudged him.

"Hand it to him, Pleasant. I want to see his eyes when he
reads what a man can do in a lawful manner. I don't rely on
orneriness and illegalities the way he does. Go on, hand it over."

Fixx took it from the sheriff's reluctant hand, but didn't
bother to look at it. He handed it through the open door. "Take
this paper, 'Livia. Toss it in your cooking-range fire."

She took the warrant and rushed into the kitchen. Moments
later, he heard the sound of the lid as she lifted it from the
cooking range. It grated loud even from this distance and above
the scream of the wind.

"Where's your fine paper now, Honus?"

He was elated seeing Rust's eyes bulging forward, threatening

to burst from their sockets, red and unnatural, marked with deep veins. "No," Rust said, as if he'd forgotten how to curse.

"Now, if you fellers ain't got nothing on me, I suggest you get on down the street. The store'll open again tomorrow morning. Come back then, and someone'll serve you."

"Come on, Honus," said the sheriff. The trio stepped down from the sidewalk, crossed the street, and entered the sheriff's office.

Redman leaned forward, watching. "They gone now, you think, Pap?"

Fixx reentered the room. "Nope. They'll be back."

CHAPTER TWENTY-NINE

Ten minutes later, Rathaus, Rust and Bowler Tallman emerged from the sheriff's office. Fixx watched through the window as they stepped onto the street, bearing shotguns.

"Here they come," Fixx said. "I'd hoped they'd go for another warrant. That would've given Enos time to get the children in the wagon and out of town. But not now."

He stepped outside, shutting the door behind him. The snow and sleet blew hard, stinging his face. The brittle pellets burned Fixx's exposed skin. The wind blew the snow sideways. He stopped at the edge of the sidewalk, rifle held across his chest.

The men walking toward him, side by side as they crossed the street, looked like ghosts, pushing through the frail screen of blowing snow, sleet, and screaming, frigid wind. His death or theirs was crossing the street straight toward him. They were packing 10-gauge shotguns, powerful weapons, enough to kill the heaviest beasts.

But Fixx felt as calm as he'd ever been in his life. In his heart and soul, though, he realized he was inhaling his last gasps of air. For some reason this didn't bother him. Not as much as he'd once supposed it would. His regret was that Enos hadn't had time to flee to safety with the children and that Olivia was in danger. If Enos had been able to reach home, he and Batch could've barricaded themselves inside the house. At some point, someone with good sense would show up, he figured.

The wraithlike men stepped closer. There'd be few survivors

from the blasts of those 10-gauge shotguns packing their heavy loads of lead.

"Steely Fixx," the sheriff said. The wind caught his words, swept them away with the snow and sleet. "You ready to give yourself over to the law? Go to jail for the murder of Jorod Rust?"

Fixx stepped to the street. He raised his hand as he did so. "Stop right there, Pleasant."

He didn't want them to step one foot nearer where their shotguns would be of a definite advantage. If they did, though, he meant to kill his cousin first thing. They'd shoot him down, he knew, but his boys might have a better chance if he stopped them where they stood. He hoped the boys had the sense to shoot from cover. For some reason, though, he doubted this. Clive might find cover, but Redman was much too headstrong for that.

"Better tell him to stop, Honus. He takes one more step, I'll shoot you dead."

Rathaus heard the warning. Fixx figured he felt safe, hidden within his personal cloud of inebriation, shielded from all gunfire by the strong confidence alcohol provided him.

Rathaus strode straight ahead. The other two men stopped. Rust's face clouded over from Fixx's warning, and because Rathaus hadn't heeded it.

Fixx threw his rifle to his shoulder, squeezed off a round. The report of the rifle was flat and dull. The wind carried it away instantly. The burnt gunpowder bit his nostrils, but briefly. The wind cast it away too.

His slug struck Rust high in the chest. He'd hoped to kill Honus with the first shot, but had missed a major spot of vitality. He took his time, aiming for the center of Honus Rust's heart, blocking out everything else.

Before he could fire a second shot, Rathaus shot him. He

grew aware of the heavy shot tearing his clothes apart. He felt the shredding of his flesh. He staggered. The blast of the 10-gauge knocked him backward. He tried to keep his feet beneath him. The backs of his knees struck the lip of the boardwalk, however, and he sat down on it in the snow that'd accumulated upon the wood planks.

The rifle weighed two tons. He did his best to raise it, but before he could do so, another heavy blast of lead tore his flesh apart. Three shotguns boomed loudly, fired off closely together. He dropped his rifle, crumpled sideways onto the sidewalk, and drifted slowly down into the deep holler, which had been his favorite hunting spot in his youth. He looked for the small dog, Tuffy. He didn't see her, although he could hear her, barking treed somewhere nearby.

"Pap!" Redman screamed. He flung open the door, rushed onto the sidewalk, raising his rifle as he ran. Olivia watched it all.

She stood paralyzed by the horrific scene that passed before her eyes.

"Pap," Redman screamed again. "Pap!"

She watched Clive follow his brother, walking instead of running, his rifle already at his shoulder as he left the building, ready to die, but to kill first. Her middle son, Redman, caught a gut shot. A blast from Bowler Tallman's shotgun killed him so sudden there was no likelihood he'd been aware the heavy shot from the 10-gauge had struck him down.

She shifted her icy attention to the deputy, watched as he hurried to reload, fingers clumsy in their haste.

All three men, Rathaus, Tallman and Rust had fired off both barrels of their weapons. They now stood defenseless, striving frantically to reload.

Clive fired. Rathaus fell on his face. It looked to Olivia that the heartless man died with such suddeness that his body failed

even to kick about it, not even the slightest twitch. Her eldest
son swung his rifle and sought a new target. She saw Honus
fumble the shells from a pocket, as he attempted his reload.
Tallman finished reloading. Clive swung his rifle, and leveled it
on him.

Tallman and Clive Fixx fired at nearly the same time. The
slug from Clive's rifle, struck the deputy in the center of his
chest, which was wrapped in a heavy coat of wool. It tore
through bone and flesh. Tallman called out one time in a weak
voice of surprise, then crumpled to the street, but Clive Fixx
himself fell backward as if someone had latched onto him from
behind and yanked him off his feet. Tallman's shotgun blast had
done its terrible damage.

Olivia felt a spasm of pleasure that Tallman hadn't been able
to derive the satisfaction of knowing he'd shot Clive. She felt it
likely the deputy's dead eyes weren't capable of registering the
street as it reared up and smacked him in the face.

Clive sat up. He groped about for his rifle—alive yet, she saw,
by will and imagination alone.

"Red . . . Redman? I can't see you. Where are you, brother?
Red."

His pleading voice tore Olivia's heart out. The heavy pellets
from Tallman's shotgun had blinded him.

When Rust saw that Clive was blind, he walked right up to
him, fearless of retaliation. He pushed his shotgun right up into
Clive's face. She saw a satisfied smile part his lips, and this was
nearly too great a burden to bear. The old man pulled the trigger. The lead shot blew Clive's head apart.

She shut her eyes, but couldn't block out the outrageous image of the death of one so worthy.

When she opened them again, Rust stood with his arms lifted
over his head, the gun still in hand. He yelled out in triumph as
if he'd collected on a sizeable bet. Olivia figured he must've felt

he'd killed all his enemies, or those of them who were an honest threat to him, and more importantly, that he'd remained alive to boast about it. She heard him cry aloud to the world his jubilation. The insides of her skull turned to flames of red fire instantly. All she could think of was revenge.

She plunged from the store without thought to her safety, caught up her husband's fallen rifle, struggled as she lifted it to her shoulder. But she was unused to firing a weapon heavier than a twenty-two rifle. It was heavy and uncomfortable. She cursed Rust for the devil she felt he truly was. Her breath spewed from her lungs in heated, steamed clouds.

Her hair fell into her eyes. The wind whipped it in and out of her face. She became a demon sprang to life from some old superstitious, deep-holler tale.

Honus, she saw, was struggling to reload. She was nearly upon him. She'd caught him off-guard. She took note of his fingers. They were fat, gore-covered, and slick as lard from the blood coursing down his arm and hand from his high chest wound. She pulled the trigger, still in a dead run, eyes blind to everything except Honus Rust. Much too hasty, she knew, attempting a duty that was better suited for her calm son, Clive. Her slug whistled past him.

She stopped running, walking now straight toward him, steadying her aim. It was as if she'd shed her earthly form and become a dispatch rider from hell. She jacked another shell into the chamber.

Rust, still struggling, dropped a shell between his feet, found another one, and slipped it into the chamber.

One shell would be enough, she realized, and sensed her own death. She watched him raise the ugly weapon. There'd be no reason for him to aim. Olivia fired first. She watched him flinch. He stumbled over his own feet, and nearly fell. Her slug struck him somewhere in the right leg. But it wasn't enough to finish him off. Rust became the recipient of the purest form of luck—one that often comes to the unworthy. She felt a head-shaking bewilderment, and had no answer as to why.

Rust's lips were flapping. She figured he was praying. Knew he had reason to pray. Again, she ejected the spent cartridge.

Honus pulled his own trigger as Olivia's empty shell casing spun off, tumbling higher and higher into the sleet-filled air. Her peripheral vision of the casing as it spun off like that somehow trapped her in a protective bubble of time, which was all that saved her from feeling the heavy lead pellets shredding her chest and midsection apart.

The blast lifted her off her feet, and flung her backward in a short flight. She struck the ground, a mere dead weight of torn, tattered flesh. The proud woman lay in total waste alongside her own gut-pile. It sprawled there, an object too gruesome for even the strongest mind to comprehend, offering up the last of her body heat to the cold wind.

Chapter Thirty

"What is that, Uncle Enos?" said Sarah Ellen. She cocked an ear toward the explosions from the furious gun battle in the street below. "What's that noise?"

Enos didn't answer. He herded all the children into the closet, raised a finger to his lips. "Don't say a word. Not a peep. Keep little Honus quiet, even if you have to clamp his mouth shut. You hear, Honus? You keep quiet and mind Sarah Ellen."

His finger, now finished delivering this warning, lingered inches from the boy's face. The rebellious child caught it, and bit down on it with teeth almost as sharp as an animal's. Enos boxed his ear hard, and slammed the door shut on his nieces and his nephew. He ran for the rifle standing by the door that led downstairs, shaking blood from his finger as he ran.

He jacked the bolt of the single-shot rifle, checked to see if it was loaded. Then, seeing the shine of brass strike his eyes, he took up a number of shells his mother had given him, stuffed them into a shirt pocket, and walked to the window, where earlier he'd witnessed the horrific massacre of his entire family.

Below him, Honus Rust walked about in short circles among the dead, still lying where the blasts of the guns had robbed them of animation. It seemed the old man was looking for something. Whatever it was, he either found it or gave up, because he cast an eye to the upstairs window, and saw Enos staring back at him. The hideous old man dropped his empty shotgun in the street.

Enos Fixx's heart seized up. He saw blood gush from the chest of the nightmare character below, saw it gush without restraint. Rust yelled out something, but the wind caught his words and carried them away. Enos didn't need to understand them to read his intent. He watched him shuffle forward, pass from his sight beneath the overhang of the roof of the porch attached to the store's front.

The loathsome creature had seen him. There was no doubt. He felt an urgent need to prepare himself. His mother had charged him with the safety of the children. He mustn't fail. This became more than another minor duty. This was much more, more in the nature of a formal contract between himself and his dead mother.

He turned away from the window—waited.

Below him, he heard Rust barge inside the store. He sounded unsteady on his feet. The old man banged into something heavy. Enos figured it was the large display case. He heard it fall to the floor. Heard glass shatter, and the contents of the case strike the floor and roll away.

He listened, breath frozen in his chest, as his father's cousin set about searching for the stairs that led up to the apartment.

"I saw you, you little bastard. I'm going to kill you," the old man roared.

Honus found the kitchen. He blundered noisily about down below.

Enos heard the door open onto the staircase.

"Now, I'll kill the damn bunch of 'em. Be rid of the Fixx family for all time. We'll see then who keeps Jorod's kids, by god." His voice boomed in the tight space of the stairwell.

The noise Rust's boots created upon the stairs caused Enos to about faint from anxiety. For a large man like Honus, he knew, to climb up so many steps must be a most difficult chore. Difficult for the heavy old man on the best of days, but now with the added penalty of his wounds, he made frequent stops to rest. These lengthy pauses tortured Enos.

He heard Honus's ragged breathing in the stairwell. The boy had witnessed the terrific surge of blood from the old man's chest. Maybe he would bleed to death on the steps. He couldn't rely on miracles, though. He had to look to himself for the safety of the children, and for his own well-being. Old man Rust was a lurid, outlandish character from the deepest recesses of Enos Fixx's imagination that had been born on the day of the hanging. His hands shook in spite of all he could do. He needed a steady hand to shoot him dead. He would aim for the head. Right between the eyes. His mother had ordered this. He heard him mumbling curses, pausing.

He started climbing again. How long could the devilish old man hang on with a wound like that one, he wondered? Again, he prayed Rust would die before he reached the door. That way he wouldn't have to face him. He recalled the commitment he'd made to his mother, however, and shame heated his cheeks.

He rose up and stood as tall as possible. But what he really wanted to do was to shrink up so tiny he could hide in the narrowest crack in the floor.

He had no idea it'd be like this. Joining the men should've been his pleasure . . . not this . . . this, instead, was overwhelming anguish.

Rust moved faster. His boots pounded louder on the steps. He stopped again. All sound ceased so abruptly it startled Enos.

But after what seemed a great amount of time, he heard those boots bang again on the steps . . . climbing toward him.

Rust reached the top landing. He was standing outside the door.

Enos heard Rust's harsh breathing. Fear climbed his body, a separate entity he had no control over, chilling as ice as it climbed higher. This, he figured, was what it felt like to die.

Maybe he could kill Rust without facing him. "I'll shoot through the door," he mumbled. "What if I miss, though?" His doubts plagued him. He decided to face him, to stand—make sure of the kill, and he needed a loaded rifle to do that. If he fired through the door and missed him, he'd be vulnerable until he could reload.

Maybe Batch would show up. This thought cheered him. Maybe he would arrive, pound up the steps, shoot Honus Rust down. Wouldn't he love to hear Batch's warning voice before killing the old man?

He heard Rust stagger forward. Enos forgot all about Batch. The door handle jiggled up and down. He heard it rattle.

A loud bang erupted, as if Honus had fallen against the thin door, and then the frightening old man fell into the room. The apartment door struck the inner wall, and bounced off.

Enos fired in anticipation of Rust's entrance.

His falling saved Rust.

The boy had expected him to enter the room upright.

He'd had no time to adjust his aim, and missed. Rust struggled to rise from the floor.

Enos worked the rifle bolt back, but the spent shell casing stuck in the chamber—jammed-up tight.

He dug at it with his fingernails, broke one off to the quick, but this didn't stop him, despite the blood that dribbled from the ripped cuticle. He felt no pain.

Rust struggled to his knees. He lunged to his feet, out of control. He lurched forward, arms raised, huge hands thrust out before him.

The man's spread fingers looked like claws. Enos's agonized senses raced faster than did his pounding heart.

He dug into his pocket, found his knife, opened a blade and went to work on the jammed-up casing.

"Got you now, you little, floppy-eared bastard." The old

man's voice wheezed loud, despite his wounds. "I got you. When I kill you that'll be the end of the whole goddam Fixx family. I'll be rid of y'all. A thing I've been fighting to do since I was a chap."

Honus stood close enough now to grab Enos. But the old man stopped and stood still as if listening to or for something.

Enos watched Rust's face twist up ugly in pain. His face twitched and contorted uncontrollably.

A short sound, cut off and muffled, sprang up from behind Honus Rust. A strangled cry came again, louder, from the closet.

"Grandpap!"

Little Honus had given away their hiding place.

The hated old man whirled. He took one forward step toward the closet. "Honus? Is that you, boy? Ring out again."

Little Honus said no more.

Enos dug out the spent shell casing, dropped it to the floor along with his knife. He slipped another shell into the chamber, slammed home the bolt, ready now to defend his nieces and nephew.

"Mr. Rust," he said.

Rust swung back to the boy, determined to fall on him, drag him down, and choke the life from him.

Enos raised the rifle, calm now. He couldn't miss again, never at this range. This was his final chance to save himself and Molly's children. He aimed the rifle. Set the sights precisely between Honus Rust's stress-filled red eyes.

He recalled the gun battle on the street. Saw again the tiny red and white bees that swarmed up from his father's checkerboard coat, watched them soar away on the wind, saw his father die. He watched again as his aggressive, impulsive brother Redman ran into a shotgun blast. Saw this through tears, as Redman fell. He watched Clive—and prayed he might pull off what his father and Redman had failed to do.

The sheriff died before the frightened boy's eyes. He watched the deputy fall into a pool of his own blood, then stared in horror, his heart all a-quake from his heartbreak, as Clive, his last hope, simply sat down in the snow, waiting there until the hated old man killed him.

Rust took one forward step toward him. Enos jerked up from his sad reverie. He faced the old man, watched his terrifying face freeze in disbelief. Rust's hoggish face turned white as chalk on a blackboard. He clutched his chest with fat fingers, and then moved his fingers to his head. The old man ran them through his hair. He wobbled on his feet. His knees crumpled beneath him. He collapsed and fell straight down and jarred the entire room. The racket sounded so loud when he struck the floor, Honus Rust might as well have fallen from the ceiling.

Enos waited—watched for a long time, fearful of a trick. After awhile, he found his courage. He stepped forward, kicked the man in the ribs. The dead weight felt the same as that of a deer he'd killed last fall. But he saw the fabric of the old man's coat lift and fall in jerky movements. Rust wasn't dead—not quite.

His mother had pled with him to kill him. He raised the rifle again, pointed it down at the helpless old man. His finger took up the slack on the trigger, ready now to carry out his mother's commandment. The closet door burst open, and the children swarmed out like wasps off a disturbed nest. They charged across the room.

"Grandpap," little Honus cried out. "Grandpap." He rushed toward the old man lying on the floor, and flung himself down onto his body. The girls too fell to their knees in a protective circle around Honus Rust.

The eldest girl looked up into Enos's face. Her large eyes filled up with fat tears. "No, Uncle Enos. You can't kill our grandpap. We won't let you."

His mother had commanded him. He owed her. He had to kill this hateful old man. He had to. He tightened the tension on the rifle's trigger until the least added pressure would touch it off, and send a slug crashing through Honus Rust's brain. The world would be better off with him gone, Enos knew this as well as he knew anything. But the children were there. How could he kill him with them there? Sweat broke out on his forehead. He owed his mother, his father, his brothers, even his dead sister. He closed his eyes to pull the trigger. The room grew dark. He needed the darkness to finish this deed. He couldn't do it with his eyes open. Not with the children here.

"No," the girl cried out. "Don't, Uncle Enos . . . please."

Enos wheeled to the sound of scuffed feet at the open doorway. Big Boy Hines stood there. He was holding a shotgun, pointed ahead of him for protection. Another head appeared— Dr. Hance.

"What're you doing, boy?" the saloon owner said. He lowered the shotgun. Dr. Hance stepped around the saloon owner, still cautious, and walked cautiously across the room.

Both men stood beside him. The children were surrounding the old man. Enos caught at his breath, couldn't find enough air to fill his needs. Tears formed in his eyes. He choked on a sob. He looked again at the old man and saw the truth. Honus Rust, he felt, had reached a safe stage of tranquility. The man was unable now to harm anyone. But what if he recovered? What other catastrophe would he bring? Dr. Hance, the saloon owner, his nephew, and most of all, his nieces were there. He couldn't do it. No matter how torn and ripped apart he felt, he was simply unable to do it.

The saloon owner reached out. He took the rifle from Enos. "There's been killing enough as 'tis, son. Move back, please. Let Doc Hance look at Honus."

Enos stepped back, far back, and watched as Dr. Hance

listened to the old man's chest through his instrument. He couldn't recall the name, but knew it was what doctors listened to the beating of a heart with.

Like magic, the room was overflowing with the people of Witness Tree Station, come to investigate. Three women stepped forward, and took the younger children in their arms, shushing their soft sobbing. They led them downstairs away from the awful, bloody scene in the apartment.

Dr. Hance peered up at the men surrounding him, kneeling at Honus Rust's side. "He's had a stroke. A heart attack as well. He had a heart attack once before this. If he lives, it'll be a miracle."

CHAPTER THIRTY-ONE

Two years later

Shortly after Dr. Hance had deemed Honus able to be moved, his nieces had begged Enos to allow the old man to stay with them at their Grandmam and Grandpap Fixx's house. He had hated to, but they had endured so much already that he had caved in to their pleadings.

Shortly after that, a letter arrived addressed to Honus Rust in care of Enos Fixx.

Enos handed the letter to Sarah Ellen, eleven years old and mature far past what she should be. She took it inside to read to her grandpap. He waited on the porch. Ten minutes passed before Sarah Ellen returned to the porch. Enos turned at the sound of her footsteps.

"Uncle Hughie is dead." She dropped her head to her chest.

These children had been through an enormous amount of tragedy. Now, here was another one. Although they didn't know the full extent of Honus Rust's ruthless madness or that their Grandpap Fixx had killed their father, he wondered how much more they could take.

"What happened to him, Sarah Ellen?"

She hesitated. Enos thought she would cry, but she lifted her head and looked him strong in the eyes. "An accident. They were moving cattle. Uncle Hughie was riding a green-broke horse. It shied and pitched him then stepped on his chest. He died two hours later."

"I always liked Hughie," he said. "He reminded me much of Pap. Looked a lot like him too. I hate this, Sarah Ellen."

Enos watched her face break apart. Her chest heaved and tears streamed. Still she issued no sound.

"Aww, Sarah Ellen." He took a step toward her. She fell into his arms, and broke into large sobs that sounded like a grownup in unbearable distress.

"It's okay," he told her.

"But what about Grandpap?" She stopped crying for a time and wiped her eyes.

"He can stay here. The nurse takes good care of him. He'll stay here until he dies or you are old enough to take over managing the ranch."

"But you don't like Grandpap."

He tried to put on an honest face, but it was a hard thing to accomplish. "A man has to learn to do things he don't really want to, Sarah Ellen. Batch says this is part of how a boy becomes a man."

Batch should've had no other thought on his mind today other than his wife and dancing. For it was their wedding day. He held Irene Murphy Batch close. He whirled her about the lawn, and heard her laughter, caught the grand scent of peach blossoms from some perfume she had put behind an ear. But his mind was restless. He knew that Hugh Rust had been a good man. He had known that from the day Hugh had hired him off the streets of Staley all those years ago. Hugh Rust had never felt hatred for his relatives. Batch had worked under Hugh's instruction for many years and had learned his trade from him.

Batch also marveled at the quirkiness of how a simple act of compassion—the day he'd ridden to the Fixx ranch to relate to Steel and Olivia the sad news that their daughter had died—had made him a defender of Enos Fixx. He'd lost a foot on his ride over in the cold that long gone day, but instead of being bitter, he felt he'd do the very same again. It was in his genes, he figured. He couldn't help himself. Honus Rust and Steel Fixx had been incapable of stopping the actions that led to the near ruin of both their families. That had been in their genes as well, sad to say.

The feud had been between two stubborn men, incapable of forgiveness. Batch held his wife closer and released a deeply held sigh. He felt warm of heart now. Not only because he'd been involved in averting the total ruin of the two families, but because he'd found a new life, and a wonderful wife in Irene Murphy.

He had added a room onto the Murphys' cabin for his future mother-in-law and Joan Murphy had taken over housekeeping duties for Enos. She avoided old Honus Rust. She forgave him because the Bible commanded her to do so, but she refused to look at or speak to him.

Batch had been with Enos when the merchant from Camp Smyth—the man, Maples—came down to announce the arrival of the railroad in Witness Tree Station. Maples had ordered whiskey on a scale so great it'd frightened Enos. They'd struck a deal. When Maples left and Enos expressed his fears, Batch advised him to do his best—and allow the rest to go to hell.

Later, sitting at ease on the porch, Batch and Enos had struck their own deal. Batch would raise the cattle, Enos would make the whiskey.

Enos Fixx sat on his front porch watching the dancing couple on the lawn. The day had been one of joy, as wedding days are supposed to be, not only for the married couple, but for all concerned. Enos's aunt and uncle from town, the Ridenours, were there, as well as many folks from Witness Tree Station, and from all over the county. Batch, by now, had become a solid member of the community. They came to wish the couple well, and to relax, have fun, for life continues despite what calamity falls.

Dancing continued to the old fiddle tunes. The men imbibed whiskey, but hid to drink it, for the act still didn't set well with many members of the community, though Enos was a whiskey-maker himself and was building his business.

Enos watched little Honus Rust scramble among the crowd on the lawn. The boy's left arm was in a sling. He'd fallen from the back of the bull, Star, and broken it. Enos figured that Star no longer held any memory of allowing the boy to ride him. Time, though, hadn't diminished little Honus Rust's memory. He made it a daily practice to try the bull. So far, he hadn't stayed on long. He had time, however. If he kept at it, he'd likely ride him one day. Enos knew Olivia, his mother, would worry her head off over the boy's actions if she had a way of knowing them, but he saw no way to stop it. Besides, he'd been the one who'd introduced the boy to this dangerous activity in the first place. How could he interfere now, and do it with any authority?

He watched little Honus scurry between the legs of the men and women gathered on the lawn, chased by other boys, some his own age, some older.

"Honus," he called out to him in reprimand because he'd nearly caused a woman to fall. Little Honus flashed him his wide grin, so much like Jorod Rust's own smile, one so captivating, so disarming that Enos felt he might be wrong about little Honus.

Honus Rust, the old man, was in his wheeled-chair where the nurse had placed him, sitting to Enos's left. Enos hadn't looked at the old man since the nurse had brought him outside. She sat close by, crocheting until she was needed.

"Honus," Enos called out to his nephew again in a sterner

277

voice. "You be careful now. See you don't knock someone down."

He heard the old man utter a sound of protest. A chill crawled through his body. He looked at him, but Honus Rust's face remained blank. He wondered if he'd really heard what he thought he had.

He looked up. The bride and bridegroom walked up to him on the porch.

Batch slapped Enos on the shoulder and said, "We'll have to keep our eyes on that Honus."

Irene, alongside her man, ruddy of face because of all the dancing they'd done, said, "He's going to be a handful, that's for sure. Together, though, we should be able to manage it."

Enos was aware that Irene had helped Molly with the boy at the Rust ranch. He figured he'd have help with little Honus, and that he would need plenty.

"Thanks," he said. "I appreciate it."

Irene turned her husband away from the porch, guided him down the steps, and flashed Enos a proud smile. "Today, though," she said. "Today belongs to me and my husband. Let's go dance, Mr. Batch. No telling when we'll have this chance again."

When the Batches were on the lawn dancing, he sat and watched all the dancers. He witnessed joy on the faces of all for they were hard-working men and women with little opportunity for relaxation and celebration.

As he was growing up, Enos had felt there would be something he should touch—something he should pass through like a portal into a new life as he shed his childhood and learned to sit with the men. Now though, since it'd happened, he felt nothing of the kind. He saw for sure now that there was no great joy, no happiness at childhood's end. Surely, he figured that the child one day folds into the man and that no one ever notices the innocence that falls to the side in the process.

Enos Fixx was young. He already knew patience, and he vowed to meet his every responsibility with cheerful eagerness. This alone, he figured, was worthwhile.

His father had once told him that a man needed to watch where he placed his feet. The rest would come naturally. He planned to do that. He turned again to old Honus Rust who sat there as mute as a block of wood.

He reached out a hand, and set it atop Honus Rust's own wide, fat one. He paused, and stared at the old man as if he were trying to read his thoughts. The wasps buzzed sleepily around their nests in the porch's ceiling.

In a soft whisper to prevent the nurse from hearing, he said, "I promised to kill you the day you butchered Mam and Pap and my brothers. I failed to do my duty. I don't see no way to ever forgive you." He paused, and sighed heavily. "So I reckon I'll promise you to do my best to keep you alive. I owe it to Sarah Ellen and the girls. Maybe I can keep that promise . . . but, then, maybe not. So far, I ain't been much good at keeping my promises.

"I can scarcely stand to look at you, Mister. I'm sure you don't like looking at me, either. So we're tied to each other for life. It's sort of like trying to swim with a heavy stone around our necks."

The old man didn't reply, neither did his expression change, nor did he blink.

ABOUT THE AUTHOR

Sumner Wilson is a retired railroad trainman, switchman and brakeman. He took up writing in motel rooms to bedevil time while waiting to "get-out" on homebound trips. He is the author of the novel *The Hellbringer,* as well as a young adult novel, *Billy in the Lowground.* Wilson's short stories have appeared in *Cappers,* in *Big Muddy, a Journal of Southeast Missouri State University,* and he sold two dozen stories to Sterling/McFadden Holdings, Inc. In addition, he has been published multiple times in *Frontier Tales,* an online magazine. He and his wife live near the Gasconade River in Phelps County, Missouri where many of his stories take place.

The employees of Five Star Publishing hope you have enjoyed this book.

Our Five Star novels explore little-known chapters from America's history, stories told from unique perspectives that will entertain a broad range of readers.

Other Five Star books are available at your local library, bookstore, all major book distributors, and directly from Five Star/Gale.

Connect with Five Star Publishing

Visit us on Facebook:
  https://www.facebook.com/FiveStarCengage

Email:
  FiveStar@cengage.com

For information about titles and placing orders:
  (800) 223-1244
  gale.orders@cengage.com

To share your comments, write to us:
  Five Star Publishing
  Attn: Publisher
  10 Water St., Suite 310
  Waterville, ME 04901